What the critics are saying

About LAST KISS

"Dominique Adair has written a very sensual love story that will enormously entertain the audience."
- *The Best Reviews*

"5 stars"
- *Sime~Gen, Inc.*

About NIGHT FLIGHT

"...a superb story, a fast read, highly enjoyable."
- *Sensual Romance*

"Not to be missed."
- *Michelle Gann, The Word on Romance*

About HEART OF MIDNIGHT

"This is a marvelous story of two wounded souls who find healing through their love for each other
- *Irene Marshall, Escape to Romance*

I love Kit Tunstall's books what ever the genre, she never disappoints. Her books are on my automatic buy list.
- *Gail, Romance Junkies*

Ellora's Cave
Romantica Publishing

Ellora's Cave Publishing, Inc.
PO Box 787
Hudson, OH 44236-0787

ISBN # 1-84360-393-4

LAST KISS, edited by Tina Engler.
NIGHT FLIGHT, edited by Cris Brashear.
HEART OF MIDNIGHT, edited by Ann Richardson.

Cover art by DARRELL KING.

Warning: The following material contains strong sexual content meant for mature readers. DARK DREAMS content has been rated R, Hard R and NC 17 erotic, respectively, by a minimum of three independent reviewers. We strongly suggest storing this book in a place where young readers not meant to view it are unlikely to happen upon it. That said, enjoy…

DARK DREAMS

Last Kiss

Written by

Dominique Adair

To Raelene, Francine, Cheetah, Bubba and the rest of the girls – wherever you are…

"I suppose they like me because I bring romance into their life for a few moments."
- Rudolph Valentino

Chapter 1

Somewhere in Colorado

It's show time!

Butterflies crowded Elaine Nichols' stomach as she climbed out of the limousine, ever mindful of her long skirt. The last thing she wanted was to land in a heap upon her arrival. Retrieving her small overnight case, she shut the door. Stepping to the side, she watched as the car pulled away, wondering if she shouldn't run after it, jump inside, and go back to the airport.

Do not pass go; do not collect two hundred dollars.

No, this was something she wanted to do. Scratch that; make it *Had To Do*. She had to pay taxes, be a good person, pay her bills, keep a roof over her head, and have sex with a stranger.

Though not necessarily in that order.

After ensuring that her half-mask still shielded her face, she straightened her spine and smoothed her damp palms over the form-fitting evening dress. Standing before her mirror at the hotel where she'd been taken upon landing in Denver last night, she'd pondered her decision to wear the body-skimming Vera Wang dress. Now, having left the dubious sanctuary of her hired car, she wished she'd worn the silk pantsuit she'd first selected. It hid more flaws than the dress.

A Rolls Royce pulled up and Elaine eyed the woman who exited the car. A brilliant gold half-mask concealed her face, but not her flame-red hair and sheer, black Versace dress. It was obvious the newcomer wore nothing underneath.

Yes, she'd chosen well if somewhat modestly, in comparison. Besides, who would wear a pantsuit, even a Dior original, when coming to a party to seduce a total stranger?

The Rolls pulled away and a silver Audi took its place as she quelled a nervous laugh. That was what they all were here for. Sex. And lots of it.

She tugged her thin shawl tighter around her shoulders and took a deep breath. Rubbing her hand over her stomach, she picked up her skirt and ascended the steps leading to the front door.

The house resembled an English castle though it boasted a multitude of lighted windows overlooking the curved drive. Discreet landscaping and an abundance of blooming roses, columbine, and impatiens added a splash of color against the severe gray stone of the house. Illuminated by the flicker of tiki-style torches, it looked warm and welcoming.

As she neared the entrance, a man standing by the door turned to her. Dressed in a formal tuxedo—Armani if she wasn't mistaken—his gaze was impersonal.

"Your invitation, Madame?"

"Oh, yes." Flustered, she turned and loosened her shawl to bare her shoulder with the small white rabbit painted on her skin. "I was invited by the host, Dirk Pren-"

"No last names," he interrupted. "Anonymity is key here. We want the guests to feel welcome so we only use first names and you may call me Nigel." His expression changed from cool to welcoming. "You must be Miss Elaine. Mr. Dirk told me to watch for you."

She tugged her shawl back into place. "It's very nice to meet you, Nigel."

He smiled as if her words amused him. "Your luggage arrived several hours ago and was delivered to your room. If you'll permit me, I will escort you there now so you may freshen up from your drive."

Elaine bit back a smile as he held out his arm toward her. He looked to be a bit younger than her own forty-one years, but his manners bespoke of a time long since dead. "Thank you, I'd appreciate that."

Slipping her hand into the crook of his arm, Nigel led her into the house. Though she'd known Dirk for almost twenty-five years, she'd never been to his ancestral home. Built in the late 1800's, Prentice House was the creation of a megalomania cal railroad baron, the first Prentice to make a name for himself. Many years ago over cocktails, Dirk had laughed about the ostentatiousness of the house and grounds. After seeing it, now she could understand.

The floor seemed like an acre of carved, Italian marble with brass inlays of railroad tracks, engines, and cattle. She stifled a grin at the sight of a particularly well-hung bull. The ceiling soared two stories overhead with two massive arches of rich mahogany interspersed with a chandelier the size of which she'd never seen outside of an opera house. The light reflecting off the numerous crystals dazzled her eyes.

The colossal staircase fit the overwhelming size of the house itself. Carpeted in a rich, wine red, the width was at least fifteen feet and ascended to a dizzying height. She allowed her fingers to trail on the polished mahogany banister as she climbed, her gaze fixed on the three towering stained glass windows at the top.

The jeweled panes caught the fading sun, casting colored shadows across the landing like jewels tossed carelessly about. The center pane depicted a golden-haired woman of amazing proportions. Clad in angelic attire complete with halo, her rapturous expression, exposed breasts, and outstretched hands decried her heavenly aspirations. Flanking panes framed the wanton creature with fat little cherubs armed with harps and mini bows and arrows. As she neared, she noted that many of the little creatures boasted impressive cocks.

Elaine couldn't prevent the laugh that bubbled up in her throat.

"Interesting piece, isn't it?" Nigel commented as he led her to the left toward yet more steps. "The original owner commissioned the piece. It's rumored that his wife refused to use the main steps, preferring instead the servants entrance."

"I can see why."

"Mr. Dirk instructed the staff to take special care of you." Nigel led her down a long hallway lined with doors.

"He did? Dirk and I have been friends for many years. I adore him." As they passed an open door, Elaine glimpsed a sumptuous bedroom suite in the process of being prepared for a guest.

Nigel gave her fingers a friendly pat before releasing her to open one of a pair of doors at the end of the hall. "This will be your room for the duration of your stay." He stepped back to allow her entrance.

Her heels sunk into thick cream carpeting as she entered the room, a sigh of pleasure on her lips. To her left, a large fireplace arranged with logs and tinder awaited the touch of a flame to bring it to life. A comfortable-looking couch covered with an array of plush pillows sat facing it. A small desk was positioned in front of a large window and next to that a large rocking chair with no arms. Directly opposite the doorway was a set of French doors leading onto a balcony overlooking the gardens.

To the right was the bed. A substantial four-poster shrouded in cream silk gauze, the king-sized bed was covered in an ivory and lilac striped comforter and a quantity of pillows.

It looked heavenly.

"This is lovely."

"I'm pleased you find your accommodations to your liking. The bathroom is through the door over there." He gestured to the open door on the far right beyond the bed. "Your maid's names are Molly and Rachel and you can reach them by dialing 9 on the phone at any time of the day or night."

Elaine ran her fingers over the comforter, luxuriating in the feel of raw silk. "Thank you for your help, Nigel."

"You're welcome, Miss Elaine. I hope this visit fulfills all your expectations."

Her gaze darted to his face but his expression was as friendly as before. He gave her a sketchy bow before leaving the room, closing the door behind him.

She tossed her clutch purse on the bed, then walked to the bathroom. Flicking on the light, she sighed with pleasure at the sight of the immaculate room. Thick peach-colored rugs covered polished marble while spotless mirrors lined one wall. A massive garden tub occupied one corner with a large stall shower complete with a built-in bench next to it. The commode was tucked into another corner along with a bidet.

On the vanity was a selection of fat vanilla candles in brass holders along with a selection of top line creams, lotions, and shampoos. A pile of peach towels awaited her pleasure on a padded stool within reach of the tub.

If there was one thing she loved, it was a spacious bathroom. When she'd bought her house several years before, she'd had few requirements—several fireplaces, a big kitchen and a spacious bathroom. She'd been lucky to find two out of three then she'd remodeled a bedroom into her luxurious bathroom.

Elaine made quick use of the facilities before moving to the vanity. Removing her sequined mask, she stared at her own familiar face.

Dark green eyes stared back from a vaguely heart shaped face. Her nose was average but her lips were full and pink. Thanks to moisturizing, her skin was good, her figure decent thanks to a love of running.

Her long brown hair was arranged in a simple twist with a few tendrils allowed to escape. Her hair had always been both a blessing and a curse to her. It was thick and, when the humidity was high, unruly. Because she'd lost her hair several years ago, she loathed to cut it short and something deep inside started screaming the moment her hairdresser ever turned in her direction with scissors in hand.

She grinned at the thought.

Some would say she was pretty; several men had even dared to call her beautiful. She turned to the side to check the line of her dress by running her hand down her side.

Yeah, not too shabby for a lady just dipping her toe into her forties.

In short, she'd have a good-looking corpse at her funeral.

She took a deep breath and straightened her spine. She wasn't going to think about that now, for it was time to make merry and, darn it, she was going to have a damn fine time even while wondering if she'd finally gone off the deep end.

She slipped her mask back into place, straightening it with the aid of her reflection. For the moment she was feeling good, looking good and that was all she needed… for now at least. Dirk had invited her to his house to relax, meet people, and, if desired, engage in consensual physical pleasures with a man of her choice. A glance at her watch told her it was time to begin the hunt.

She paused long enough to touch up her lipstick before turning the light off and exiting the bedroom, careful to close the door behind her.

When Dirk had extended the invitation to his weekend party, she'd been shocked. In all the years she'd known him, she'd never dreamed he threw such soirees consisting of an entire weekend of hedonistic indulgences: sex, great food, fine wines, and stimulating company. She knew he ran with a much more sophisticated crowd than she did, but she'd never dreamed of such occurrences, certainly not with her friend playing the host. Not that she was a prude, not by a long shot. But Dirk hosting a weekend of illicit sexual encounters for a houseful of guests? She stifled a chuckle as she moved down the central staircase.

The entry hall was crowded with partygoers, each sporting a mask that covered at least half of their faces. The men were almost uniformly clad in tuxedos while the women were dressed in every color of the rainbow. Many of the dresses were the same seen at any New York cocktail party, while others were downright non-existent. She looked away from a woman who appeared to be clad in a scarf and nothing else.

A soft chime caught her attention and her comrades in sex began filing through a doorway and out of sight. As she reached the bottom of the steps, Nigel appeared at her side. "Miss, if you will please step into the ballroom." He gestured toward open doors. "Mr. Dirk will be welcoming his guests and you can partake of the refreshments."

She gave him a smile of thanks and hurried into the room, one of the last to arrive.

Overhead, chandeliers were dimmed, casting a muted, golden glow over the guests. Joined with the soft light from a variety of floor candelabras and the scent of exotic incense, the effect was an aura of indulgence.

Along the far wall, arranged against the windows, was a large table filled with a vast array of finger foods and, in the center, a fountain flowing with champagne. Waiters and waitresses dressed in togas circulated the room with trays of wine and canapés if the participants didn't wish to serve themselves from the impressive spread. Elaine eyed the mountain of cocktail shrimp. A few of those would hit the spot right now.

At the far end of the room stood a dais with two ornate chairs draped in yards of red silk and black velvet. Dirk sat in one of the chairs like a King surveying his subjects. She recognized him, not because he wasn't wearing a mask for he was, but for the rich spill of his hair. Too pale to be called blonde, he wore it long, several inches below his shoulders. Normally he wore it clipped or tied back, but tonight it was free, pale as moonlight against the black of his tuxedo.

As the bell sounded for the final time, he rose to his feet, effectively shushing the group with his presence alone. Dressed from head to toe in black, he looked like an angel who'd taken a wrong turn and she smiled at the image that formed in her mind.

A waiter approached bearing a tray of champagne and Elaine had to force her gaze away from his well-filled loincloth. Smiling her thanks, she accepted a glass before stepping back to lean against the wall and listen to her friend.

"I wish to welcome everyone to my home this evening." Dirk addressed the forty or so attendees standing in a semi-circle near the platform. "Many of you have been here before, while for some of you, this is your first time. Here in Eden, the normal societal rules do not apply with the exception of one. No means no. If something makes you uncomfortable, speak up and everyone in this house will heed your wishes. For this weekend, the only hard and fast rule is to enjoy yourself and indulge your wildest fantasies." Nervous twitters sounded from several women as a few men tugged on their ties.

Elaine's gaze swept the crowd and she grinned. Yes, this was going to be an interesting few days. Her skin prickled as the hair on the back of her neck rose to attention.

Someone's watching me.

She slowly scanned the room, looking for the source of her discomfort. Standing in the back as she was, she couldn't see anyone paying her the slightest bit of attention until she looked up.

To her left, a balcony ran the width of the room and a man stood in the center, his gaze fixed on her.

His raven-black hair was long and loose, trailing below his shoulders. He looked quite tall with long legs encased in black leather knee boots and tight black pants. A burgundy velvet jacket covered impossibly wide shoulders while white ruffles from his shirt peaked through the open front. A simple black mask covered most of his face, but not his mouth. Unsmiling, he looked firm and commanding.

She looked away, willing her breathing back under control. She was being foolish. It couldn't be *him* because *he* didn't exist. He never had.

For as long as she could remember, she'd had dreams about a tall raven-haired man who was her lover. The dreams had started when she was in her late teens and they'd begun innocently enough. Every three or four months, she'd dream of walking under a full moon, his hand in hers, of stolen kisses that curled her toes under the cool, blue light. They would laugh, talk, and lie in fields to stare at the stars.

As she grew older, the dreams changed and increased in frequency. They were almost always sensual or erotic in nature, leaving her damp and aroused when she woke. On most occasions, she'd been aroused to the point that a simple touch from her hand would bring her the satisfaction she craved.

She glanced up once more and their gazes connected. He nodded, sending a shiver of anticipation through her as she saluted him with her glass and a big smile.

She'd rarely sustained a long-term relationship because, as crazy as it sounded, she'd always had the strange feeling that she'd been cheating on her dream lover. Face it, no real man had ever measured up to her nocturnal visitor.

What time she'd wasted being faithful to a figment of her overactive imagination. The man on the balcony probably wouldn't measure up either, but she might have fun finding out.

A waiter dressed in a white loincloth distracted her when he offered her a mouthwatering selection of mini-quiches. Though she didn't want one, she selected a mushroom quiche and nodded her thanks as he left. After nibbling her treat, she took a leisurely drink of her champagne before returning her gaze to the balcony.

He was gone.

Chapter 2

It was her, it had to be.

Count Alexei Romanov ran a shaky hand through his hair as he stepped into the seclusion of a small lavatory, taking care to lock the door behind him. No other woman had that smile or air of confidence that *she* possessed. When she'd tilted her head to the side while listening to Dirk, he knew he'd seen that head tilt before.

Even now, after seeing her in person, it was hard for him to believe it was her. He'd seen her photo in Dirk's office, but his friend had been remarkably tight-lipped about Elaine. It had taken four years of haunting Dirk's every move in pursuit of the woman in the photograph. And finally, she'd turned up at this event. He'd known that if he stuck close to Dirk long enough, the elusive Elaine would appear. And she had.

So many years had passed since he'd last seen her but he knew his memory to be true. To be sure, there was one more test, one sure way to find out if it really was her. With any luck, he'd know within a few short hours.

He tipped his head back, his eyes stinging with tears of joy. After all these years, his quest was almost over. He closed his eyes and offered a silent thanks to the Universe for showing him the way to his love.

* * * * *

Elaine turned away from the balcony, disappointed. Where had the stranger vanished to so quickly? She could only hope he'd reappear later and she'd get the chance to chat with him.

A round of applause brought her attention back to Dirk. "Dinner will be served in one hour. Until then, please partake of the wines, canapés…and anything else you might...desire."

Elaine smiled as his voice dipped and he gave the crowd a slight bow. Stepping down from the dais, he headed toward her, pausing to exchange a word with one of the guests. Her heart swelled as his face broke into a broad smile when he reached her side.

"Darling!" He swept her into a hug. "I'm so pleased you made it."

"And I'm pleased you invited me." She returned his hug with a big squeeze. "Thank you."

"You're welcome." He released her and stepped back to look her up and down, his gaze warm. "You're looking well, my dear."

"I'm feeling well." She smiled. "Very well in fact."

He caught her hand and gave it a quick squeeze. "I've been worried about you."

She caught the glimmer of concern in his eyes and her heart tightened. One of the hardest phone calls she'd ever had to make was to tell Dirk of her returning illness. Together they'd fought the same battle five years before and now it was back with a vengeance. Homemade soup and hand-holding wouldn't save her this time.

She widened her smile and gave his hand a squeeze. "Don't worry about me, not this weekend anyway."

His smile reappeared. "You're right. This weekend you're well and, for that, we shall be thankful." He nestled her hand in the crook of his elbow, leading her from the room. "For the next few days, I only want you to think about pampering yourself. I've arranged for a daily massage at 1 P.M. in the privacy of your room." When she made a noise to object, he shushed her by placing a finger over her lips. "No, dearest, let me do this for you." He replaced his finger with a quick kiss. "I know how important it is that you be as relaxed as possible."

She nodded, her eyes stinging with unshed tears. "You've been a good friend to me, Dirk."

"And you to me." His expression turned serious. "Elaine, I wanted to—"

"Mr. Dirk," Nigel approached. "I'm terribly sorry to interrupt, but we have a slight problem in the kitchens that requires your immediate attention."

"Oh bother." Dirk rolled his eyes theatrically. "I'll be there in a minute." He steered Elaine toward a large set of open doors. "I want you to see my new acquisitions in the gallery. I shipped many of the paintings from the New York apartment to make room, however, I bought a new one specifically for this house." He raised her hand to his lips and pressed a warm kiss to her knuckles. "I think you'll enjoy it."

"I'm sure I shall."

Elaine couldn't prevent a smile as Dirk moved away. He was such a kid, spending his outrageous inheritance with his usual dash and style. Which was not to say that he was indiscriminate, he wasn't. He donated much of his money and free time to various charities. The reality was that he was so darned rich he didn't know what to do with it. She'd always thought that he had more money than sense at times and she loved him for it.

Stepping into the gallery, the noise of the party faded behind her. Here, only a few drifted around to view the impressive collection. She wandered past a Gustav Klimpt that Dirk had acquired almost twenty years ago, one of his first serious purchases. They'd been in Germany when the painting had come up for sale and he'd been determined to buy it.

Next came a Degas in pastel, a group of young dancers. Then a lesser-known Manet hung beside a series of Picasso's work from the later period. An impressive collection of small Monet's were hung above a delicate gilt table topped with a vase of flowers.

He had exquisite taste in art.

She spied the new painting at the end of the room and she turned toward it, eager to see what gem her friend had found. Before she could get a good look at it, a couple entered the gallery, their laughter disturbing the calm of the room. Elaine stepped to the side, ducking behind a potted fern as the man's gaze swept the room.

"We're alone, darling." He spoke to his companion.

"Smashing, just smashing." The woman grabbed his arm and led him to a padded bench near the center of the room. Pushing him down, she zeroed in on his lap, concentrating on releasing him from his trousers. Pulling her voluminous skirt up, she climbed into his lap, impaling herself with a squeal on his erection.

So much for foreplay.

As the woman set to work, Elaine clapped a hand over her mouth to thwart her laughter. Heavens, what did she do now? She couldn't very well step out of her hiding spot and make her escape. They'd see her and know she'd been watching them. Maybe she could—

Their shared groans escalated and she bit her lip, trying desperately not to laugh. Just a few feet away were the terrace doors. Maybe she could sneak through there and make her escape into the garden, then around to the front of the house. She could only hope the alarm wasn't armed.

She shot a glance at the amorous couple and noted they were oblivious to anything around them. Holding her breath, she moved the few feet to the door and curled her fingers around the handle. With a quick, silent prayer, she opened it with nary a sound and she slipped outside into the darkness, careful to quietly shut the door behind her.

Backing away, she allowed a wild giggle to escape. That had certainly been a new experience for her. She'd been caught in quite a few embarrassing moments in her life, but this one took the cake. Dirk would get a laugh out of this and she couldn't wait to tell him just as soon—

She stumbled as she backed into something solid, throwing her off balance. Pin-wheeling her arms, her breath caught as hands descended upon her shoulders, hauling her back into a broad chest. Warm breath tickled her neck as her unexpected companion leaned down to speak in her ear.

"Shh, don't make a sound. We don't want to disturb our friends."

A shiver ran down her spine and those strong hands guided her back across the terrace. Once she was sure they were safe from detection, she turned to face her rescuer.

It was *him,* the man from the balcony. He smiled and her breath caught. As he captured her hand and raised it to his mouth, a jolt of awareness raced up her arm and her throat went dry.

"Allow me to introduce myself, I am Alexei." He kissed the back of her hand, then raised his head, his gaze meeting hers. "And you are?"

She swallowed hard. "E-E-Elaine. My name is Elaine."

A spark of amusement lit his eyes at her nervous stammer.

Great! She meets the most handsome man on the planet and she'd just proven she was a nervous Nelly who can't even say her name successfully.

"A beautiful name for a beautiful woman."

His accent was faint and yet somehow familiar. Did her dream lover have an accent? In her dreams, she couldn't actually say that she'd heard him speak. It had always seemed like she just *knew* what he was saying.

She shivered as he turned her hand over and pressed a kiss to her palm. "Where are you from?" she blurted.

"Here and there." He rose, still retaining his grip on her hand. "I am from Moscow originally, but I have lived all over the world."

"Since Russia fell?"

He smiled as if her question amused him. "You could say that."

She bit her lip and his gaze immediately dropped to her mouth. Disconcerted, she parted her teeth to release her flesh as his thumb stroked her palm, causing a shimmer of heat down her spine.

"So what brings you here?"

Great Elaine, we all know why we're here.

His smile grew. "I am here for a variety of reasons, mainly to visit my friend, Veronique."

Elaine nodded. She guessed he was talking about Veronique LeMonde, Dirk's lover. They'd been together for years.

"Ah, so you know her as well?" he asked.

"Oh yes, I've known Dirk for most of my life and I remember the day he and Ronni met." She grinned. "He mowed her down on his rollerblades in Central Park."

Alexei laughed. "I remember that. She had to appear onstage at the Fall Fashion Preview with a bandage on her forehead."

"And still managed to look stunning." Elaine chuckled.

Their laughter faded, the night sounds enveloping them as their eyes met and clung. Shadowed by the mask, she couldn't tell what color his were but she felt the heat of his gaze as it swept her, scorching her from the inside out. Her breasts tingled and her nether regions involuntarily clenched. Already she knew that she wanted him. With only a few words and a touch, he'd managed to move past her defenses and firmly plant himself in her psyche. The next question was how to get him into her bed? She licked her lips. Was he even interested?

A loud cry from the amorous couple within the gallery brought a rush of heat to her cheeks, forcing her to avert her eyes.

He squeezed her hand, jerking her attention back to his face. "They are very… energetic, yes?" He nodded toward the doors, his eyes gleaming with amusement.

Elaine couldn't prevent her smile. "You could say that."

"He makes too many mistakes." Still retaining hold of her hand, Alexei urged her to walk with him. "He's hurrying too much and doing a disservice to his woman."

Alexei stopped to lean against the stone railing, turning her so she faced the house. From their new position, she could see directly into the gallery and the couple writhing within.

"I don't think we should…" She tugged at her hand but he refused to relinquish his hold.

"Shh, watch and learn."

He pulled her into his arms, her back to his front. She had to part her legs to accommodate his feet as his hands slid down to grasp her waist. His big hands cupped her hipbones, pulling her snug against him, the press of his erection evident despite the layers of clothing that separated them. Lust unfurled in her gut, moving lower to pool in the apex of her thighs.

That answers that question…

A rush of feminine power hit her at the thought of bedding this handsome man.

"He's greedy." His voice sounded in her ear, pulling her attention from her buttocks where he pressed against her, back to the couple. His breath tickled her neck as his chin brushed her skin, eliciting a shiver from her.

"See how he eats her alive?"

She focused on the couple. The woman sat astride the man, her fingers tangled in his blond hair as she rode him with short, jerky movements. His hands grasped her voluminous breasts through her open dress-front, nimble fingers flexing her white globes as they ate at each other's mouths.

Elaine winced. The man's grip looked painful to her, but his partner didn't seem to mind.

"He'll leave marks on her flesh." Alexei said.

She swallowed. "His partner doesn't seem to notice." Her voice came out low, husky, and aroused.

"No, she doesn't seem to care." His lips brushed her neck and her eyes slid shut as a gush of warmth flooded her vagina. "When we make love, I'll not treat you in such a cavalier fashion. I'll handle you as one would a prized possession. You are a woman to be worshipped." His lips moved up her throat to tease the skin just behind her ear, sending shivers down her spine. "Every inch of you, I shall explore and cherish with all of my body."

She barely managed to contain her groan as powerful images washed over her. This dark Russian in her bed, his hands on her body, as he made love to her. It was all so…familiar. She bit back a moan as his right hand moved to her stomach, his pinkie following the waistband of her panties through her dress.

"For hours, we will delight in one another as we explore our deepest, most carnal fantasies." His teeth grazed her skin. "Time will be of no importance, for lovers such as we shall have eternity."

Her eyes opened slowly, her blood sluggish with desire. She licked her lips. How well she knew the bondage of time. She'd been fighting it for years and, now, she was almost out of it. While he might have an unlimited supply of time, she did not.

She turned in his arms, leaning into him, relishing the feel of his strong body against hers. His arms slid around her, nestling her breasts against his broad chest. Her gaze met his as she leaned in to brush her mouth against his lips. She caught the feverish glitter of his eyes shadowed by the mask as she repeated the motion. This time, his mouth opened, his tongue teasing the seam of her lips, requesting entrance.

Her fingers curled over his shoulders as a sigh slipped from her and she opened to him. His taste, potent male, forbidden desire, exploded in her system as their tongues curled around one another. His grip tightened as the kiss turned urgent. She moaned as he sucked at her tongue, sending shivers of delight through her body. Her breasts ached and she shimmied against him, trying to appease her hunger, relishing in the groan sounding from his throat.

His hands slipped to her hips, pulling her tight against him as they feasted. Her fingers tangled in the silk of his hair as he nibbled on her lower lip before kissing the corner of her mouth. She tipped her head back to give him better access as he seduced her chin.

Dimly she was aware of sounds coming from the other couple as they reached completion. Their ecstatic cries mingled with the rapid beat of her heart. His hand cupped her breast, his thumb brushing her beaded tip eliciting a sigh of pleasure. She'd felt desire, even love, in her life. But never had she felt anything like the white-hot, fast burn that was consuming her now and she never wanted Alexei to stop.

Her limbs were leaden with desire as he nibbled a path of awareness down her throat to nuzzle her collarbone. His lips were heated against her skin; the rasp of his faint beard teased her senses and stood her hair on end. The edge of his mask brushed her neck, shattering the illusion of intimacy and bringing her back to earth with a thud.

What was she doing making love to a stranger in public? She couldn't relinquish herself to a complete stranger within moments of meeting him, what was she thinking?

Wasn't that the reason you attended the party?

Yes.

No.

"Stop."

Shaken, she pushed out of his arms, staggering as he freed her to stand on her own. Their gazes met and she saw desire change to concern.

"What is it, Elaine?"

"I-I-I think we're moving too fast." She stepped away from him while her mind screamed for her to take a leap of faith and beg him to make love to her. She ran her hand over her hair, unable to met his gaze. "I realize that this is the norm for a party such as this, but—"

"Shhh, no explanations are necessary." He straightened and reached for her, one finger tipping up her chin. "Perhaps we've been a bit hasty, and this after I told you I would worship you as a prized possession." He chuckled. "Yet I find that I can't keep my hands off you. I've behaved no better than that lout inside."

She smiled as a sense of calm descended. He understood at least and for that she was grateful. "Thank you."

"You're welcome."

The deep chime of a gong sounded.

"Sounds like we are being summoned. May I escort you to dinner?"

She ran a shaky hand over her stomach and tugged her shawl back into place, trying to cover as much skin as possible. "Yes, I think I'd like that very much."

He took her hand, their fingers lacing together as if they'd walked as such a thousand times before. Upon entering the gallery, Elaine was pleased to see that the couple had left, leaving behind only a white silk garter on the floor as a silent testament to their passion.

Chapter 3

Nothing could dim his awareness of her. Now that they'd kissed, her taste resonated through his body to tease nerves he'd thought long dead. It was a painful process, this reawakening, and he relished every moment of it.

The thrill of victory ran through Alexei as he watched Elaine chat with Dirk and the lovely Veronique. It was her, his love reincarnated. While he still didn't have concrete physical proof, he didn't require it when his heart was telling him what he already knew.

During dinner he'd sat by Elaine's side, pushing unwanted food around his plate as he'd inhaled the scent of her perfume. She'd driven him crazy as she'd laughed and flirted shamelessly with another guest who'd been old enough to be her father. He'd barely managed to quell the urge to smash his fist into the other man's face when he saw the interest clearly written there.

It was accepted—even expected—that the men and women who attended these parties entertained multiple partners, but Elaine was his and his alone. She just didn't know it yet.

As dinner wound down, he'd escaped outside for a few minutes to pull himself together. He didn't want to frighten her with the savagery of his feelings. He must move cautiously if he hoped to win her once more. He'd spent the past fifty years looking for her, and he was determined not to lose her by being impetuous.

On the balcony overlooking the ballroom, he watched her from afar. The subdued lighting gleamed on her thick hair, contorted into a sleek twist with soft tendrils escaping into ropy curls long enough to brush her bare shoulders. His fingers itched to release the silken mass from its torturous arrangement. He longed to see it spread across his pillows as he seduced her into mindless abandon.

At some point she'd lost her shawl, exposing a large expanse of her back to his gaze. He would kiss her curving line from nape to tailbone before taking her from behind, spreading her thighs and entering her with a slow thrust.

He contained a groan at the thought of her nude body beneath him. Lust gnawed at his zipper as his cock swelled and he silently cursed the tight pants. Damn things were in danger of emasculating him if he kept imagining making love to her much longer.

He turned away, his breathing harsh as he struggled to control his desire. He wanted her as he'd never wanted another woman and once would never be enough. If they spent the rest of this weekend in bed, it would be but a start. He would settle for nothing less than eternity this time.

He walked to the stairs, taking them in an easy stride to the main floor. Ignoring the interested glances from women and even a few men, he set his unwanted drink on a tray and advanced across the room to claim his woman.

Her laughter sent a trickle of awareness down his spine as he reached her side. Placing a hand on the small of her back, he caught the tremor that rippled through her as he dropped a small kiss on her bare shoulder just above the painted rabbit.

"Miss me?" he asked.

She smiled and he noted the flush that swept across her skin, her desire as tangible and heady as her perfume. "What do you think?" her voice was low, husky.

"I'll take that as a yes." He gave her a small smile.

"I wondered where you'd wandered off to," Veronique said. "Dinner was over and you escaped like a man released from jail."

Her tone was questioning, but he ignored it. Veronique was a great friend and a shameless gossip. "I stepped outside for a smoke."

"Are you still smoking those Greek things?" she asked.

"I have Turkish with me this weekend." He didn't miss the gleam of interest in Veronique's eyes. He withdrew a silver-plated case from his pocket. "Would you care for one?"

"I'd love one." She accepted his offering, then linked her arm through Dirk's. "Come, lover, let us slip outside and indulge in an illicit smoke."

"Take good care of Elaine, she's very dear to me."

Alexei looked down at the woman in question, amused to see her accepting another glass of champagne from a waiter. Her gaze was locked on the young man's toned backside as he turned to offer a glass to someone else. He glanced back at Dirk. "And to me as well."

The other man gave a solemn nod before allowing Veronique to steer him toward the terrace doors.

"What was Dirk talking about?" Elaine asked, raising her glass to her lips.

"You, my dear. We were talking about you." Her eyes widened and she took a gulp of her drink. Unsettled was she? Good, he wanted her off balance when it came to him. "Shall we dance?" He reached for her glass. "It's been over two hours since I've held you in my arms."

She flushed again and he wasn't sure if it was from the alcohol or his words, but he hoped it was the latter. Wordless, she nodded and gave him the glass, which he abandoned to a table in favor of escorting her to the dance floor.

As she moved into his arms, he released a breath that he hadn't realized he'd been holding. They were well matched with her head coming to his chin, her soft curves melting into him without urging. She felt natural, familiar in his arms. He rubbed his cheek against her soft hair, wincing as the soft strands caught on his faint beard.

"I fear I shall have to shave," he said. "I wouldn't want to mark your tender skin."

She tipped her head back, her eyes glittering behind her mask. "Aren't you presuming a bit?"

"I don't know." He raised his hand and drew a finger down her jaw, marveling at the softness of her skin as he traced the curve. "Am I?"

"You might be—"

He leaned down and brushed his lips across hers, halting her words as he fought the urge to devour her. A soft sound escaped her as his tongue slipped out for a taste of her, sending a surge of lust to his loins that threatened to curl his toes. He smiled as she turned her head slightly, his offering landing on the corner of her mouth. He nibbled on the fold as a shudder ran through her body. She was still shy, but soon enough she'd feel at ease in his embrace as if she'd been there forever.

He raised his head, taking in her beautiful face—what wasn't hidden by the mask—and her dazed expression. "So, what do you think so far?"

She blinked, her desire-laden gaze clearing. "What do I think of what?"

"The party, this weekend."

"Well..." She glanced about the room, then leaned in to whisper. "It isn't quite what I'd expected."

"How so?"

"I think I expected...more."

"More of what?'

"Sex." She ducked her head, unable to meet his gaze.

"You expected an orgy, you mean?"

She nodded and he bit back a shout of laughter. "And you came anyway? How very brave of you."

She tipped her head back, her brow raised. "I'm more adventurous than I might seem."

"I'm sure you are." He drew his thumb along the curve of her lower lip. "In fact, I'm counting on it." He dropped his hand to her waist, pulling her snugly against him where she belonged. "Are you disappointed in the lack of an orgy?"

"No." She laid her hand over his heart. "I just didn't know what to expect."

"Well, I can't say that it's never happened, but group sex isn't a regular occurrence. However," he dipped his head, his lips brushing the delicate curve of her ear. "You might want to knock before opening closed doors. You could very well walk in on more than you bargained for."

She chuckled. "How many of these parties have you attended?"

"Too many. Veronique invites me every time and I can't refuse her."

"You have a problem saying no to a beautiful woman?"

"I make it a policy to never say no." A soft blush spread under her skin and he wanted to press his mouth to the telltale warmth.

"So why did you attend this weekend?" she asked.

Why did he attend? Could he tell her he'd seen photos of her in Dirk's office and he'd been obsessed ever since? Pumping Dirk for information had led to nothing fruitful, so he'd decided to stake out all of Dirk's parties. If they were really close, as close as Veronique had implied, he'd known that sooner or later she would turn up and he'd been right.

"I came to find you."

She lifted her head, her gaze startled, then she smiled. "You're teasing me."

He fought to keep his expression grave. "I would never tease about a matter as important as this."

"I'm serious." She shook her head as if she couldn't figure him out. "Why would you attend something like this? You're obviously handsome—"

"Thank you."

"You have an accent that could melt butter on a cool spring day. I can't imagine you having problems finding female company under normal circumstances."

Suddenly uncomfortable, he shrugged. "I have many reasons for attending this weekend. But, regardless of what brought me here, I'm delighted to have you in my arms. That's what counts. Right here, right now, and not what brought us to this moment."

Her expression turned serious and he caught a glimpse of sorrow in her gaze before it was quickly subdued and she gave him a brilliant smile. "You're right, nothing else matters now."

He smiled, absurdly pleased with her words. "Now, my lovely, let us lose ourselves in each other and see where it leads us, yes?"

* * * * *

The rest of the evening passed in a blur to Elaine. She stifled a giggle. He'd been right about one thing; from now on, she would knock before entering rooms. Earlier she'd been looking for the ladies room and, instead, she'd found a man sprawled on a divan with one woman sucking his impressive erection and another woman seated on his face. Oblivious to her unexpected presence, she'd managed to slip out of the room and close the door without interrupting them.

Sheesh, didn't anyone think of locking a door?

Numerous glasses of champagne later, Alexei was now escorting her to her room.

Her room.

She swallowed hard, her palms suddenly damp. Throughout the evening, Alexei had remained by her side, never farther than an arm's length away. Through her lashes, she looked up at her handsome escort as he led her down the hall toward her room. His mask was still in place, hiding half of his face from her gaze. Only the strong line of his jaw, shadowed by dark stubble, and his mouth were visible. She longed to remove the mask and feast her eyes upon him. Was he as handsome as she thought he'd be?

"Which room is yours?" he asked.

Mute, she pointed to the left door at the very end of the hall.

"Ah, so you have access to the balcony as well?"

"Yes, I believe so."

"It is my great fortune to have the room located next to you."

"Really?" She glanced at the door next to hers, only a few feet away. "That is, indeed," she swallowed, her throat suddenly dry, "fortunate."

He raised her hand to his mouth. "It will be daylight in a few hours, yet I loathe to let you go so soon. Shall we meet on the balcony for a final nightcap?"

She hesitated. Would she be able to resist him in the privacy of her own room? Did she really want to?

"I promise, you can retire alone, if you wish. I have no desire to rush you into anything you aren't ready for."

"I'll meet you on the balcony in five minutes." She spoke before she could change her mind.

He smiled and opened her bedroom door, allowing her to scurry through the opening. Her breath came in pants as he closed the door and she leaned against it, her knees shaking. Through the wood she heard his door open, then close.

Silence.

What was she doing? She raised a trembling hand to her mouth. Alexei was the most gorgeous man she'd ever met. Handsome, cultured, educated, he was everything she'd ever looked for in a partner and she wanted him. They didn't have much time, so what was she waiting for?

She pushed away from the door and stalked into the bathroom, throwing on the light as she tugged her mask off. Other than the flush that colored her cheeks, relieving her usual paleness, she looked the same as she had a few hours earlier. The only noticeable difference was the excited sparkle in her dark eyes that hadn't been there before. The sparkle attained by a woman after she'd received The Kiss.

She made quick use of the facilities, then wasted precious moments contemplating whether or not to keep her panties on. Opting for modesty, she kept them. It wouldn't do to appear too eager.

With a giggle, she grabbed a drawer and opened it, her eyes widening as she caught sight of the array of sex toys contained in the vanity.

Oh my…

She picked up a large purple vibrator and flicked the switch. A soft hum sounded as the vibrator worked, wiggling gently between her fingers. She flicked it up a notch and the vibrations increased. Then she tried the third setting and almost dropped her new-found toy as it ripped into high gear.

Heavens, this thing could hurt someone.

She turned it off and looked into the drawer. Nestled in the array of toys was a small plastic case of rechargeable batteries. She grinned. At least Dirk was environmentally conscious. She put the purple fiend in the drawer and selected a fat pink dildo. Turning on the switch, she blinked as the top half began to rotate in her hand. Goodness, she'd never seen a real penis perform that trick.

A soft knock startled her and she dropped the dildo in the drawer. Still on, it vibrated against the other plastic toys and made a loud racket before she could turn it off. She shoved the drawer shut, her cheeks inflamed. She grabbed her mask and covered her face as she walked to the balcony doors and the shadow that awaited her.

Opening the door, her heart was pounding wildly as she stared at the man about to become her lover. Alexei had discarded his burgundy jacket and was clad in only his white ruffled shirt, tight black pants and knee boots. All he needed was a parrot and a sword and he'd pass for a pirate.

"I couldn't wait five minutes." He gave her a devilish grin and her heart stuttered.

"You're incorrigible."

"You don't even know the half." He handed her a small glass filled with yellowish liquid.

"What's this?" She lifted the glass and sniffed the contents.

"It's an Italian liquor called Strega. It is created from seventy different herbs. The name means witch."

"Is that so?" She took a small sip, pleasantly surprised at the refreshing herbal flavor that treated her palate. "Mmm, it's lovely."

"I'm glad that you like it."

She took another sip and noticed he wasn't drinking. "You aren't having any?"

"Being with you is far more intoxicating than any liquor on earth."

She laughed and stepped onto the balcony. "You flatter me." The air was cool and fresh and she took a deep breath. In the gardens, many of the torches had burned out, leaving the blooms shrouded in night. Only the gazebo was still lit with tiny electric lights.

"Tisn't flattery, merely the truth," he said.

"Uh huh."

She took another sip, enjoying the flavor coating her tongue and warming her stomach. She turned and leaned against the railing. Before she could speak, he reached for her. His fingers tangled in her hair and he started removing her hairpins. "I've been wanting to do this all night," he said. He tossed them over his shoulder to land carelessly on the balcony with faint metallic plinks. She couldn't prevent a groan as his strong fingers dug into her scalp, massaging it as her hair tumbled to her shoulders.

Her eyes closed as he rubbed a particularly sensitive spot that had been jabbed with a pin repeatedly during the evening. "That feels lovely," she moaned.

"It looks even better."

She opened her eyes. The mask shadowed his face, but failed to hide the deep glitter of desire in his eyes. Desire unfurled low in her belly and she clenched her thighs together as she grew damp. "Kiss me," she whispered.

"My pleasure." He removed the glass from her hand and set it to the side before taking her fully into his arms.

His mouth touched hers; his tongue teased her lips until she opened for him. The taste of warm male sent a shiver over her skin as their tongues tangled. Slipping and sliding, she tentatively took over the kiss by nipping his lower lip with her teeth. Growing bolder as a muted groan burst from his throat, she slipped her hands down his sides to reach around and cup his buttocks. Firm and tight, she gave them a gentle squeeze, pressing his erection against the damp apex of her thighs. She shifted, spreading her legs ever so slightly, a sound of pleasure building as he applied pressure to her damp heat.

His fingers released her hair to venture south, dipping into the low back of her dress. She released his mouth with a soft, wet sound.

"I need to touch you." His breathing was ragged.

"Please."

Without a word, he swept her into his arms and carried her into the bedroom. Compared to the moonlight outside, the room was dim and shadowed, a perfect setting for lovers to indulge their senses.

Alexei sat her on the edge of the bed then dropped to his knees. Reaching for her ankle, he placed her foot on his thigh. Nimble fingers unbuckled the tiny straps, allowing her sandals to fall to the floor before moving to her other foot and repeating the process.

Strong hands caressed the back of her calves, tortured by the sexy footwear. She moaned as he massaged his way to the back of her knees, then down again before he rose.

He slipped his hand under her arm and her dress loosened as he released the hidden zipper. Her bodice sagged to reveal her strapless blue lace bra and she heard his breath catch.

Alexei sank to his knees once more, pressing forward between her legs. He placed a kiss between her exposed mounds before taking her dress into his hands. Silent, he urged her hips up to allow him to remove the garment. She leaned back, arching her hips to allow him to slide the dress off her body.

"Christ, woman." His jaw closed with an audible click when he saw the barely-there matching thong. "You're going to kill me.

Hidden beneath her mask, Elaine felt bold as she reached for him. "You'll die a happy man," she murmured.

She tangled her fingers in his hair as he kissed her just above her belly button, curling her toes as his tongue dipped inside. He reached for her hands, twining their fingers as he pushed her back on the bed. Soft kisses trailed heat to her mons where he nuzzled the blue lace and soft curls contained there.

"Alexei?" her voice trembled.

His grip tightened urging her to slide toward him, spreading her thighs to accommodate the width of his shoulders as she bared herself to his touch. He nuzzled the thin material of her panties aside and, with the first swipe of his tongue, sent fire through her blood. As he settled in to suckle her tight bead of sensitive flesh, she bit her lip to prevent herself from crying out at the delicious sensations he was creating. Heat raged through her body as the tension built beneath his mouth.

She made a sound of protest when he stopped and raised his head, their gazes clashing.

"Sing for me," he said. "I want to hear your pleasure."

He lowered his head once more and she dropped back to the bed. As he teased her sensitized flesh, soft moans poured from her lips. Vaguely, she was aware of the animal sounds but paid them no mind. He wanted to hear her, to let him experience what his touch did to her.

He released her left hand, sliding down to tease at her nether lips before inserting one thick finger into her tight channel. She arched her hips as he filled her with a second finger, his tongue never losing its persuasive rhythm.

Tension pooled low in her gut as Alexei stroked her needy flesh, her cries increasing in volume. Her breath caught as her world exploded into spasms of delight against his mouth. Deep and convulsive, stars showered against her closed eyelids as release raged through her body. It seemed to go on and on until, finally, their intensity lessened and she sagged against the bed, her breathing ragged.

She was vaguely aware of Alexei as he rose from the floor. She heard the sound of a drawer sliding then he stalked around the bed. He opened and shut another drawer, muttering under his breath as he did so.

Feeling as if she were drugged with pleasure, she forced her eyes open to see him standing at the foot of the bed, a frustrated expression on his face.

"What's wrong?"

"No condoms."

She gaped at him. "You don't have any in your room?"

"No, I checked earlier."

She blinked, then began to laugh.

"I don't think it's very funny," he growled.

"I don't either." She bit her lip until her merriment was contained before she continued. "I was thinking that I have an entire drawer of sexual hardware in the bathroom and not one condom to be found. Talk about lack of planning." She burst into laughter.

He moved around the bed to stand between her spread thighs. "This lack of planning will kill me."

"So you keep saying."

She sat up and grabbed his pants, her fingers dipping into the waistband mere inches from his thrusting erection. She pulled him down, fully clothed, to cover her, raising her legs to cradle him. He moaned and gave an involuntary thrust, his cock grinding against her sensitized core.

"Not the optimum answer, but it will do in a pinch," she panted.

He caught her mouth in a searing kiss as her fingers captured his hips, guiding him into the perfect rhythm. She twined her legs around his hips, giving herself up to the sensations he aroused in her.

She came again, hard. Fast.

He paused only long enough for her to catch her breath before he started again, his thrusts hard and short. Urgency raced along her skin and, within seconds, she peaked for a third time, her cry thin and high. Her eyes closed as a myriad of sensations poured through her body.

"Can you take more?" His strained voice sounded harsh in her ear.

She blinked, seeing his face, only a shadow, so close to hers. His tone told her he was in agony. She'd been multi-orgasmic for as long as she could remember, she usually outlasted her male partners every time. But she'd never seen a man last as long as Alexei did.

She released her grip on him and snaked her hands between their bodies. The front of his pants were damp from her arousal and she unzipped them, eliciting a strangled groan from him as he angled up, allowing her to free him.

His breath hissed through his teeth as she stroked his impressive erection from root to tip. Silk over steel, she marveled over the size she felt but couldn't see. He thrust against her hands, gentle involuntary movements she knew he couldn't prevent.

She cupped the head, running her fingers along the sensitive underside of his cock, glorying in the mix of ecstasy and pain that sounded in his groans. Was she hurting him? Was he so sensitive she was causing him pain? She repeated her movement and he growled deep in his throat as he thrust against her hands, harder this time.

"Alexei," she whispered. "Do you like this?" She cupped his balls with one hand, her other tracing a ring around his tender tip.

"Yes," he panted.

"Alexei. Come for me."

His breathing grew ragged as her fingers curled around his shaft. A sound of near-pain escaped his mouth and she reluctantly released him. He lowered himself against her lower belly, sealing his steel between them as he began thrusting.

Once...

Twice…

A cry dragged from his soul as he came. Warmth gushed over her skin where their bellies pressed together. Glorying in the sensation of his release, she slid her arms around his shoulders as he sank against her, his breath hot against her neck as he trembled with the force of his release. The scent of warm male and shared sex perfumed the air and she released a lusty sigh. She was replete.

"I'll supply the condoms tomorrow." He pressed a lazy kiss to her neck.

"Mmm, today. It's already tomorrow."

"Okay, today."

"A big box," she prompted.

He gave a half-hearted nip at her throat. "A huge box."

She grinned as a thrill of possession ran through her. Relaxed, she stretched her legs out, stifling a laugh when she realized they hadn't taken time to remove her stockings or her bra.

Next time…

Chapter 4

She was wearing his gift.

Alexei watched Elaine as she chatted with two tall blonde women, twins he suspected, each dressed as lusty barmaids, exposing more skin than was covered by their clothing. Elaine had a glass of champagne in one hand and a huge smile on her face, her green eyes sparkling from behind her burgundy half mask.

The rich wine-colored silk of her full skirt licked the top of her black leather button-up boots. As she turned to wave at Dirk, Alexei caught a glimpse of her white, lace-trimmed petticoats. The black velvet corset made her waist look impossibly tiny while pushing her normally adequate cleavage into bountiful proportions.

He licked his lips as he took her in shoulders, clad in fine white linen. She'd added the shirt under the corset to cover some of her exposed skin, no doubt. He wasn't disappointed. If anything, her modesty only added to her allure. A narrow band of onyx stones encircled her throat and she'd tossed a brightly colored scarf over her arms to cross the middle of her back

With this gift of the clothing, she looked like the beautiful Russian gypsy he remembered. He closed his eyes and entertained an image of Elaine dancing under a full moon, her feet bare, her hair tangled with wildflowers.

Tonight was the night to find out for sure if she was the one, and to do this he had to strip the outfit off her body. He opened his eyes, his gaze fastening on her. It was a tough job, but he was just the man to do it.

* * * * *

Elaine's breath caught in her throat as she saw Alexei make his way toward her. Tight black leather pants clung to every inch of his legs, accentuating his muscles as he moved. A long-sleeved, oversized royal blue shirt fluttered as he moved, the chest open, leaving his rippled stomach in view. Around his slim waist, he'd tied a burgundy silk scarf that matched her skirt. Tucked into that was a jeweled dagger.

He looked dangerous, and he was all hers.

She tightened her thighs as a spurt of warmth sprang to life. Tonight was the night…

"Oh my, I just *have* to sample that one…" With a swish of her tan skirts, Sabrina, one of twins walked toward Alexei, an exaggerated swing to her walk. She shifted her shoulder, allowing her blouse to slide off, revealing pale skin. "Well, hello there."

Alexei gave her an abbreviated nod and stepped around the predatory blonde. Elaine's breath left in a rush as he curled an arm around her waist and hauled her into his arms. His mouth descended and he took her in a kiss that was powerful and earthy at the same time.

She leaned into him, sliding her arms around his shoulders as he insinuated a strong thigh between hers, pressing against the damp apex of her thighs. She squirmed to get closer, anything to appease the ache of need he alone kindled.

"I missed you," he growled.

A laugh bubbled in her throat. "And I, you."

"Come." He glanced around the outdoor party before meeting her gaze. "Let us find someplace quiet."

She nodded and, together, they turned and arm in arm, walked toward the doors and the gardens outside.

"Did you see *that*?" Sabrina said in a mock-stage whisper.

"I most certainly did," her twin Serena said, the laughter evidence in her voice. "You, my dear, were just kicked to the curb."

Elaine's grip tightened on Alexei's waist. He'd claimed her in front of the entire assemblage. She considered herself a liberated, modern woman, but there was something to be said for caveman tactics and she couldn't deny the thrill that possessed her as he kissed her.

The sounds of the party faded as they entered the formal gardens. Tiki torches were positioned at regular intervals along the path, lighting the way through the darkness. The scent of night blooming jasmine and lavender swirled about her head as he led her toward the small gazebo in the center of the garden.

Her heart thudded painfully in her chest as he drew her into the shadowed interior and into his arms. His mouth was soft, warm as he kissed her. His touch tender, worshipful. Gone was the man staking a public claim. Here was Alexei, simply a man.

Her hands stole about his waist as he kissed her, seduced her senses and sent her mind twirling into oblivion. He nibbled her mouth as he removed her shawl to stroke her shoulders through the linen.

He broke the kiss and leaned his forehead against hers. "I want you," he breathed.

"You can have me." She pressed a kiss on his chin, noting that he'd shaved recently.

A shudder ran through him and he kissed the edge of her jaw before leaning down to nibble on her neck. Nimble fingers ran along the edge of her exposed bosom. "You look lovely," he mumbled against her flesh.

"I think it's false advertising."

He gave a startled laugh, then gave her a hug. "There is nothing false about you, my dear."

Oh, I wouldn't be so sure about that…

Elaine pushed the intrusive thought away as she curled her fingers in his shirtfront to pull him into a kiss that was sensual. He was fully aroused, his erection strained against her belly. She was hungry for him, aching and empty. A gush of warm wetness between her thighs had her straining upward so that she could cradle his hardness where she needed him so badly. Her breasts grew taut, her nipples hard, her skin slick with need.

Alexei backed her against one of the gazebo supports, pinning her against the column with his big body. He broke the kiss, his breathing harsh as he leaned into her. Catching her thigh, he lifted her leg, hooking it over his hip. Her breath left her in a rush as he thrust against her mons, sending a rush of heat straight to her toes.

"I can smell your arousal," he breathed.

She moaned as he dipped his fingers into her corset, teasing her nipples with his fingernails. His scent swirled about her head, hot and musky, blending with the perfumes from the garden blooms.

"And I can smell yours." She nipped his jaw.

He growled, thwarted from touching her by her tight-fitting corset. "I need this off."

She gave a throaty chuckle. "That may take a while."

"No, it won't." He withdrew the knife from his waistband.

She tensed, relaxing only when he examined the laces of the corset. "You'll ruin it."

"I'll buy you a dozen more just like it."

Elaine was amazed at the speed with which he handled the knife. Within a few seconds, he'd cut the laces in the back and the corset fell away, her once-mountainous bosom resuming its former position. Already she missed her abundant cleavage.

Stripping the linen aside, he cupped his hands over her breasts as she sighed with delight. He wrapped an arm around her backside and lifted her higher, his mouth hungry on her exposed skin. He sucked at her flesh, her fingers curling in his hair, holding him tightly to her as wave after wave of sensation rocketed through her.

Abruptly, he released her and set her on her feet. She leaned against the column, barely able to stand, her senses in turmoil. She watched with drugged eyes as he tore his pants open and released his turgid staff. In the dimness of the gazebo, she couldn't see him well. He was but a shade among the shadows. But she knew his proportions well as she'd dreamed of him while sleeping. She heard the tear of foil and the soft snap of latex, then he reached for her again, twining her skirt in his fist.

He tore her panties from her unresisting body before he picked her up, resuming their former position. She arched her hips, his fingers moving over her damp flesh until he found her opening, then he sank one finger deep. She moaned, her hips moving against his invasion. She shuddered, her fingers digging into his hair as he stroked, preparing her for his entry. When he could stand no more, he removed his hand and replaced it with the broad head of his erection.

She moaned as he pushed into her, stretching her heated flesh with his. With slow, stroking motions, he entered her, each motion taking him deeper than the last. She moaned, pressing against him, wanting him deeper, yet fearing she wouldn't be able to take him. To her amazement, he sank deep, his breathing harsh in her ear.

His grip tightened on her hips, arching her to take his thrust as he began to move. She was open, vulnerable as he pressed into her. The inexorable rush of desire swept over her, her body straining against his as a low cry built with the tension in her body.

Then a shudder swept her body as her orgasm burst through her. It was so strong that reality faded away and there was only Alexei and herself. On and on she spasmed until she triggered his release as well. Head thrown back, a cry burst from his mouth, his grip punishing on her hips as they traveled to the heavens together.

* * * * *

"We're missing the party."

Alexei watched as his woman took a bite from a slice of fresh peach. A single drop of juice glistened on her lip and he fought the urge to lick the sweetness from her skin. Instead, he propped his head on his hand, comfortable in her spacious bed.

"Are you sorry you're missing it?"

Elaine licked her lips and shook her head. "Not a bit." She selected a ripe strawberry from the bowl of fruit. "Are you?"

"Not in the slightest." He smiled. "I'd much rather be here with you."

A soft blush stole across her cheeks as she chewed. They'd removed their masks hours ago and he couldn't stop staring at her. The golden glow of candles scattered around the room made her skin appear golden. Her hair was unbound, the thick sable locks below her shoulders in waves of silk. Her deep green eyes were dark and surrounded by thick lashes. Her mouth was full, her lower lip soft from his kisses.

She wore a silk robe while he remained bare to her gaze. He'd been sorry she'd elected to don the garment but he didn't want to push her. Soon enough, she'd feel comfortable to remain nude with him and he was a patient man.

"You're staring again," she said.

"I can't help it, you're beautiful."

She dipped another berry into a bowl of whipped cream. "No, I'm not." She licked the white blob with tiny cat-like motions.

His groin tightened as he thought about her licking him the same way. "Why do women always say that?"

She dipped her berry in the cream once more. "I don't know why other woman say it." She shrugged. "I am what I am. I can't take responsibility for genetics."

"Is your mother beautiful?"

"Was. She was very beautiful." Elaine licked the berry clean before taking a small bite. "She was a singer and she met my father on Broadway. Oh, the scandal of it all..." Her eyes gleamed with amusement

"Do tell." He wanted to know everything about her. Her past, her lovers, her family, her dreams as a child, her favorite color and what delights her future held.

"My mother was Rachel White and her stage name was Rachel Martin. She was a chorus girl in New York in the late fifties. She worked hard and was finally awarded a part in *Fiddler on the Roof.* It was during this stage production that she met my father." She tossed the stem on the tray, her nose crinkling in his direction. "Are you sure I won't bore you with this?"

He shook his head. "Please, continue."

"My father was the heir to a bread fortune or a fortune in bread, depending upon how you want to look at it. You've heard of Downing Mills?"

He hadn't, but he nodded in agreement anyway.

"He was born with the proverbial silver spoon in his mouth. He and some college friends escaped from their dorm rooms and came into the city. He took one look at Rachel and that was it. He fell madly in love and set out to possess her." She selected another berry. "He sent her flowers, gifts, came to see her every weekend and they called each other every other day. They were married eight months after meeting."

"Were they happy?"

She turned the fruit over in her hands, her expression thoughtful. "What's happy? They had one child—me. They lived a life of wealth and privilege, but my mother never forgot where she came from. My father's family looked down on her for being an actress and I think that bothered her a lot." She shrugged. "She loved my father and she loved me. But I always had the impression she felt she was missing something in her life. Maybe she should have continued with her acting? She talked about doing some small roles, but never got the chance. She was killed when I was thirteen."

He brushed his fingers over her knee. "I'm sorry."

She tossed the berry onto the tray untouched. "It seems like a lifetime ago."

"Doesn't lessen the pain any. What happened to your father?"

"He remarried and has a new family. Three girls and a boy."

He stroked the tender skin of her inner knee as he spoke. "Do you see them?"

"Several times a year. Father moved them to California, said he couldn't stay in New York any longer. There were too many memories on every corner."

"What happened to little Elaine?"

The smile she gave him threatened to curl his toes. "Little Elaine grew up to become devastatingly beautiful." She rose to her knees and moved closer. "She became a legend with scads of handsome lovers..." She rolled him onto his back and slipped her leg over his, seating herself across his thighs. "All of whom she cast—" She dipped her head and pressed kisses to his chest as she spoke "—aside, one by one."

He chuckled and laid his hands over her knees. "Is that so?"

She raised her head and gave him a devilish grin. "Mmm, until now, at least."

"That's reassuring." He stretched to give her better access as she nibbled her way south. His breath caught as her hair brushed his groin.

There was something almost painfully erotic about watching a woman pleasure her man. His eyes narrowed as she nipped the sensitive area just below his belly button. Her fingers curled around his cock and his eyes almost crossed with the power of lust. He murmured his acceptance and his eyes slid closed, giving himself over to her magic touch.

Her tongue rimmed his sensitive head and he fought the urge to lunge for her when she stroked a particularly sensitive spot. Sensation curled in his stomach as she licked his cock, her touch soft yet assured.

She paused, then something cool touched him and his eyes flew open.

Elaine held the bowl of whipped cream and was liberally coating the head of his cock with the mixture. Once covered, she put the bowl back. After licking her fingers clean, she picked up the bowl of chocolate syrup. Dipping her fingers, she then drizzled the liquid over the tower of white, laughing as his cock twitched, threatening to topple its white covering.

"Are you quite through?" he asked, amused in spite of himself.

"Not yet." She licked her fingers clean again and reached for the bowl of fruit, extracting a cherry. She placed it on top where it wobbled precariously. "Now I'm done." She shot him a heated smile. "I guess dessert is on you this time around." She lowered her head.

"Take your robe off," he said.

Her brow rose, her gaze heated as she tugged the silk tie and the material slid open to reveal her body. Her breasts were firm and high, her skin creamy pale and the small raspberry-colored heart-shaped birthmark stood in relief against her pale skin.

His throat tightened. She had the birthmark. She was The One.

Her hips were slim, her legs long and strong as she tossed the robe out of her way. A soft thatch of dark hair covered her feminine mound, mere inches from his cream-coated cock.

She leaned forward to nibble the warming cream and he suppressed a groan as her lips brushed the sensitive underside of his head and she lapped at the melting cream and chocolate.

"Mmm," she purred. "Delicious. I could eat this all night long."

He groaned. There was no way he'd last all night, not at this rate. She licked him clean, taking small cat-like laps as she cleaned him from root to head before taking him fully into her mouth. He was so big that she couldn't take much, but she made good use of her hand and, within minutes, he was straining beneath her.

"Elaine, I'm going to explode," he rasped.

She made quick work of a condom before rising over him, her slender fingers guiding him to her damp entrance. He dug his heels into the bed as she rubbed the broad head of his cock against her slick opening. Her eyes closed, her expression rapturous as she rocked her hips. Positioning him, she sank, his fists clenching as she clasped him in her honeyed heat.

He slid his hands to her waist as she moved slowly, languorously. Bracing her hands against his chest, she rode him to completion. Her orgasm triggering his, their cries mingling as he came in slow spurts, from deep inside his gut.

He managed to open his eyes as she sank to his chest with a sigh. Wrapping his arms around her, he rubbed her spine in a long slow sweep, complete for the first time in half a century.

Chapter 5

Silently cursing, Alexei reluctantly slipped from her bed. The sky outside her window ripened with the coming morning and he had to remove himself to his lair within minutes or face the painful consequences.

Nude, he gathered his scattered clothing, tossing it carelessly over his arm as he moved about the room. His fingertips brushed the stiff velvet corset and he picked it up. Her scent rose from the fabric as a stab of desire shot to his loins. His fist knotted around the hard plastic stays. He raised the corset to his nose, inhaling her perfume, the scent of her skin. A soft shudder ran through him and his arm dropped as if his muscles were suddenly unable to support even the slight weight of the garment.

He'd always been weak where she was concerned. With each incarnation, his desire for her grew and each time he lost her, he'd been devastated. No matter how hard he'd tried, he'd never succeeded in saving her life. With each loss, he'd lost another piece of himself until he often wondered if anything remained of the human he'd once been.

He dropped the corset on the back of a chair and looked at his lover. Elaine lay on her stomach, the covers twisted about her long legs, her back exposed. Her hair was tangled from his fingers as they'd made love, her lips swollen from his kisses. Rosy with life, her skin glowed with contentment.

His lips tightened. She was his, for now and forever and, this time, he was determined to never lose her.

* * * * *

The low throbbing in her head took her from sleep to full wakefulness in seconds. Elaine opened her eyes, her heart constricting at the dimness in the room. A cry locked in her throat as she sat up in her nest of silken sheets and her hand moved to her forehead where the grinding pain was centered.

"No..."

Her knees collapsed as she tried to get to her feet and she slid to a heap on the floor by the bed. Her hands shook uncontrollably as tears of desperation filled her eyes.

Not now, not yet.

Threatened tears spilled over and she covered her eyes with her fists, trying to stop the tide. Alexei's scent swirled about her, filling her with a sense of yearning so powerful that she nearly crumpled beneath the onslaught. For a split second, she failed to breathe, her heart thudding so hard she thought it might explode from her chest. What she wouldn't give to have his arms around her for five more minutes more. A bitter laugh escaped her. Who was she kidding? Five years in his arms would never be enough.

He must never know...

She sank into the carpeting as helpless sobs ripped through her. She barely knew him, but she had the strange sense that they'd known each other forever. Never had she met a man whom she'd felt immediately comfortable with, whom she'd felt she could tell almost anything and he wouldn't bat an eye. Alexei seemed to understand her better than she did herself. What a cruel twist of fate it was to meet The One just as her life was ebbing.

She stifled her sobs with her hands, crying until she could cry no more. Her throat ached and her headache had intensified though it wasn't unbearable for her to reach for the pain pills she carried with her everywhere.

Not yet.

Dr. Peach had told her this would probably be the way she'd die. The tumor that was slowly destroying her brain would take first her sight, her consciousness, and her life in short order. There was nothing she could do, the tumor was inoperable and, this time, it would kill her.

The last time she'd dealt with this demon was almost four years ago. After a long and painful round of radiation, chemotherapy then finally surgery, Dr. Peach had declared her cancer free. But she hadn't made it to that magical, five-year mark, had she?

So close and yet so far.

She bit her lip, hard. She'd come to Dirk's house to have one last fling with a handsome man. At the time of her diagnosis three months earlier, she hadn't been dating anyone and, after the diagnosis, she hadn't felt it fair to become involved with a man knowing he'd only lose her. No one knew how long she had left to live.

This time it really was it.

She rubbed her eye with the heel of her left hand. She couldn't complain... Well, she could, but who'd listen? With the first diagnosis, her chances had been less than fifty-fifty and she'd defied the odds and survived four years. It had been a wonderful... no, make that magical four years and she'd relished every moment of it.

She'd been lucky to have the financial resources to live as she wished thanks to a trust from her paternal grandmother. She'd traveled, seen almost everything she'd wanted to see, spent time with friends, volunteered for various charities, and now she was writing the final chapter to a wonderful life.

What would you give for one more day?

Anything, anything at all.

She sniffed, tears threatening again at the thought of Alexei. No, it was better that she left now, before he knew she was ill. For a while he'd wonder what happened to her, why she'd left without a word, but this was for the best. She never wanted him to know she was sick. She wanted him to remember her as she'd been last night, hale and hearty, laughing in his arms.

She braced her hands against the carpet and pushed upright. Keeping her eyes closed, she leaned back against the bed, needing a moment of darkness to steady herself. As long as she kept her eyes closed, she could fool herself into being normal for a few seconds longer. Whenever she'd closed her eyes, it was always dark, right? But it was when she opened them that her world was forever altered…

She blinked, her heart in her throat.

The room was lighter.

She blinked again, barely daring to believe her eyes. Outside the window, a gray rain was falling and the sun was struggling to break through the dissipating clouds. Stunned, she struggled to her knees and crawled across the ocean of carpeting in pursuit of the faded patch of sunlight streaming through the windows. She was barely aware of the faint whimpers escaping her throat as she reached the door, her palms pressed against the cool glass as the sunlight, stronger now, cascaded over her.

Tears dampened her cheeks as her vision wavered. She blinked away the wetness and the scene sharpened. The rain slowed to a fine mist and the sun broke through the clouds, illuminating the gardens outside her windows.

Her gaze darted madly, flitting from the brilliant roses to the tangled mass of spiky columbines. The fat cherub in the center fountain continued pouring water from a big vase, a silly grin on its face. Rows of brilliant green hedges glistened with rain in the strengthening light as a feeling of joy clutched her heart.

I'm not going blind. It was the rain, only the rain.

Laughter bubbled and she tilted her head back. Tears streamed down her face and the sun was warm on her face as she gave silent thanks for another day.

* * * * *

He couldn't take his eyes off her.

Alexei glanced over his shoulder in time to see Elaine duck under an overhanging branch, her seat sure and steady in the saddle. Her horse, a soft gray mare, walked easily behind his as they rode into the dark Colorado night. The air was cool but her thick sweater should keep her warm enough.

He looked forward. Until he could warm her, that is.

When he'd arrived at her room, mere moments after sunset, she'd thrown herself into his arms as if she'd feared never seeing him again. He was pleased by her reaction. It reminded him of the woman she'd been before. Always open and loving, this incarnation of his love was far more guarded than she'd been in any other lifetime.

Then again, she was older than she'd ever been as well. He pondered that for a second. In this lifetime, she'd lived to be older than in any other lifetime. Maybe, on some cosmic level, she'd been waiting for him as well?

He liked that idea a lot. Soon, it would be time to tell her about their lives together. For now, he still had work to do. The more attached she became to him the smoother the transition would be when it came time to enlighten her.

Or so he hoped.

He pushed the thought away. He would succeed; the universe couldn't be so cruel as to take her away from him again. This evening he wasn't going to worry, for he was about to show her the eighth wonder of the world and he couldn't wait to see her reaction.

The trail grew steadily rockier, but the horses handled the path with ease. No doubt they'd followed the trail to the grotto on many occasions.

A few minutes later, a rocky outcropping surrounded by trees came into view. He pointed his horse to a sheltered area between some tall trees before speaking. "We'll dismount here." He reined in his horse and dismounted before turning to assist her. Born to the saddle, he'd ridden since he was three years old.

"Are we still on Dirk's property?" she asked.

"Yes." He slid his hands around her waist and guided her to the ground. "We've barely scratched the surface of his holdings. However, our destination is just ahead."

She tipped her head back, her expression teasing in the moonglow. "So secretive."

"Just wait and see what I have in store for you." He wiggled his brows in a mock-lecherous look.

She blinked, then her eyes narrowed. "That street goes both ways, my friend."

"I'm counting on it."

He retrieved a backpack and pulled stakes from a side flap. Pounding them into the ground, he staked the horses so they had room to graze. When done, he slid the pack on his back, adjusting it until it was comfortable. "Come." He held his hand out toward her.

She laced her fingers through his and he led her into the woods.

"It's dark, how can you see?" she asked, stumbling over a branch.

"Follow my steps and you'll be fine. I've been here many times and I know the way by heart. Don't worry, I won't lead you astray."

She gave a throaty laugh. "That's too bad as it's exactly what I was hoping for."

He gave her hand a squeeze as they neared the rocky outcropping that sheltered their destination. Sliding around a cluster of bushes, Alexei led her into the darkness of a narrow crevasse in the rock.

"Where are we going?" There was tension in her voice.

"Patience, it's well worth the journey." He gave her hand a reassuring squeeze.

They traveled twenty feet, twisting and contorting around knobs of rock in the tight passage. He led her around a narrow corner and the trail opened into wonderland. He stepped to the side allowing Elaine to follow. He heard her intake of breath as she stepped into the light.

They stood on a small ledge overlooking a large hot spring. The ochre red walls glowed in the flickering light from dozens of torches illuminating a spring ten feet below. Large flat rocks hung suspended over the water, forming a series of ledges and steps enabling people to move about the pool. Heat radiated from the spring as steam drifted upward in lazy tendrils. Overhead, the sky was laid out like black velvet strewn with millions of diamonds. The ochre rock walls soared twenty-five feet over the base like an oddly rounded coffee cup contained the heat from the spring.

"I've never seen anything like it," she said.

Alexei smiled, pleased with her response. "I've been to almost every country in the world and I, too, have never see anything like it." He looked at her awed face. "Come, let us partake of its delights."

He led her down a winding path of stones that led to the floor. Elaine scampered to the edge of the pool and dropped into a crouch to dip her fingers in the water, a look of extreme pleasure on her face. "This is amazing. How deep is it?"

"Thirty, forty feet or so." He slid the pack off his back as he walked to a large, flat rock. Through the soles of his boots, the warmth radiated to the bottoms of his feet. "It is amazing and the best part is that we're all alone."

She rose and sauntered to him as he set the pack down. "How fortuitous." Her fingers wrapped around the bottom of her sweater and she pulled it up slowly, torturing him as she exposed each delectable inch before finally pulling it over her head. Beneath the bulky wool, she wore a scanty emerald green bra that barely covered her breasts. "It's getting warm, don't you think?" She asked, her expression mock-innocent.

"Yes." He licked his lips. "It's getting warmer every minute." He sat, making himself comfortable, eager to see what she would do next.

She spread out the sweater on a heated rock before continuing her journey toward him. Her deft fingers undid the button on her jeans, then unzipped them. She stopped before him then raised one foot, placing it square between his legs, inches from his arousal.

"Can you help with my boots?"

He smothered a smile as he tugged the laces with one hand while the other slid as far up her pant leg as possible to touch the softness of her skin. Her eyes narrowed as he removed one boot, then her sock, stopping long enough to give her instep a slow rub with one finger.

A smile curved her mouth as she lowered one foot and raised the other. He repeated the process, this time lingering over the fine bone of her ankle. He smiled as she shivered and pulled her foot away, careful to move away a safe distance before shimmying out of her pants. Her panties matched the bra, and they were ridiculously skimpy. He licked his lips as he devoured her with his eyes.

"Like what you see?"

He looked at her face. "What do you think?"

She approached and dropped her gaze to his crotch. He felt his cock leap under the heat of her gaze. "I think you're enjoying yourself, or at least *he* is."

He reached for her, pulling her into the vee made by his legs, then pressed a noisy kiss to her stomach. "What am I going to do with you?" he mumbled against her sweet skin.

She laced her fingers through his hair and tugged his head back, her gaze dark, slumberous. "Everything, I hope." Dropping her head, she caught him in a kiss that was sizzling and loaded with promise. Her tongue tangled with his as her taste exploded through his nervous system, setting his senses on high alert.

She released him and moved away, and he had to restrain himself from reaching for her again. He wanted more, much more, but they had time for that. All the time in the world.

Her gaze never wavering, she reached up to release her sable hair to fall in thick, soft waves on her shoulders. She ran her fingers through the silk and he caught the scent of herbs and knew it was her he smelled.

"Come join me?" she asked.

"In a minute." He wanted time to gather himself before joining her in the pool. In his current state, he'd be on her in a minute and he didn't want that. He wanted it to last and last.

She nodded and turned away, presenting him with a nicely rounded backside framed by her thong panties. He swallowed hard as she walked, an unselfconsciously sexy sway in her gait. She approached the edge and, without a pause, dove into the water with very little splash.

He released the breath he'd been holding. She was lethal and he adored every inch of her. He rose and made quick work of emptying the pack. He laid out a blanket and a bottle of wine swaddled in a thick layer of insulated material. Next was an assortment of cheeses and meat with crisp crackers. A snack for her later as he knew he wouldn't need one.

All he needed was her.

She was splashing around the pool as he pulled off his clothing, laying out his garments as she had on the heated rocks. Stepping to the ledge, his gaze locked with hers before he dove into the water to claim her.

Chapter 6

Despite the heated water, Elaine shivered as she watched his nude body cut through the pool. Already she could feel her nether regions filling with desire, her breasts aching and there was a strange tightness in her chest that threatened to steal her breath.

Alexei came to the surface without a sound. His head rose from the water, inches from her. They'd removed their masks last night and yet, each time she saw him, she was astounded by his masculine beauty all over again.

Wet black hair was slicked back on his head and streamed over his broad shoulders. His dark chocolate brown eyes were flecked with gold and framed with sooty lashes. His nose was straight and smooth, his nostrils flaring slightly as he filled his lungs with air depleted from his underwater journey. His skin was olive-toned, unusual for a Russian unless he had Romany in his background.

Her gaze drifted over the exposed expanse of his chest. Yes, she could certainly see him as a gypsy. Under the lightly furred skin, his chest muscles were sharply defined. His mouth was firm and set in a straight line as he regarded her with a serious expression, his chin jutting out.

"Give me a kiss," he demanded.

He wanted to be in charge, did he? She hid a grin. "Okay, I'll give you a kiss, but first you have to close your eyes."

"Why?"

"Because I said so."

His eyes narrowed as he considered her words.

"I'll make it worth your while…" she teased.

His eyes widened, the spark of desire deep in their chocolate depths. He closed them, a faint smile of anticipation smile curving his handsome mouth.

Elaine moved closer to her lover. Raising her hand, she dripped water on his shoulder yet didn't touch him, her eyes greedily taking their fill of Alexei. She moved behind him and placed her hand on his shoulder, guiding him down until the ends of his hair floated on the surface of the water.

On the top of his left shoulder, she saw a small hook-shaped scar. She pressed her lips to the old wound and caught the shudder that ran through his big body. A sense of power invaded her at the thought of bringing this man to his knees.

She leaned in to whisper, her lips brushing his ear. "Regardless of what I'm about to do to you, you cannot touch me, do you understand?"

He opened his mouth as if to object and she silenced him by nipping on his lobe. His breath sounded loud as he sucked in air, her movement taking him by surprise. He nodded.

"Good."

She took his hand and led him to the edge of the pool nearest a small waterfall. A cool mist filled the air from the falling water, a sharp contrast to the heat of the water below. She settled him on a low rock, the water rising to just below his nipples.

"Close your eyes," she whispered.

After he obeyed, she moved behind, trailing her fingers over the expanse of his shoulders. The heat radiating off him was astounding. Never had she met a man who was so consistently hot. With trembling fingers, she removed her bra and tossed it to the side.

Elaine curled her arms around his shoulders, pressing her erect nipples into his back. Relaxing her knees, she sank, her breasts never losing contact with his back. He groaned as she rose, repeating the motion in reverse.

She looked over his shoulder and into the clear water. His hands were clenched on his thighs and from the thick thatch of hair stood his cock.

Alexei is ready to come out and play.

Dropping a kiss on his shoulder, she moved to stand in front of him. His eyes flickered open, his pupils dilated with lust. She spread her thighs and sat in his lap, his cock tight against her silk-covered crotch. His hands came to rest on her legs, his thumbs digging into her sensitive flesh. Sliding her fingers around his wrists, she pulled his hands away and curled his fingers around his staff. At his perplexed look, she brushed her lips over his.

"I want to watch," she whispered.

He cleared his throat. "You want me…to pleasure myself?"

She licked her lips and nodded, her throat suddenly dry.

A devilish smile curved his mouth. "Your wish is my command."

Alexei released his turgid flesh and snaked his arms around her waist. Rising, she shrieked as he carried her to a rocky ledge and set her down. Her nipple grazed his chin and he couldn't resist taking it into his mouth. She moaned as he suckled her flesh, her thighs tightening on his waist. He released one and moved to her other, lavishing it with the same attention.

"This isn't what I had in mind," she panted.

He licked the water from her skin between her breasts. "You told me to pleasure myself and I am." He ran his tongue along the fold below her breast and she arched against his mouth.

Trailing kisses down her stomach, he wrapped his fingers in the narrow elastic band of her panties. Urging her hips up, he stripped off the material to feast his eyes on the mound of soft dark hair between her thighs. He dipped his head to tease her belly button before blazing a path of kisses farther south.

As he sank, her thighs opened to reveal her moist entrance. He draped her thighs over his shoulders as he parted her lips and supped on her hot, pink flesh. Closing his eyes, he lost himself in the heat and scent of her arousal as he stroked, teased, and cajoled her into release.

He lost count of her cries of completion when he finally rose. His blood ran thick in his veins, his cock hard and straining for release. Elaine lay on her back, eyes closed. If he didn't know better, he'd think she was asleep.

As his fingers closed around her wrist, her eyes opened. He stepped close and pulled her upright into his arms. Without asking, her legs twined around his waist and he picked her up to carry her to the rock where it had all began.

He groaned as she sank onto his cock, her aroused tissues surrounding him like a glove. Rooted to the hilt, he stared deep into her emerald eyes.

"Do you believe in love at first sight?" His voice was low, husky.

Her eyes widened and he was caught by the pain in their depths. She looked away, her neat white teeth digging into her lower lip.

"Elaine—"

She rolled her hips, breaking off his words. She turned to gaze deep into his eyes. "I believe in this." She rolled her hips again. "I believe in this as well." Her fingers curled in his damp hair as she pulled him into a kiss that was sensual, earthy.

His arms slid beneath the water and around her waist. Their joined movements were slow, sensual.

"I think," she panted. "At this moment, we have more than most people ever have in their entire lives. That's what I believe in."

I love you.

In his mind, he said the words over and over as they moved together. Each moment a shining drop of brilliance in his mind as they teased each other into completion. Their cries mingled with the mist from the pool to swirl into the heavens above.

* * * * *

"What did Dirk say when he found out about the altered wine?" Alexei drew his fingertip in a lazy trail down her arm, marveling in the silken feel of her. They lay on the warm rocks, long limbs entwined. The torches burned low and the heat from the rocks kept them comfortable in each other's arms.

She gave a soft laugh. "He said he'd rather we cut his heart out than tamper with his wine."

Alexei grinned, reveling in the changes wrought by their time in the pool. Soft and warm, Elaine lay beside him unconcerned about her nudity. The shifting moonlight painted her skin silver and, with her tangled dark hair, she resembled a temptress of old. His beautiful gypsy.

"I want to paint you," he said.

She blinked, a soft flush moving across her cheeks. "Me?"

"Yes, you. Do you not know how beautiful you are?"

She shrugged. "I am what I am."

"So modest." He lifted her hand and raised it to his lips. "Will you sit for me?"

She hesitated.

"Please?" He kissed her palm.

"Someday."

He nodded. "Fair enough. Now I have another question for you." He slid his fingers around her slim wrist, marveling in the delicacy of the bones beneath her skin.

"I might have an answer for you." She purred as he pressed a kiss to the inside of her wrist, her pulse fluttered beneath his mouth.

"What do you think of vampires?"

"Do you mean theatrical vampires or literature vampires?"

"Neither. I mean the real thing."

"Vampires don't exist."

"Says who?"

She shook her head. "It's physiologically impossible to survive on blood alone. It can't be done."

"If you're human, it can't be done. But what if a human was changed on a molecular level? Their metabolism is frozen in time with their digestive system. All they need is a dose of fresh blood, say once a week, to keep their other systems functioning normally."

"I think you should become a writer as you have quite an imagination." Her tone was dry.

"I'm serious here."

"So am I."

"Would it be so bad, being a vampire?"

Her eyes narrowed, her hand tensing beneath his. "Do you believe you're a vampire?"

He saw the doubt in her eyes. She wasn't ready for the truth yet and, if he uttered the one word that would set him free, he would lose her.

"I'm open to the possibility of vampires is all I'm trying to say," he said. "There is a lot in this world that we can't even begin to explain."

"You're right about that." The suspicion faded from her eyes.

He pressed another kiss to her wrist and she sighed. "Do you believe in destiny?" he asked.

"Hmm, destiny as in people being destined to be something or a predetermined course of events?"

"Yes, to both."

"Well, I guess so. But I also believe that people can alter their own destiny by their actions, or non-action."

He nodded and twined his fingers through hers, his gaze lifting to meet hers. "What about reincarnation?"

She frowned, small wrinkles distorted her brow and he wanted to kiss them away. "I like the idea of it. I mean, we live our mortal lives and, when we die, we can do it all over again. That next time around, hopefully, we don't make the same mistakes though."

"Can you imagine us doing this over and over again?"

"I think we already did." She wiggled her brows.

"That's not quite what I meant," he chuckled.

Her expression turned surprised, then thoughtful. "Do you think we've been here before?"

"Can't you feel it?' He untwined their fingers to lay her hand over his heart, his hand covering hers. With his free hand, he covered her heart, the beat familiar against his palm. "Your heart knows mine as well as mine knows yours."

She covered his hand with her free one and her eyes widened. "Oh my," she breathed. "They beat in rhythm. How is that possible?"

"We've been here before. On a physical level, you don't remember, but your heart does, as does your soul."

Her expression was doubtful. "Do you really think we've been here before?"

"I have no doubt in my mind that we have been here many times before."

For a few seconds she was silent and he could almost hear the wheels turning in her head. "Do you think…?" Her expression turned sad. "Did we ever get it right?"

He pressed a kiss to her palm. "I think we got it right every time. How could this be wrong?" He watched her eyes fill with tears. Alarmed, he pulled her into his arms. "Why are you crying?"

"If only it were true," she sniffed. "It's a beautiful thought."

He hugged her. "Who said it wasn't true?"

"Imagine an eternity of this." She slid her arms around him and squeezed.

He smiled into her hair. He didn't have to imagine it, he'd lived brief episodes of it several times, but she didn't remember. He felt a pierce of sadness that she didn't remember all the times they'd had together. When the time was right, he would tell her what she didn't remember. But first, he needed to retrieve something.

"The party is over tomorrow," he said.

Silent, she nodded, her tightening grip telling him exactly what he needed to know.

"I need to leave here and get something for you, something I forgot."

She pulled away, puzzlement written across her features. "How could you forget something for me when you didn't even know me?"

"Let's just say that I knew I would meet you here." He smoothed away the frown from her forehead with a fingertip. "Will you wait for me? I'll be but a day, two at the most."

"You want me to wait here?"

He nodded.

"What if you don't return?"

"I'll return for you."

"Yeah, you say that now, but what if you don't? How long do you expect me to wait?"

"I promise you this, I will return for you. It will be two days at the most."

Her gaze searched his face as if she could find evidence of his promise stamped there. Finally, she nodded and he tugged her back into his embrace, tucking her head beneath his chin.

Soon she would learn that not even time could keep them apart.

Chapter 7

He was gone, both from her dreams and her bed.

Elaine lay still in her bed, the faint throbbing in her head causing a twisting pain in her stomach.

No, not now…

She raised her hand to massage the base of her skull, her mind willing her body to relax and release the pain. She rolled to her side, groaning as her thighs, overworked from a night of lovemaking, protested the movement. Her eyes flew open to have the liquid sunshine sear the backs of her eyes.

That's exactly what it was… lovemaking.

Everything she didn't want to happen had occurred in the past forty-eight hours. Their relationship had progressed to the next level, no, beyond that, beyond lust and into happily ever after.

Except there would be no such thing for her.

She stretched out her arm, her fingers rubbing the indentation in the pillow where Alexei had laid his head. Even her dream lover had abandoned her. A constant companion, he'd failed to make an appearance since Alexei had entered her life. She missed him. She didn't realize how much she'd depended upon his nocturnal presence in her life. He'd been with her every night, no matter how complex her life had become and, now, he was gone too.

Unutterably sad, she closed her eyes, her fingers continuing the slow massage on her neck. Here, four days from her forty-second birthday, she'd met the real, flesh and blood man of her dreams only to realize that she would lose him.

Her disease was progressing. For the past few weeks, she'd awakened with the headache that marked the passage of time for her. It wasn't a simple hangover nor due to a lack of sleep, it was her cancer coming back to claim her for the last time.

Elaine opened her eyes, fixing her gaze on the sun-drenched outdoors. Had she ever seen anything more glorious than a golden Colorado morning? The sky was a brilliant blue without a cloud to be seen and the flowers in the garden were blooming profusely thanks to the recent rains. Only the sight of love reflected in Alexei's eyes could stir her more than the Colorado landscape.

Alexei.

Her heart gave a painful twist at the thought of her absent lover. It was entirely possible that she would never see him again, never touch him, never be touched by him.

But you have been touched by him, and with that you have to be content.

She sat up. Why? Why did she have to be content with only a small slice when she could have had the entire pie?

Because that's all you can have…

Her shoulders slumped. A few days weren't nearly enough, nor were a few years. With the way she was feeling now, eternity wouldn't satisfy her.

But you don't have eternity, do you?

If only Alexei were right and they had an eternity together. If she knew that in her next life she'd have a chance at the same type of ecstasy she'd known in the past few days, she would face her death with greater bravery knowing that somewhere in the future, he awaited her.

What a beautiful dream that was.

But reality was that she was dying, slowly, day by day as her life slipped through her fingers. She only had today, that she knew. For her, the future was no more than five minutes ahead. More than that, she couldn't count on.

* * * * *

Clouds obscured the sun as Elaine stood with Dirk on the deck, a glass of chardonnay in her hand.

"It's beautiful here." She sipped from the drink.

"It is, but I never appreciated it when I was younger. I saw only the ostentation of the place, never the beauty and the quiet it offered."

"Youth is wasted on the young." She shook her head. "We spend our childhood racing to grow up. We spend our twenties trying to make our mark in the world, our thirties looking for the perfect mate only to find that no one is perfect and it's all a matter of what we can put up with."

He laughed. "You're right. But what happens when we hit our forties?"

"I don't know, Dirk." She looked up at him, his face as familiar to her as her own. "You'll have to figure that out for me." She longed to take back the words as she watched his smile fade. She wished she could've made some glib remark and let the moment pass, but she could never do that with Dirk, he always saw through her.

He set his glass down and pulled her into his arms. "I can't imagine my life without you, little sister."

She rubbed her forehead against the soft cashmere of his sweater. "And I, you."

His grip tightened. "All the money in the world and I can't help you."

She closed her eyes and inhaled the scent of her best friend, a mixture of sandalwood, tobacco and memories. Tears stung her eyes at the thought of leaving him behind. They'd been friends for more years than she cared to count. Every major event in her life, Dirk had been by her side and she by his.

"I need a favor from you," she sniffed.

He dropped a kiss on her head. "You only have to ask."

"When the time comes..." He stiffened in her arms. "I want to know that I can depend on you to take care of the arrangements. I've outlined what I want for the funeral and the internment. The documents are in my New York apartment safe and my lawyer has a copy as well."

"Shall I hire a brass band?" His voice was raw and his chest shuddered beneath her cheek. She knew he was crying.

"Nope," she sniffed. "Keep it simple, you know what to do and who to invite."

She felt him nod.

"Don't forget to call Jeff."

Dirk gave a broken laugh at the mention of their drag-queen friend. "Okay."

"He can come only if he promises not to wear a red boa and I don't want anyone throwing themselves on the casket, either."

"Now there's an image." Dirk gave her another squeeze before releasing her. She looked up at his dear face, streaked with tears, his expression uncharacteristically serious. "What am I going to do without you, Laine?"

She smiled as her vision wavered and her eyes filled with more tears. "You're going to marry Veronique and be blissfully happy. Then, in a few years, you'll start squeezing out some pups, buy a mini-van, run a soccer camp and retire to the country in domesticated bliss."

A look of abject horror crossed his face and she laughed.

"You're an evil woman," he said.

"Yes, I am. I will be watching you, every step of the way and I'll be taking notes. When you die… " She turned away and pointed to a fat cloud on the horizon. "I'll meet you there and we'll share a bottle of celestial wine and compare notes."

"That sounds like a plan to me." He laced an arm around her waist.

"Can I ask you a question?"

"Sure."

"Tell me, do you believe in destiny?"

* * * * *

Elaine slipped into the cool silence of the gallery, grateful for the only oasis of stillness in the house. The partygoers were leaving and the constant stream of cars, luggage, and people saying goodbye to their host was giving her a vicious headache. She shut the glass doors behind her, entombing herself in silence.

All day long she'd been plagued with the ache in her head. Not enough to completely disable her, but enough to remind her that time was running out. As if she needed to be reminded of that.

She pushed that thought away. Some people lived day by day. She'd learned to live hour by hour.

She drifted past the masterpieces by Monet, Picasso, and Dega. Committing each one to memory before moving to the next, every one was a treat to the senses. The silence soothed her aching head as well as her soul.

At the far end of the long room, she found the new painting Dirk had mentioned. Sealed behind glass, she had to step closer to get a good look. Not much larger than a sheet of writing paper, the images were dark and erotic in tone. The subjects, a man and a woman, clasped in a torrid embrace. The man was shown only from the back, his hair long and dark as he bent over his companion to feast on her exposed breast. She blinked as she took in the woman's face, her ecstasy painted for the world to see.

My, it looks like me!

Startled, she stepped back, her hand going to her throat. Well, it really wasn't her but there certainly was a strong resemblance. The hair was lighter in color and much longer than she normally wore hers. But the heart-shaped face and the small birthmark on her breast were exactly the same. She gently rubbed the matching spot on her own breast, aware of a faint tingling sensation just under her skin. Was it possible that an ancestor had posed for the portrait?

Do you believe in destiny?

As if he were standing next to her, Alexei's voice echoed in her mind. She wrapped her arms across her chest as a shiver ran down her spine. Had he known about this painting? Was that where he'd hatched the idea that they'd known each other in another life?

Beneath the painting was a discreet brass plate proclaiming the title and painter's name. She was dismayed to find that it contained only initials, *Redemption by A. R.*

Alexei?

She stepped back to study the painting. Judging from the clothing, the portrait was painted around the turn of the century, give or take twenty years. The woman's burgundy skirt was long, ankle length and with the man's thigh insinuated between hers, the hem had crept up to reveal her white stockings and button-down shoes. Her eyes were half closed, her lips parted in ecstasy as she enjoyed her lover's attentions.

Not unlike her and Alexei…

She switched her gaze to the man. His shoulders were broad, his hips narrow and he wore knee boots, like Alexei.

It certainly looked like him…

No. A lot of men could resemble Alexei from the back; it couldn't possibly be him as people simply didn't live for hundreds of years. It defied modern science.

Unless he really is a vampire…

She rubbed the tense spot between her eyes. What did this mean? Her rational mind wanted to scream to be reasonable while another part, a big part of her wanted it to be true. She was shocked to find she wanted to acknowledge that this painting was the proof that Alexei was right, they had been together in another life.

She drew her fingers over the glass that covered the painted lovers. She wished he were here right now. He'd help her untangle her confused feelings and possibly have a good laugh over this. But he wasn't and wouldn't be back for at least another day.

She turned away from the painting and the disturbing images it brought to mind. She needed to go back to her room and lay down for a while. Dirk was planning a quiet dinner for them and she wanted to be in tiptop form for it. It would be a great opportunity to ferret out information on Alexei.

Chapter 8

All night long she'd dreamed of Alexei. One such dream was a vision of him playing a guitar under the full moon while she danced barefoot in the grass. Dressed as gypsies he'd looked devastatingly handsome as she twirled to the music he'd enticed from the instrument.

Her skirt had contained the colors of the rainbow, her white peasant blouse barely hiding her breasts as golden bracelets sang with her evocative movements.

Breathless and flushed from the sensual dance, she'd gone to him, putting aside his instrument, and they'd lain on the grass and made love, their cries echoing among the woods.

It wasn't real…

But it *seemed* so real. Even now, she could almost taste the heady wine of the night air, the feel of his hands on her skin as they'd seduced and teased one another, journeying to the heights together. In her mind he lay beside her, whispering all the erotic things he wanted to do to her, with her, and she'd only been to eager to obey.

The dull throb in her head brought her from sleep into full wakefulness. She didn't have to reach for the other side of the bed to know she was alone. Rather than face the empty space, she rolled toward the windows.

The room was dim, the sun obliterated by thick clouds and a thin gray drizzle. The weather certainly suited her dark mood and heavy head.

The phone rang.

She squinted at the clock, but the room was too dim to see what time it was. Fumbling for the receiver, she mumbled a greeting into it.

"Did I awake you?" His voice poured over her skin like warm fudge, welcome and warming her from the inside out.

"No." She was startled by the husky tone of her voice. "I was awake."

"Are you still in bed?"

"Yes."

He gave a purr of pleasure. "I like imagining you in bed thinking of me."

She gave a low laugh. "How could I not?"

Her answer must have pleased him for he made another sound, this one lower, more sensual. "I miss you," he said.

Elaine swallowed hard, struggling for a calm voice. "And I, you."

"I just wanted to hear your voice."

Her throat tightened. How long had she waited for the right man to say those very words? It felt like forever. She rolled onto her back and the low throbbing in her head drew her attention away from the man she loved. She clamped a hand over the base of her skull, silently willing the pain to go away and give her yet another chance at life.

"I had a dream about you," she blurted.

He chuckled. "You did? What was your dream?"

"We were outside and dressed like gypsies and you were playing a guitar for me."

"What were you doing?"

"Dancing. I was dancing just for you. It was night and the stars were overhead. I twirled round and round until I became quite dizzy." She chuckled. "Then I took your guitar away from you and we made love in the summer grass." She sighed. "It was lovely."

The only sound from the other end of the phone was his ragged breathing. She frowned. Wasn't he going to say something? "Alexei?" she said.

"You're beginning to remember our shared past." His voice was hoarse. "I know that dream."

Her heart gave a queer little jerk. "It was only a dream—"

"It is and it isn't," he said. "In some ways, it's much more than just a dream. I have so much to tell you, but I need to be with you, not over the phone like—"

Voices in the background caused Alexei to break off his words. He covered the mouthpiece and spoke to someone else then returned. "Elaine, I have to go. I'll be back tomorrow before you awaken."

She was struck with the sudden fear that she would never speak to him again. "Promise?" Her voice wobbled and she despised herself for the sudden weakness.

"I promised you, did I not?"

She sniffed, fighting to stave back the tears that threatened. What the devil was wrong with her? She wasn't normally such a leaky faucet. "Alexei?"

"Yes, angel?"

"I know this sounds crazy, we barely know each other but…" The words stuck in her throat.

"No, it isn't crazy. Tell me, I want to hear it from you, I need to hear it." She caught the sense of urgency in his voice and something in her broke free.

"I love you, Alexei."

"And I love you, Elaine, more than you'll ever know. I have so much to tell you that I don't know where to begin."

She gave a watery laugh. "Me too."

"Tell Dirk to take good care of you until I return. I'll see you in a day."

She sat up, tears running unheeded down her face. "And you take care and come back to me, Alexei."

"Nothing will stop me from reaching your side, remember that. Nothing." With that, he hung up.

Trembling, Elaine replaced the receiver then rubbed the tears from her face. He would return to her. She knew that as well as she knew her own name. Alexei was a man of his word.

Shoving the tangled sheets aside, she got to her feet and stumbled into the bathroom, flipping on the switch as she walked. Headache or not, she needed to take a shower, then find some breakfast, albeit it would be a late one…

Why was the room so dim? She frowned and turned to stare at the light switch. She'd turned the lights on…

Her image in the mirror was cloudy as if it were coated in steam from a hot shower. She frowned and approached the mirror, raising her hand to lay her palm flat on the cool, dry glass. She rubbed, but there was nothing to obliterate her image. She rubbed harder, but her vision didn't clear, not one bit. Her hand stilled then clenched as the reality of her situation sunk in.

Time had run out. She was going blind.

Her knees wobbled and the room swayed around her. A cry broke from her lips as her knees gave way and she fell onto the cold marble floor. She barely felt the bruising jolt as her hip struck the corner of the tub.

Horror spread beneath her skin like ice water as she struggled to breathe. In her mind, she kept hearing a game show buzzer, over and over again. A soft moan escaped her as she melted into the floor, pressing her cheek into the cold stone.

Alexei…

Dirk…

Pain clawed her heart as she forced herself upright, her breath coming in pants. Head throbbing, she forced herself to crawl to the in-house phone. It took her several attempts, with shaky fingers, to dial the numbers and then she waited for someone to answer.

"Dirk, I need you."

Chapter 9

Alexei stared in disbelief at Nigel.

"What do you mean, she left?" Alexei asked.

"Mr. Prentiss left last night with Miss Veronique and Miss Elaine." He frowned. "I don't think Miss Elaine was feeling well as he carried her out to the car."

A spurt of panic bloomed in his chest. Was she ill? Was it serious? Why hadn't she told him?

"Where did they go?"

The butler shook his head. "I don't know. Mr. Prentiss didn't inform me as to his destination."

He ground his teeth in frustration. "Did he have his cell phone with him?"

Nigel nodded. "Of course."

"If you hear from him, tell him to call me immediately." Alexei turned and stalked to the limo that awaited him. Climbing in, he grabbed his phone and punched in Dirk's number. The phone rang several times and he growled as voice mail picked up. "It's Alexei. Call me as soon as possible."

He slammed the phone shut and tossed it on the seat beside him. "Back to Denver, Reg," he said to the driver.

The car pulled smoothly away from the house and Alexei let his head fall back against the butter-soft leather of the seat. Why had she left? Damn. He knew he should have returned last night. He'd had the feeling when he spoke to her that something wasn't right. His gut had screamed at him to return, but he hadn't. He'd waited because he'd wanted the moment to be perfect.

A bitter smile twisted his mouth and he pulled the ring from his pocket. A one-carat emerald surrounded by diamonds glittered between his fingers. It was the ring he'd never managed to give her the last time they'd been together during the war. She'd died before he could reach her side.

His hand fisted around the ring, the prongs cutting into his skin. Not this time. He loved her, he'd always loved her and he'd meant what he said. Nothing, not even time itself, would keep them apart this time.

* * * * *

Dirk ran his thumb over her knuckles again, his gaze glued on Elaine's sleeping face. His best friend was dying and it had happened so fast. Just two days ago, they were making plans to take a short cruise to the Mediterranean next month and, now, it was almost over.

Even as she lay in her drug-induced sleep, she was suffering. From time to time, a soft sigh would escape her lips and her forehead would pleat as if something reached through her morphine-clouded slumber to disturb her.

He'd panicked when Elaine had called. It was too soon to lose her. Too soon for the world to lose her mercurial laugh and wicked sense of humor. Eyes dry, he raised her hand to his mouth and brushed a kiss over her cool skin. He'd cried himself dry in the past twenty-four hours and he was exhausted. He just didn't have any more tears left in him.

Thank the Gods for Ronni. She'd been a rock. She'd stepped in and made arrangements to get them back to New York in record time, not to mention the twenty-four hour a day nurses and the transformation of Elaine's bedroom into her sick room. Ronni had filled it with flowers and soft classical music played on the stereo. The hospital bed was covered in silk sheets and Elaine was dressed in her favorite emerald silk kimono.

Elaine was right. He loved Ronni. Why had he waited so long to tell her? He shook his head. All that wasted time. He wanted to marry her, have children with her and, yes, he'd even buy a damned mini-van and drive the kids to soccer practice if she wanted him to do so.

He dropped his head onto the bed beside her arm. "Damn, if you weren't right all along, Elaine."

She stirred. "Bout time…" she slurred.

He raised his head, a smile on his face. "Doesn't it just figure you'd wake up when I said that."

She gave a slight chuckle. "Must be dyin', never thought I'd hear that in my lifetime…"

Her voice trailed away as she slipped back into her drugged sleep. She had moments of lucidity, but they were rapidly becoming farther and farther apart. Her doctor had been in a few hours earlier and his diagnosis was that they had a few days at best.

He swallowed hard. Damn, he wasn't ready to let her go yet.

The door opened and he turned to see Ronni enter. She looked as tired as he felt. Her normally perfect coif was scraped back into a ponytail, her face devoid of makeup and she wore oversized sweats and a white t-shirt.

He'd never seen her look more beautiful in his life.

"Alexei called again and he's quite frantic," she said. "We have to tell him something, Dirk."

He shook his head. "She doesn't want to see anyone, especially not him. She doesn't want him to remember her like this."

"Well, guess what, Dirk. He told me he loves her and not telling him is tearing him apart. If he doesn't learn the truth he'll end up hating her forever. Does she want that instead?" She laid her hand on his shoulder. "He deserves the chance to say goodbye and she deserves to hear that he loves her one last time."

Dirk's gaze swung to his sleeping friend, her image burned into his mind. What was the right thing to do? Follow Elaine's edict or bring the man she loved to her side for one last time?

What would he want? Would he want Ronni by his side as he lay dying?

Yes.

His gaze never wavering from Elaine's face, he spoke. "Bring him to New York."

Veronique dropped a kiss to his check. "I love you."

His throat tightened. "I love you."

She turned to leave.

"Darling?" he said.

She stopped, her expression questioning.

"Tell him to hurry."

Chapter 10

"She has cancer of the brain and it's inoperable." Dirk ran his hand through his long pale hair.

Dying.

Alexei closed his eyes, sorrow lancing his soul as his mind screamed, *NO*! He couldn't lose her again, not this time.

Blindly he turned and started down the hall, his only thought to reach her side as soon as possible. A hand on his arm halted him and he looked back into Dirk's tormented gaze.

"She's known the end was near and that's why she attended the party. She knew her death was eminent and she told me she wanted to feel alive one last time." He released his grip on Alexei's arm. "You did that for her. You made her feel more alive than I've seen her in months."

Alexei swallowed hard, his eyes stinging fiercely.

"I know what you are," Dirk continued. "Ronni told me several years ago and I didn't want to believe her. It was only when I saw the evidence with my own eyes that I realized you really are a vampire. After that, I thought you were a monster and I'm sorry for that. You've been a good friend to me and I forgot about that. Irregardless of your…"

"Dining preferences?"

Dirk's smile was faint. "Well said."

Alexei cleared his throat. "How is she?"

"She's sedated for the most part, but she has moments of lucidity. She's blind, but the medications are keeping the pain under control for now. At this point, all we can do is make her comfortable."

Dirk's anguish was written on every line in his face. Right now, he looked far older than forty-three. Making Elaine comfortable might be all Dirk could do, but Alexei could do more.

"I love her you know."

Dirk nodded. "She needs to hear that now."

Alexei's knees wobbled and he straightened them, forcing them to lock. Elaine needed him to be strong and strong he would be. He gave Dirk a swift nod before walking down the hall.

She might not remember their lives together, but her house told him a different story. Soft fabrics covered overstuffed furniture in bold, vivid colors. Cozy nooks filled with books and candles invited him to sit for a respite. The scent of flowers filled the air, but he'd expect no less from his beautiful gypsy woman.

He heard Veronique's soft voice as he approached the half-opened door. Through the wedge, he saw her sitting in a puddle of lamplight. Her gaze was fixed on a book in her lap as she read aloud.

He pushed the door open and his breath caught as his gaze locked on Elaine in the narrow bed.

She looked much the same as she had when he'd left her side three days before. Her hair was neatly brushed and tied with emerald ribbons. Her skin was pale, her lashes barely covering the shadows under her eyes.

Dressed in a vivid green kimono, she looked like a sleeping angel.

She can't be dying.

On the nightstand stood a variety of bottles, syringes and other sickbed implements that voided his thoughts. Next to the nightstand sat another woman dressed completely in white, a nurse no doubt. Her pale blonde hair was pulled into a neat bun and she sat bent over knitting. The pale pink yard fairly screamed baby blanket.

Veronique rose from her chair, her expression solemn. "I'm glad you're here, Alexei."

He caught her hand. "So am I."

"Maddy, let's leave them alone."

The nurse nodded and quickly gathered her things, pausing only to check Elaine's pulse before leaving the room.

Veronique laid her hand on his arm. "Let me know if you need anything, Alexei."

He nodded, his throat tight as she left. He wanted to scream at her to stay, but he didn't speak.

As he moved toward the bed, his gaze locked on her face. She was so impossibly beautiful and he needed to touch her, hold her. He stretched out beside her, pulling her into his arms, shocked at the sudden fragility of her body in such short a time. She curled into him with a soft sigh.

He stroked her back, a repetitive motion that soothed his scattered thoughts.

"That first time, I fell in love with you the moment I saw you. You were so young, so beautiful. You were always the gypsy, your feet bare and your hair tangled with wildflowers. Your mother was forever yelling at you to comb your hair, but an hour later it would be tangled again." He chuckled.

"Your name was Natasha in that life and I lost you too soon. Less than a year after we married, you were dead with our child inside of you."

He pressed a kiss to her brow. "I was devastated and it was then that I became a vampire. I know what you're going to say, vampires don't exist, but they do. I left the mother country, too many memories for me to stay there any longer. I traveled for several years and ended up in the Carpathian mountains. It was there that I was transformed."

He sighed. "I was forever doomed to walk the years of darkness in pursuit of you, my love.

"I found you next in the French countryside. I could barely believe my eyes when I saw you in the middle of a field of mustard with a cluster of children around you. It was dark and you were teaching the children about the animals that came out only at night. I fell in love with you all over again."

He tangled his fingers in her hair. "We were happy, living in the country. We'd make love all night long, talk for hours and laugh. You were everything to me and, yet again, I lost you less than three months later."

He closed his eyes at the memory of the crushing blow of her death. She'd fallen from the barn roof and broken her neck.

"I searched and searched for you. If you were returned to me once, I knew you would be yet again. It was almost thirty years before I found you once more. This time I was in England during the time of the War. You were working for the British Red Cross nursing wounded soldiers. The first time I saw you, you'd been cutting bandages and were covered in lint and your feet were bare." He chuckled. "My beautiful Elise, you never could keep your shoes on.

"I lost you less than three weeks later. The Germans bombed London and you were killed while ushering several small children to safety. You always did put everyone else's safety before your own.

"You don't know this, but I first saw your picture in Dirk's office. Do you remember the photo with you and he when you went fishing in Canada?" He chuckled. "In that photo, your feet were bare and your face was mostly covered with a big floppy hat, but I knew it was you. I didn't even have to see your face and I knew.

"It took me the longest time to get Dirk to even tell me your name. He's very protective of you.

"When you walked into the ballroom, I couldn't breathe. I'd dogged Dirk's steps for almost four years waiting for you to appear. I knew you would, it was only a matter of time. Then I came here." He sighed, his grip tightened on her sleeping form.

"For the first time in fifty years, I felt like I could breathe. You were by my side once more and this time I was going to make you mine." He reached into his pocket and withdrew the ring.

"I bought this for you just hours before you were killed in London. We were to meet for dinner and I was going to ask you to marry me, but I was too late." He slipped the ring on her finger and his heart gave a jerk at the sense of rightness. The emerald was finally where it should have been placed years ago. "Marry me," he whispered.

* * * * *

His words filtered through the cloud of morphine and she absorbed the enormity of what he was telling her. This explained the dreams that had plagued her for her entire life and had only grown worse with each passing year. It all made perfect sense now.

Or she was stoned, maybe too stoned and he wasn't really here at all. She poked his chest with her finger. He certainly felt real.

"Alexei." Her voice came out as little more than a croak.

His chest jerked beneath her cheek. "Elaine?"

"You're crazzzeee."

He cleared his throat. "How am I crazy?"

"Vampires don't exist," she whispered.

"How can you doubt your own heart? I think you know as well as I do that we've lived and loved before."

She did. She knew it as well as she knew her own name. They'd been together before, but… a vampire?

"Follow your heart, my darling."

She swallowed. "I know that I love you. I don't need to know anything else."

"Marry me."

"I can't." Her voice came out as a sob.

She felt him pull away and she knew he was looking at her even though she couldn't see him as he was, only how she remembered him. Now, he was reduced to a silhouette of dark on light and she'd never see him again. Her eyes misted and she blinked madly to keep the tears from falling.

"Why not?" he asked.

"News flash, I'm dying."

He chuckled. "And this is more important than marrying me? You wound me."

"No." Her smile felt rusty. "Nothing is more important than loving you."

"Do you mean it?"

She nodded and laid her head on his chest, unable to bear not being able to see him, only his shadow. "I'm so tired. I want to sleep now."

"I know you do, darling, but you need to stay awake for another minute. I need to ask you something."

She raised her head. "I wish I could see you." Her tone was wistful.

"For now, it is enough that I see you, hold you in my arms as well as my heart."

"You say the sweetest things."

"Will you marry me?"

"If only I could."

"If you could, would you marry me and stay with me forever?"

Her threatened tears spilled at his words. "That is my greatest wish. To marry you and remain by your side for however long we could."

"You can do that you know."

She ducked her head. "You're not to tease me at a time like this, I can't take it."

"I'm not teasing you, my love. I am truly a vampire. I'm immortal."

"I don't think—"

He shushed her by pressing a finger to her mouth, then caught her hand and raised it to his mouth. Brushing a kiss across the back, his breath warm on her skin, then something pricked her finger and she jerked her hand away.

"What was that?" she asked.

"My teeth."

"Your teeth?" She frowned. "Are they real?"

"As real as you and I."

She laid her hand on his cheek. Stroking, she ran her thumb along his lip then inside, to inspect his teeth with the lightest of touches. His front teeth were even and strong. She ran her finger along their edge, then stopped when she hit an obstruction. Closing her eyes to concentrate, she ran her finger over the barrier. It was on the left side of his mouth where his canines should have been. Smooth, she followed the hard surface up to his gums then down to the sharp point.

It was definitely a tooth.

She moved to the other side of his mouth and found the matching one.

"I feel like a horse," he said around her fingers.

She pulled her hand away. "Why didn't I see these before?"

"They retract."

"Uh huh…"

He led her hand back to his mouth and placed her index finger on a tooth. Then she felt them shift and shrink. Within seconds his teeth felt normal beneath her touch.

Shaken, she pulled away. He really was a vampire. All of her life, she'd prided herself on being open-minded and, now the man she loved was a vampire. Talk about mixed relationships!

"Do you believe me now?" he asked.

She nodded, not trusting her tongue to be able to speak.

"Does this change how you feel?"

Did it? He was still Alexei, warm, funny, intelligent, passionate. He was just a great deal older than she'd imagined. And definitely not a vegetarian.

"No." The moment she said it she knew it was true in her heart. It didn't matter if he was Vlad the Impaler. She would still love the man she'd come to know so well.

"Tell me that you love me and will stay with me."

She caught the desperation in his voice and it called to her. "More than anything in the world, I want to stay with you. I love you, Alexei."

"I don't know that this will work," he said.

"What are you going to do?"

"Transform you."

She tensed. "Does it hurt?"

"No, it feels… strange but it doesn't hurt. And the best part is…" His finger ran down her cheek eliciting a rush of warmth through her body. "If it works, we will be together forever."

"And if it doesn't?"

"You'll die."

"I'm already dying." She shivered and his grip tightened. Eternity or death. She was afraid, very afraid. She was afraid to transform, but she was more afraid of dying and never being in his arms again. "If I die, will you come for me in my next life?" she quavered.

"Death will never part us. We are destined." He dropped a kiss to her hair.

"Alexei," she whispered, "kiss me one last time."

"Of course, my love."

His lips brushed hers then settled, a mark of possession as his taste exploded in her nervous system, far more potent than the morphine and much more desirable. Their tongues tangled as she clung to him, their hearts beating as one. Head spinning with the power of his touch, he nibbled the line of her jaw and she tipped her head back, offering him free reign over her body and soul.

Her fingers twined with his as he caressed a blazing trail to the base of her throat, the movement as intimate as any embrace they'd ever shared.

Her breath left in a rush as his teeth pierced her skin, his offering of eternity or death, and she raced to embrace her destiny as the world faded away.

Epilogue

New Orleans, 2030

Alexei inhaled the fragrant smoke from his clove cigarette, its scent blending with the crush of human bodies, spilled liquor and utter decadence that was Mardi Gras.

How he loved this gracious old city with it's myriad of wrought iron balconies, hidden gardens and colorful personalities. But now he had more essential things to do than admire the architecture. He had an important meeting to keep.

He crushed the remains of the cigarette under his heel before moving into the crowd. Music swirled through the dark sky as costumed revelers made their way down the street. A Crewe parade was in full force as he moved through the throng, resisting the lure of the music that beckoned his gypsy soul. He left the wildness of Bourbon Street and walked down Orleans to Jackson Square. Few people were in the square and he scanned the area for the person he sought above all others.

Then he saw her and his heart almost stopped.

Standing near the fountain, she was a vision in full gypsy getup. Her long sable hair hung in wild ringlets to the small of her back and a daisy crown adorned her head. Her pale shoulders were bare, the sleeves of her peasant top pulled low to expose her skin to the kiss of the moonlight. A vividly colored scarf encircled her waist and hung to lick the hem of her ruby-colored skirt. He smiled when he saw her feet were bare.

She was looking away, her profile a perfect cameo as he approached. She turned, her gaze curious and unalarmed.

He gave her a sketchy bow. "Madame, at last we meet."

Her brow arched. "Do I know you, kind sir?"

"No, but I know you."

Her eyes widened and she gave a half-step backward, one hand fluttering to rest at the base of her throat.

"Don't be afraid." He held his hand out. "I would never hurt you for I've been looking for you for years."

She tilted her head to the side. "How many years?"

"Almost thirty."

She rolled her eyes. "Not nearly long enough I think." Then she turned away.

He grabbed her about the waist, startling a laugh out of her. "Not long enough?" he growled, dipping his head to kiss the base of her neck.

"The last guy told me three hundred years." She sighed as he licked the sensitive patch just below her ear.

"Are you trying to drive me crazy?" he asked.

She gave a throaty chuckle. "Is it working?"

"Yes."

"Good." She twisted in his arms to face him. "Are you glad to be back in New Orleans?"

"Yes, very." He brushed a stray lock of hair out of her face. She never could keep her hair under control and it didn't bother him a bit. "What would you like to see first?

The parade? Listen to some Blues? Or maybe visit with Dirk and Veronique and their multitude of great-grandchildren?"

"Seven great-grandchildren do not make a multitude."

"It does when they all gather in the same room."

"I have a better idea." Her playful expression softened. "How about we inspect the bed in our suite instead?"

He wiggled his brows at her. "I like the way you think. We have eternity to examine the charms of the city."

She tipped her head back to expose her throat to the moonlight and his gaze as she laughed. At the base was a tiny scar, a memento of Elaine's last moments as a human, their last kiss. How close he'd come to losing her. He brushed his finger over the mark, then pocketed the unwanted thought. This time, he'd won—they'd won.

As he pulled her into his arms for a kiss, he knew that an eternity would never be enough for them, but it would do for a start.

About the author:

Dominique Adair is the pen name of award-winning novelist, J.C. Wilder. Adair/Wilder (she chooses her name according to her mood - if she's feeling sassy and brazen, it's Adair - if she's feeling dark and dangerous, it's Wilder) lives just outside of Columbus, OH where she skulks around town plotting her next book and contemplating where to hide the bodies (from her books of course - everyone knows that you can't really hide a body as they always pop up at the worst times).

Night Flight

Written by

Margaret L. Carter

Chapter One

A siren wailed through the clear night air.

Gillian eased off the accelerator, downshifted and steered her vintage Corvette onto the freeway shoulder.

About time! Where are the cops when you need them? She had started to think she would have to drive halfway to Los Angeles to run into a speed trap.

She braked, then turned off the ignition just as a California Highway Patrol car pulled up behind her. *Dinnertime!* Gillian got out of the driver's seat and stood by the open door, assuming a "lost waif" expression. Or as waiflike as a woman almost six feet tall could look. Her elfin-thin face and boyish figure helped.

The officer emerged from the patrol car and strode toward her. He was blond, broad-chested, and tall, at least two inches taller than Gillian. Good, she preferred males she didn't have to bend over uncomfortably far to nibble on.

"What's wrong, officer?" she said in a breathy whisper, to force him to approach closer to hear her. His clean scent sharpened her appetite. This hunting method snared much more satisfying prey than she would catch by cruising bars. "I didn't think I was speeding."

Brandishing his notepad, he said, "Miss, you were doing at least eighty-five."

"Oh—I'm sorry. I must have been daydreaming." She stretched out a hand to brush his collar with one fingernail, while her eyes held his gaze. She knew he saw pinpoints of crimson glowing in their depths. She made no attempt to hide this inhuman trait, for his vision was already glazing over. Even though still young for one of her kind, she had no trouble casting a glamour over any human subject who wasn't prepared to resist.

"Daydreaming. Not a good idea on the freeway."

"I know. I'll never do it again. You don't want to give me a ticket, do you?" she murmured. Her touch intensified the effect of her hypnotic stare.

"Not really—" His hands dangled, barely keeping a grip on the ticket book.

She pressed her fingertips to the warm flesh on the side of his neck, relishing the throb of the pulse beneath the skin. "Let's go back to your car."

After guiding the man into the driver's seat of the police car, she slipped into the passenger side. She gently turned his head so that his eyes focused on hers again. The car's radio crackled, unheeded by either of them. "Now I'm going to kiss you. You want that, don't you?"

He slowly nodded.

She scattered feathery kisses over his cheeks and temples, avoiding his lips; somehow that contact seemed too intimate, despite what she was about to do. His breathing quickened. His skin temperature rose, sharpening her appetite. Strong emotion added spice to the blood, and sexual desire flavored it most intensely. Her empathic sense drank in his rising passion. The background noise of distant traffic blurred to an oceanic roar in her ears. Gripping the back of his neck, she unbuttoned his collar and fastened her mouth on his throat. Her tongue flicked rapidly, teasing both him and herself while the enzymes in her saliva augmented the painkilling effect of her hypnotic spell.

He gripped the edges of the seat. When her razor-edged incisors pierced his skin, his hips arched. The salt-sweet gush of blood sent heat surging from her mouth to every cell of her body. The thrill rippled through her taut nipples and the hypersensitive flesh between her thighs.

For a second she almost stopped drinking. *I shouldn't feel that way.* Normally, her pleasure was diffused throughout her body, radiating from the spot where she luxuriated in the taste of her prey. She didn't expect such intensely localized sensations.

Never mind. Think about it later. She yielded to the ecstasy.

Her victim groaned aloud as she sucked and licked the tiny wound. She dropped her free hand to the zipper and ran her open palm along the hard ridge that angled across his lap. He thrust into her strokes. She drew one last, long swallow of hot blood and pulled away. She pressed against the wound to stop the bleeding, meanwhile lightening the pressure of her hand.

His moan of frustration reminded her of the final step she needed to take, according to the rule she'd learned when her need for human blood had first awakened: "You have to pay them back for your meals, even if it's with pleasure they'll have to forget the source of. That's only fair." Her memory recited the words in the voice of her mother, Juliette. Smiling, Gillian wondered how it would feel to be—intimate—with her prey.

What am I thinking about? Just take care of him and get away from here!

Massaging the back of his neck, she murmured, "Shh, it's all right. In a minute you're going to take a little nap. When you wake up, you'll forget you ever saw me. You pulled over to rest for a minute and fell asleep. All you'll remember is a dream, a very nice dream."

Inch by inch, she pulled down his zipper, while the fingernails of her other hand skimmed the nape of his neck. His erection sprang free. She circled his shaft, meanwhile nuzzling his throat without quite reopening the wound. He arched his back, rising out of the seat, as he thrust into her palm. Engorged with blood, his organ felt on fire to her. "Yes," she hissed against his flushed skin. "You're in the arms of your ideal woman, plunging into her. She's wet and hot. You've never been so stiff before, you've never come so hard."

His hips pumped. With the frantic acceleration of his movements, his heartbeat thundered in her ears. His heat and musk filled the car like a cloud of incense. At his moment of release, she nipped the skin of his throat and tasted one more drop of blood. Her own body echoed the climax as he erupted.

She licked her fingers before wiping them with his handkerchief, then pressing the square of cloth into his lap. Semen had a flavor tantalizingly similar to blood.

"Now," she whispered, "close your eyes." Leaving him to the fantasy she had planted in his mind, doubtless a thrill more intense than he'd ever shared with a human female, she returned to the Corvette and drove away.

Now if that were Paul, she thought, *I might not mind getting a little--closer.* She squelched the image, annoyed at herself for letting it arise in the first place. Her association with her collaborator Paul Shelby had to remain businesslike; anything else could be dangerous. She mustn't even let herself wonder how he would taste. In fact, she'd made a point of feeding well tonight because she had a meeting with Paul the next day and she didn't want to be hungry when she saw him.

Lately she'd caught herself thinking of Paul more and more, outside the boundaries of their writer-photographer partnership. She'd felt oddly restless in the past few weeks, even dreaming about him several days in a row. Her nonhuman neural patterns required only a few hours of REM time per week, vague, fleeting images that evaporated upon waking. The vivid scenarios that haunted her weren't normal. Those tantalizing visions wrecked what should be peacefully dreamless day-sleep.

Rolling her window all the way down, she let the desert wind blow through her short, curly red hair. The feeding had infused her with energy; she wanted to banish pointless worries and enjoy the sensation. She took the next exit and reentered the freeway southbound, headed for her home in El Cajon, a suburb east of San Diego.

Chapter Two

Half an hour later, she breezed into her townhouse still high on her victim's blood and passion. Just inside the foyer, she stopped short, her exhilaration flattened by an all-too-familiar metallic scent in the air. Extending a telepathic tendril, she brushed the surface of the intruder's thoughts. Only the surface; hard, smooth, and cold. Despite the blood-bond they shared as mentor and pupil, he never allowed her into the depths of his mind. *Lord Volnar.*

She drew the front door shut and fastened the deadbolt. She didn't need to ask how he'd got in, since he had a key. But she couldn't imagine why he was visiting, with no prior notice. Now that she was too old to need constant supervision, she saw her adviser only a few times a year, a schedule of which she heartily approved. And their last meeting had occurred only nine days earlier.

She marched into the living room, folded her arms, and glared down at the man seated on the low, sea-green sofa. In the dark room, his eyes gleamed red. "What are you doing here? I'm not a kid anymore. You can't just barge in anytime."

With a tight smile, Volnar gestured at the other end of the couch. "Sit down, Gillian."

As she did so, perching stiffly on the edge of the cushion with her hands clutching each other in her lap, his nostrils flared, and his thick eyebrows arched. Not for the first time, she observed how much he looked like Stoker's description of Dracula in the original novel—aquiline profile, high forehead, iron-gray hair, thick moustache, eyebrows meeting over the nose. She knew there must be a story behind that resemblance, one he'd never told her.

"At least you could've called first."

"Pointless," he said. "You would have wasted time trying to persuade me to stay away."

"You bet I would. I don't need you hovering over me anymore. So what's wrong? I haven't done anything I can think of."

His smile widened to bare his teeth. "Why do you assume I'm here to chastise you? I have good news."

Suspicious of Volnar's idea of "good news," Gillian didn't quite relax, but she did sit back and unclasp her tightly entangled fingers. "What's going on?"

"Last time I visited, I noticed a change in your body chemistry, your—fragrance. Now it's more obvious. I'm sure of it—you're about to go into estrus."

"What?" Her heart accelerated. She drew a deep breath and willed her pulse to a slow, even rhythm. "Happy, happy, joy, joy," was *not* her first reaction. "That's impossible. I'm only twenty-six. I shouldn't start for another four years."

"That's the typical pattern for our species. You are not typical. You're one-fourth *Homo sapiens*, completely unpredictable."

"I did start needing to feed on—human prey—younger than normal. But this—I'm not ready. Can't you do something to stop it?" She realized the silliness of that plea almost before the words emerged from her mouth.

"Stop it? Child, this is an unprecedented opportunity. With your human genes, anything is possible. You might even be fertile at your first heat. If so, we mustn't waste it."

Her throat tightened with anxiety. *Maybe he's right. The way I reacted to that policeman –*

"If I really am going to be fertile a week or two from now, the last thing I want is to get pregnant. You know how I feel about that stupid breeding program of yours."

"Young lady, without that 'stupid program', you wouldn't exist. I've lavished enormous amounts of time and energy on you. I expect cooperation. You know how our birthrate has dropped over the past few centuries."

"Of course I know. You never let me forget it. Human DNA is going to revive our gene pool, I have a duty to the race, yada, yada." Momentarily she wondered where she got the nerve to be rude to her adviser, the most ancient of their kind.

He showed no anger. With his power, he didn't have to squander emotion. "I never let you forget it because it's important. You can certainly spare a little of your time for the good of your people."

"A little time!" She jumped to her feet and paced around the room, fists clenched at her sides. "Eleven months of pregnancy, three or four years of breast-feeding—"

"Out of a lifetime that will last for millennia. Calm yourself and think rationally. You have to mate with someone. The compulsion is irresistible. So you may as well accept my choice."

"Your what?" That couldn't mean what it sounded like.

"Unless you already have someone in mind? No? I assumed not."

Her nails dug into her palms. She flexed her fingers to ease the muscle spasms. "You're not saying you've picked a mate for me?"

"Of course. If you're capable of conceiving, we can't leave the father to chance. Since you have little or no background to base a choice on, it's logical for me to make that decision."

"Now wait just a minute!" She choked down the rage boiling up in her throat. She knew her aura must be sparking like a thundercloud. His remained as serene as ever. "I pick my own mate! Females of our species always do. You can't take that right away from me."

"You are not an ordinary female. While it's unlikely that you'll ovulate the first time, in view of your heritage—"

"Damn my heritage!" Lightheaded with anger, she breathed deeply until the red mist cleared from her vision. "Those human genes you keep lecturing about come from my father and he hates the whole idea of this selective breeding crap as much as I do. He wouldn't put up with this for one minute."

Volnar's eyes hardened. "He has nothing to say about it. In view of his human mind-set, I've allowed him an unusual involvement in your upbringing. But not something this important." He stood up, though he didn't approach her. "Don't you want to know whom I've chosen?"

"Doesn't matter, because I won't do it."

"Luciano Rossi. A good bloodline, proven fertile, but he hasn't yet sired enough offspring to cause problems with future inbreeding, if he should succeed in impregnating you."

"You've got to be kidding." A futile outburst, since her adviser never joked. She visualized Luciano, slightly over five centuries old, born in Italy, with dark, wavy hair in dramatic contrast to his vampire-pale skin. Attractive, no doubt about it, probably a ravishing success with human females.

"I know what he thinks about `half-breeds' and `lap dogs who pretend to be wolves' and contaminating the gene pool with lower life forms. I overheard him ranting about it once, not that he tried very hard to keep me from listening. I can't stand him."

"That's irrelevant," said Volnar with a dismissive wave of his hand. "It's not as if you're expected to marry each other, like ephemerals. One night and you never have to see him again."

"Yeah, well, one night is about twelve hours too long." She flung herself down on the sofa. "Why are we arguing about it? Luciano would never want me, anyway."

"On the contrary, he has already agreed."

Her pulse stuttered in renewed shock. "You asked him without even talking to me first? You—" When she'd forced her emotions back under control, she said, "Oh, I understand. He wants to get on your good side. The Prime Elder favors interbreeding with ephemerals, so Luciano decides to have a change of heart. That's the only reason he could possibly have to mate with a half-breed."

"His reasons shouldn't concern you. The point is that he's a superb physical specimen, with enough experience to give you a pleasant initiation."

"Right, about as pleasant as being staked out in the desert at high noon." A possible escape occurred to her. "Why don't you mate with me yourself? Like you said, I have to do it with somebody. You're bound to have more—experience—than Luciano."

"Out of the question," Volnar said. "I've already sired more than enough offspring. The purpose of this project is to increase our genetic variety, not subtract from it."

"Then let somebody else do the increasing. I won't let that man near me."

Volnar's lips quirked in amusement. "What will you do about your needs, then?"

"Maybe I won't have to do anything. You said yourself; all bets are off because I'm one-fourth human. Maybe my estrus will be weak enough that I can ignore it, ride it out by myself."

"You don't know what you're saying, young lady." Sitting beside her, he took her hand. "That's extremely unlikely. And if you find yourself overcome by the full force of the compulsion, with no mate available—I would not want you to suffer that agony."

His cool touch sent an unexpected shiver up her arm. She snatched her hand away. Her skin felt too tight, and her head began to pound with tension. "I'll worry about that when it happens. Now that you've ruined my night, get out of here!"

He started for the door. Pausing on the threshold, he turned toward her and said, "I can feel it approaching already. You must certainly be aware that your physical response to me isn't normal. Soon, Gillian—probably within the week. Be prepared to accept Luciano."

Only after the door shut behind Volnar did she work up the nerve to snarl, "The hell with that! I'd rather mate with an ephemeral."

Abruptly Paul's image flashed into her mind. A flood of heat rushed over her.

I have to get out of here. At this rate I'll never be able to sleep tomorrow.

Hurrying out the back door of her condo, she threaded her way through the townhouse complex to the open desert behind it. Ice plants crunched under her sandals. Jogging up a steep hillside to the top of a ridge, she inhaled the deliciously cool breeze that blew toward her. After stripping off her clothes, she spread her arms wide and yielded to the electricity that danced over her skin. Silken fur sprouted on her arms, back, and face. Her teeth sharpened. Wings erupted from her shoulders. She shuddered with the thrill of the change.

Launching herself into the air, she glided over the open land. Her flight wasn't true flying, but levitation, with the wings to steer and provide balance. Regardless of the technicalities, the sense of delirious freedom swept away her anxiety and rage. She knew she shouldn't fly this near a populated area, but tonight she didn't care.

An hour later she returned home and retreated to her darkroom, immersing herself in work. By dawn, she had tired herself enough to sink into the deathlike daylight sleep.

Chapter Three

The clock radio woke her at four p. m. She dragged herself out of bed groggy and crabby, knowing the sun would shine for hours yet. *Maybe I should spend the summers in Patagonia.* Only the prospect of a meeting with Paul made facing the summer afternoon bearable.

She had dreamed of him again, of flying through the desert night sky with him in her arms, like a scene from a "Superman" comic. His image refused to fade from her mind—copper-gold hair a few shades lighter than her own, blue eyes, the ruddy aura of a man in prime health, a masculine aroma clean of any trace of disease or tobacco smoke.

Her teeth tingled, and the cilia in her palms itched with the yearning to caress warm human flesh. She cursed aloud. Her feeding the night before should have appeased that need. In the shower she ran her hands over her breasts. The friction made the tiny hairs bristle and her nipples harden. For a vampire, whose erogenous zones weren't localized like an ephemeral's, both sensations were equally tantalizing.

Ripples of pleasure spread over her bare skin, sensitized by the torrent of hot water from the shower. Though she knew she couldn't satisfy her own craving—she needed the blood and passion of a human donor for that—she couldn't resist nestling a hand between her thighs. The hidden bud swelled and throbbed. Normally she felt sensations there only when she fed, and only as a small part of the whole-body rush. Now she felt compelled to stroke that spot.

The frisson that arced along her nerves surprised her. Again she had to face the fear that Volnar might be right about her—premature development. She rubbed harder and faster, but no relief came. Gritting her teeth, she teased herself until her veins felt on fire, her stomach cramping and jaws aching. Finally, her throat dry with frustration, she turned the shower to full cold and stood under it until the hunger faded, banishing Paul's image whenever it floated to the surface of her mind.

I've been mooning over him like a lovesick heroine in one of Juliette's romances! Her mother, Professor Julia Frost in the English department at the College of William and Mary, also wrote historical romances under the name "Juliette Fontaine." Reviewers praise the authenticity of the author's mid-Victorian settings, never guessing, of course, that she'd lived through that era. Gillian had always read her mother's novels as a source of humor. Strictly for ephemerals, who made an endless fuss over their mating rituals. Now she'd started acting like one of them.

* * * * *

Wearing a light summer dress and a wide-brimmed straw hat with polarized sunglasses, her arms and face coated with factor 30 sunscreen, Gillian headed west on the freeway to Paul's ranch-style faux adobe house in La Jolla.

Beside her in the front seat lay a portfolio of recent photographs, sample illustrations for their latest book proposal. Paul augmented his income as a zoology professor at the University of California, San Diego, by writing wildlife picture books for children. Gillian supplied the photos.

As a team, she and Paul specialized in California's nocturnal fauna. They'd worked up a plan for a new series, stories instead of straight nature reportage. The first book, if the publisher they'd approached offered a contract, would be *Chico the Coyote*.

By the time Gillian reached Paul's home, driving straight into the setting sun most of the way, she had a pounding headache. The anticipation of seeing him made it worthwhile, though. He opened the door almost a soon as her finger touched the buzzer. She heard his heartbeat stutter when their eyes met. With that mutual attraction, seducing him would be fatally easy.

She pushed the thought into a corner of her mind, but not without pausing to savor his fragrance, soap and shampoo spiced with the warmth of his flesh. She noticed that his golden-red hair still curled damply from the shower.

"Gillian, hi! Got the pictures?—great, come right in." With a light grip on her wrist, Paul led her into the combination living room-dining alcove. Aware of her sensitivity to the sun, he'd left the curtains almost completely shut. When she removed her sunglasses, the pastel blues and greens of the decor soothed her eyes.

She immediately caught sight of a bottle and two glasses on the coffee table, which was carved from a tree stump and varnished to a deep chestnut gloss. "What's this, something I should know?" she said as she plopped her portfolio, hat, and purse on the couch.

Paul's smile widened. He handed her an e-mail printout. "I was planning to make a big production of it, but why wait? Here—message from Jan this afternoon."

Their agent. Gillian scanned the sheet of paper. The publisher had offered a contract for the picture book series. She had to read the amount of the advance twice. Though she could have all the money she ever needed from Volnar for the asking, she preferred the independence of earning her own.

"Yes! Of course I had a feeling they wouldn't turn us down, but—Paul, this is great!"

"Caldecott Medal, here we come!" He threw his arms around her in a bear hug. His heart pounded against her breast, his rapid breath ruffling her hair. Almost involuntarily she returned the hug. For a second her cheek rested against his. By tilting her head at a slightly different angle, she could press her lips to the side of his neck—

She eased out of his arms. Paul avoided her eyes like a flustered teenager. He bent over the champagne bottle, clumsily picking at the foil cap. Grateful for the distraction, Gillian sat down on the couch and picked up one of the empty glasses. While he opened the bottle, her eyes wandered to the terrarium in the corner where his pet boa constrictor coiled in its usual torpid condition.

A tempting fantasy flitted through her mind. Could a man who liked snakes accept the truth about a human-shaped predator who fed on blood? She smiled to herself at the idea. Surely she wouldn't seriously think of revealing her true nature to Paul? Ephemerals receptive to the companionship of vampires were far more than vampires themselves.

The pop of the cork interrupted her reverie. After filling their glasses, Paul toasted their future success. Sipping, she gazed into his eyes and fantasized about the flavor of his essence instead of the tart fizz of champagne. *I have to stop thinking this way!*

He lounged beside her on the sofa, refilling both goblets. "Come on, I want to see your latest masterpieces."

Grateful for the diversion into a professional mood, she took the photos out of the portfolio. Paul fanned them on the coffee table. Scanning Gillian's candid shots of coyotes, raccoons, chipmunks, jackrabbits, and pocket mice ignited an appreciative glow in his aura that warmed her almost as much as his leashed desire for her. "Your night photography never ceases to amaze me. These belong in *National Geographic*."

"Someday," she said, not altogether kidding.

"How do you get so close without spooking them? Raccoons, okay, you practically have to fire a shotgun to scare them away, but these others—"

Gillian shrugged. She couldn't very well explain how she used vampiric influence to lull the creatures into submission or, alternatively, cast a psychic veil to make herself "invisible" to them. "Just a knack, I guess."

"These raccoons look like you posed them that way."

She said nothing, since she couldn't admit she had done just that.

"Maybe we should use them for the next book. They're familiar animals, so kids should enjoy reading about them, plus we could use the story to educate them not to try petting or feeding weed species."

Gillian laughed. "I hope you don't plan to call them that in the book! Kind of undermines the cuteness factor."

They finished off the bottle while discussing possible raccoon-centered plots. Though their agent had persuaded the publisher to sign a multibook contract, the exact number of books remained to be decided. Paul suggested they should have several proposals ready to demonstrate their ability to follow through on a long-range series.

"How about bats?" After a moment's thought, he said with a self-deprecating laugh, "Don't know if I'd want you crawling through caves full of guano, not to mention taking chances with rabies."

"Bats wouldn't bite me," she said absentmindedly, provoking a quizzical glance from Paul.

"How about staying for dinner to celebrate?" He held up a hand when she started to protest. "Yeah, I haven't forgotten your allergies. I got a couple of things you can eat, and the rest of the time you can just talk to me."

Gillian had refused every previous invitation, partly because the "allergy" excuse would stretch only so far, but partly to keep a cautious distance from Paul. If she accepted this invitation, she'd set a hazardous precedent. Yet she couldn't bring herself to refuse this time.

He took her silence for acceptance. "Great, I'll just put my steak under the broiler."

After she'd watched him start dinner, he said, "Time to feed Naga. Want to help?"

"Sure."

While he fetched a white rat in a small cage from his home office, she lifted the glass top off the terrarium. The snake languidly raised its head to stare at her. "You know," said Paul, dangling the rat by its tail, "you're the only woman I've ever had over here who'd watch this, much less do it, without screaming or gagging."

How many women has he invited over? she thought. The pang of—could it be jealousy?—astonished her. "That's silly. It's part of nature."

"Red in tooth and claw," he misquoted. "Most people don't like to confront that fact too closely." He dropped the rat. The snake's coils whipped around the rodent and squeezed. A minute later, the fanged jaws unhinged and engulfed the victim. Paul and Gillian watched while the rat disappeared into the snake's mouth in spasmodic jerks, tail last, and became a lump in its gullet.

While Gillian replaced the lid, Paul returned the cage to the other room. The sight of the reptile devouring its prey roused her own appetite. *Ridiculous, I shouldn't be hungry at all tonight.* Maybe the anomaly had something to do with her approaching estrus. She pushed that thought aside; she wanted to forget the problem for a few hours.

Paul dined on steak, baked potato, and salad—with garlic-free dressing, in consideration for her "allergies." He shared a first course of beef broth with her, and she drank milk in addition to a glass of the burgundy he opened. She knew he tactfully restricted her wine intake because she had to drive home. She couldn't explain that her inhuman tolerance made the precaution unnecessary. With the scent of his rare steak tantalizing her, she wished the alcohol could dull her senses.

"There's something I want to ask you," he said as they moved from table to couch with after-dinner shot glasses of sherry. The rose-pink of his aura dimmed and flickered, reflecting his nervousness. She noticed how he sat closer to her than usual. When he put down his glass and touched her hand, not quite clasping it, his heartbeat accelerated. "You must know I'm interested in you, as more than a collaborator."

She nodded. The near-formality of the statement intrigued her. Most of the human males who'd tried to seduce her in the past, allured by her innate vampire magnetism, had used much more blunt language. Or else they'd bypassed words altogether. Paul, in comparison, acted like a knight from King Arthur's court.

"I don't want to push you into something you're not ready for, but I don't want to wait forever, either. So—" He shook his head with a rueful smile. "Good Lord, listen to me babble. The hell with the prepared speech. Would you like to spend this weekend with me in my cabin at Big Bear?"

She stared at him. This wasn't quite the approach she'd expected.

Apparently taking her stunned expression for reluctance, he said, "It can be just companionship, if that's all you want. Just take it a step at a time. How about it?"

Gillian shook her head. Even if it weren't dangerous to get too close to an ephemeral she actually liked—the risk of addiction was too high—spending a whole weekend with him, day and night, held the potential for disaster. Not to mention that he would see her failing to eat enough to keep an anorexic twelve-year-old alive, he might catch a glimpse of her asleep. Her daytime dormancy looked enough like death to scare him witless and destroy any illusion that she was a normal woman.

He emitted disappointment like radio static. "Can you tell me why? Is it that you could never feel that way about me, or is this just not the right time?"

"I can't explain it, Paul. I do like you, but—intimacy—wouldn't work." His unwavering look told her that he wouldn't accept this non-explanation. She gazed back at him and snared his eyes with her hypnotic power. "Don't worry about it. We can stay friends, just as we've always been. You don't need to know my reasons. You trust me."

He stared unblinkingly into her eyes. "Right. I trust you. I don't need to hear your reasons."

She felt a needle-prick of guilt. How silly most of her kind would think she was being. Ephemerals existed as prey, tools, or at most pets. Superior beings had no obligation to them. *But I'm part human, and Paul is my friend.* Her half-human father, at least, would say she was right to feel guilty.

Well, it couldn't be helped. She had to squelch Paul's curiosity if she wanted to keep working with him.

While ruminating over the problem, she unconsciously kept her eyes fixed on his. He leaned toward her, as helpless as the rat swallowed by the snake. His aura glowed a deeper red as excitement replaced his disappointment. His hand, still holding hers, squeezed tighter, and he traced circles in her palm with his thumb.

Her pulse speeded up to match his. *I'll let him go soon; just let me enjoy this for a minute or two.* Even while her brain made that sensible resolution, her body inched closer, and her lips drifted toward his neck.

His mouth intercepted hers. Though entranced by her psychic power, he hadn't lost his erotic skills. He teased her lips apart. Her tongue flickered to meet his. The moist heat of his mouth made the roots of her teeth burn. Strangely, a similar heat welled between her thighs.

She ran her fingernails down the nape of his neck. When he shivered in response, her own body echoed the reaction. She had never kissed a man before—lip contact was irrelevant to feeding—and the effect on her appetite astonished her.

Just once. What can it hurt? He won't remember a thing. She licked and nibbled her way down the side of his jaw. His breathing roughened, while one of his hands massaged her back in languid circles, and the other fondled her breasts.

When she pierced his skin, he let out a sharp gasp that mirrored the spike of arousal her bite evoked. One caress from her fingers, she knew, would trigger his release. But that didn't seem right, not in a hypnotically-induced daze.

She sipped from the tiny wound until the hot, tangy taste had fully appeased her hunger. Intoxicated with the half-awake sensuality he projected, she almost wished she could let him remember, maybe wake him and let him enjoy the climax he craved.

No, the very idea was insane. Stroking his hair and forehead until he sank into light sleep, she whispered, "I have to leave now, Paul. You won't remember any of this." A reckless impulse seized her. "Except the kiss. Remember the kiss. After that, we said goodbye, and I left. Understand?"

He slowly nodded, his eyes closed.

"After I left, you crashed on the couch. In a little while you'll wake up and remember just what I told you. Okay?"

"Yeah," he murmured.

"Tonight when you go to sleep, you'll dream about me, and it'll be totally—fulfilling." If caution wouldn't allow her to have a real-life relationship with him, they could at least share it in fantasy.

Chapter Four

When Paul woke up, he found himself lying on the couch, alone. Where the heck was Gillian? Oh, yeah, they'd kissed, and then she'd gone home. What was the matter with him, letting her escape so easily? Though she'd turned down his invitation, that kiss had been too hot to let him believe her "just friends" line.

At least, what little he remembered of it was hot. His groin tightened at the mere thought of her mouth on his. Why was the memory such a blur? He stood up and his head spun.

What's going on ? I didn't drink that much!

He stumbled down the hall, leaning on walls for balance. He couldn't believe he'd passed out on the couch without even walking her to the door. Real smooth. He'd finally had Gillian in a position to do something more intimate than discussing their books, and he'd blown it.

Lots of men might not be turned on by a tall woman with a greyhound-slender body. Their loss. He loved to watch her perky little breasts under clinging T-shirts, and for months he'd fantasized about having her long legs wrapped around him.

Cold water on his face didn't clear the mist from his head. He staggered from bathroom to bedroom. Groaning, he shucked his clothes and crashed on the bed. *Maybe I'm coming down with something?* The fog thickened in his brain and he drifted off.

Fire and ice spread over him, painlessly searing every inch of skin. He opened his eyes to meet Gillian's, gleaming silver with radiance like a cat's. Her lips teased his. When he opened his mouth, her tongue flickered like a flame. Hugging her naked body to his, he felt her peaked nipples against his chest. Her mouth moved downward to brand his neck like a red-hot coal. Pressed against her satiny flesh, his erection grew painfully hard. She arched her back and drew him in. Her moist head squeezed him in a n accelerating rhythm that drover the pressure to unbearable intensity. His rod felt a foot long. He plunged into her and shot off with a roar of mingled ecstasy and anguish.

He woke alone, drained. *Oh, man, what a dream!* Only a wet patch on the sheet gave evidence that one aspect of the dream had really happened. He felt spent but not satisfied. He craved Gillian in real life, not only in dreams. And he realized he wanted her for much more than a night or even a weekend. Maybe forever.

Chapter Five

Gillian arrived home with her head spinning. She'd done everything she had continually promised herself not to do. Encouraging Paul to expect anything beyond friendship was the worse kind of folly.

Over and over, Volnar and every other adult vampire she knew had cautioned against preying on people she worked with. Constant association with a donor would make it too easy to slip up and let the ephemeral suspect her nonhuman nature. The more often she had to mesmerize a human companion into forgetting little anomalies in her behavior, the greater the hazard that the mental control would come unstuck.

At least, she thought, *I still had the sense to turn down that weekend invitation.* On top of Volnar's revelation the previous night, this evening's indulgence with Paul left her dizzy with confusion. Mate with Luciano? Not until California slid into the ocean, and maybe not even then. Now, if Luciano were anything like Paul—

Have you lost your mind, girl? He's an ephemeral. A food source—or at most a pet.

She needed advise, and not from her official adviser. Volnar had already made his position clear. Her half-human father, Roger Darvell, a psychiatrist in Maryland, would understand her predicament. Ordinarily a male vampire had no role in his offspring's life beyond the genetic one, but as hybrids, Roger and Gillian didn't conform to the standard rules. While growing up, she had spent several weeks each year with him.

After checking the time on the East Coast, she punched in her father's phone number. Since it was well after 6 p.m. there, he ought to be awake. Curled up on her bed, she drummed her fingers on the nightstand through four rings, until he answered. She felt illogically comforted by the sound of his cultured New England accent. In a rush of words, she poured out her distress at Volnar's ultimatum.

"I'm surprised you didn't call Claude," Roger said. "He's so much closer to you geographically. Or Juliette." Roger's brother Claude had a home in Los Angeles and spent most of his time there.

"Neither of them would really understand. Sure, they'd try to sympathize, but they don't have the human viewpoint on sex. They'd wonder what I'm making such a fuss about. Even my mother—Lord Volnar picked you as her mate, and she went along with it."

"He didn't try to override Juliette's veto power, though," Roger said. "She wanted a child and accepted me of her own free will. Besides, it wasn't quite the same thing. We never actually had intercourse; it was done with artificial insemination."

"How?" Gillian asked. "I mean, if you couldn't become fertile without being stimulated by a female—"

"I was." Embarrassment tinged his voice. "In the room with her, under the influence of her scent, I ejaculated repeatedly until Volnar decided we had enough of a specimen for conception. After he performed the insemination procedure and I left, I understand Juliette inserted a cervical cap to prevent contamination, so to speak, and then mated with him to satisfy her—needs."

"Okay, probably more than I wanted to know," Gillian muttered.

A pause, while Roger spoke to someone in the background. The extension at his end clicked on, and Gillian heard the voice of Britt Loren, Roger's office partner, bond-mate, and donor. "Did I hear right?" the woman said. "Volnar *ordered* you to mate with a male you can't stand? I'd think any vampire would be shocked at that. Doesn't the female have an absolute right to choose her own—uh—stud?"

"Usually," said Gillian. "But in this case, according to him, the fact that I'm a hybrid outweighs the established custom. It's my duty to breed for the good of the species." She knew her voice sounded bitter but didn't try to soften it.

"I got exactly the same argument," Roger said. "Not that I regret having fathered you, but at the time I resented the pressure."

"Don't let them push you around, girl," said Britt.

Roger dryly commented, "That's easier said than done. We're talking about Gillian's adviser, who also happens to be head of the Council of Elders."

"Then don't you have any suggestions at all?" Depression settled like fog around Gillian.

"One possible counterattack," said Roger. "If you had an alternate choice to offer…isn't there anyone you'd want, if you were left to your own preference?"

"Not anybody who's available. I'd trust Claude, but he's totally committed to his human lover, just like you and Britt. Besides, he's too closely related to me. There are a couple of other males nearer my age that I wouldn't mind mating with, but they have the same drawback—attached to human bond-mates."

Soft laughter from Britt. "Why are all the good ones taken? I thought that was strictly a problem for *human* females."

Gillian sighed. "I'd even accept Volnar as my initiator. I suggested that to him. He turned me down, of course—didn't want to `waste' my fertility. Not that I expect to be fertile the first time anyway. I think he's making a big deal out of nothing."

"If you don't want to become pregnant," Roger said, "that's entirely in your own hands, isn't it?"

"Sure, I could mentally block an embryo from implanting. But I'd rather not be faced with the situation at all. Why can't I just skip the whole thing?" She pulled a pillow into her lap and hunched over it.

"From what I hear," said Britt, "it doesn't work that way. When you go into estrus, you have to—relieve the pressure, so to speak. Right, Roger?"

"How would I know?" he said with a tinge of impatience. "As far as I've been told, yes. You're one-fourth human, though. Your experience might not be typical."

Gillian's depression lightened a degree. "I've thought about that, but I was afraid it might be just wishful thinking. If I could keep from going into heat at all—

Maybe if I don't let any male vampires near me, it won't happen. Or it'll be weaker, not completely unbearable. Once I've ridden it out and it's over with, I won't have to worry about it for another couple of years at least."

Britt said, "And you can't…well…handle the discomfort yourself, can you?"

"I don't think so. I tried, sort of, earlier tonight. It didn't help." She caught herself squirming at the memory.

"I could have told you that," said Roger, "and I'm more human than you are. All it does is make you hungry."

"That's what I found out." Gillian caught herself sighing aloud again, as her thoughts drifted back to her evening with Paul. "What if I wanted to mate with a human male?"

"Aha," Britt said. "I have a feeling that question isn't hypothetical."

Gillian froze in embarrassed silence.

"Well?" Roger said. "Should we assume you're thinking of getting involved with an ephemeral?"

"I don't know about `involved.' I do have a friend—" She wasn't sure, herself, whether she would seriously consider intimacy with Paul.

"You're very young and inexperienced for that," Roger said. "The pitfalls of getting entangled with a human partner who'll have to be told what you really are—"

"Oh, Roger, don't give her a hard time. Gillian, do you think this man is attracted to you?"

Roger didn't give Gillian time to answer. "How could she be sure? Colleague, you know as well as I do that our kind are irresistibly seductive whether we're trying to be or not. You've commented on the phenomenon often enough."

"True," Britt said. "Unless you're consciously suppressing it, you project that magnetism all the time, especially when you're hungry."

Gillian recalled how she had been reacting to Paul lately. "Every time I get near him, I'm hungry."

"Uh-oh," Britt said.

Roger echoed her tone. "Have you fed on him yet?"

"Once, earlier tonight." She half-consciously kneaded the pillow with her free hand.

"You're in serious danger of getting fixated on this man. I can hear it in your voice. That will cloud your perception even more."

If she'd been human, Gillian would have started crying. "Do you mean I'll never be sure whether he likes me or he's just…hypnotized by me?"

"The point is," Roger said, "you have to be very careful. That's where your lack of experience comes in."

"You're bonded with Britt. So is Claude with his human mate. You made it work, and you're not the only ones." Noticing that one of her nails had torn the pillowcase, she relaxed her grip.

"All of whom are significantly older than you," Roger said. "And I know of some vampires equally experienced who've failed disastrously at such relationships."

"Don't be such a wet blanket," Britt said. "Not that he doesn't have a point, Gillian. You have to consider not only how this man will react to the truth about you, but also how he'll adjust in the long run. You're immune to sickness and almost impossible to kill, and you'll never age. How will he feel about that when he's turning into a decrepit old man?"

"You're doing okay so far," Gillian said, knowing she must sound like a sulky child.

"Not without some adjustment problems over the years," said Britt.

"And don't overlook the restraint you'd have to exercise," Roger said. "To keep him healthy, you'd have to content yourself with small sips and make up the difference with animal blood or warmed-over blood bank products. True, the quality more than makes up for the limited quantity. But don't underestimate the problem."

"Then are you telling me it's impossible?"

"Of course not. I only want you to make the decision with your eyes wide open," Roger said.

Britt added, "Back to the short-term problem, if you take a human male for a mate, you have to expect certain…deficiencies, compared to a vampire. With one of your own kind, your pheromones keep him up to the challenge, so to speak. An ordinary man can't ejaculate eight or ten times per hour. If he's young and healthy, and he's been celibate for a while, he might perform three times in the twelve hours you'll be in active estrus. With, uh, encouragement from your hypnotic powers, he might go as high as five or six times. That's a physiological limit you can't get around."

"Roger, your mother mated with a human lover," said Gillian, "or neither of us would be here. Too bad I can't asked her about it." Gillian's grandmother had been lynched, along with her human husband, in 1940.

"Yes, and she's the only one I know of. There's a good reason why most long-term interspecies liaisons involve a human female and a male vampire."

"For a human female, that special…technique…is absolutely unforgettable."

"Britt, please!" Roger said.

She laughed softly. "You're so uptight sometimes, colleague."

"I'm human enough to have a residual distaste for discussing my sex life with my daughter, even indirectly."

Gillian had the feeling that the conversation was racing out of her control. She'd received all the useful advice she could reasonably expect. "Thanks—I'll think about what you said. I'll be careful."

If it's not already too late for that, she thought as she hung up the phone.

Chapter Six

To distract herself, Gillian spent the next hour sorting piles of photographic prints into file folders, each labeled for a different prospective book. If she couldn't indulge her desire for Paul, at least she could immerse herself in the work they shared. Still left with too much time to fill before dawn, she turned on the computer to check her e-mail.

As she scrolled through her in-box, the doorbell rang. Walking toward the living room, she extended her empathic sense to check on the visitor. She touched the mind of a vampire, but not a familiar one. The intrusion puzzled her. Solitary predators didn't make social calls for the fun of it, and why hadn't the visitor phoned ahead? The presence on the other side of the barrier radiated no hostility, but she switched off the alarm and unlocked the bolt with wary deliberation, opening the door only as far as the chain allowed. She scented the metallic aroma of a male vampire's flesh.

"May I come in, Gillian?" Luciano's voice, smooth as melted chocolate, made the hairs on her arms prickle. Through the gap she scanned his face, strikingly pale against the mane of black hair. Traces of red glinted in his silver-gray eyes.

"What for? I don't have anything to say to you."

"Surely you don't want me to shout through the door." His voice had a foreign lilt, too vague to be called an accent.

Removing the chain, she stepped out of his way. "Okay, but make it quick."

"You won't be asking for that in a few more nights," he said, gliding past her to take a seat, uninvited, on the couch. He flashed a smile that verged on a leer, a gesture she'd never seen from a male of her own species before. "Lord Volnar informed you of our arrangement, didn't he?"

She remained standing, to keep whatever advantage she could. "Why, Luciano? You don't like me any better than I like you."

His grin broadened. "As a favor to the Prime Elder. And what makes you think I don't like you? Human females, from what I've seen, are ready and willing all the time. With your first estrus on top of that—"

"Oh, so that's the attraction?" She didn't care to waste breath explaining that she didn't share this human trait. "You want to copulate with a prey animal? A taste of bestiality?"

"And perhaps a taste of your part-human blood. Call it what you wish. I'm sure we'll enjoy each other."

A pain in her jaw made her aware that she was grinding her teeth. Struggling for a courteous tone, she said, "No, because it isn't going to happen. Go back to Volnar and tell him the `arrangement' is off."

The feral smile vanished. "As I understand it, you don't have any say in the matter. And you should consider yourself lucky that I offered to initiate you. Not many eligible males would consent to mate with a half-breed."

Her heart sped up, and she tasted acid. Swallowing the vileness, she reined her anger until her pulse slowed. "That's my problem. You'd better leave now."

"Not until we've discussed the logistics. Where do you want to consummate the union? Here, or on neutral ground? Perhaps a luxury hotel. Unless you're worried about the staff hearing you scream?"

Her fingers involuntarily curled, clawlike. "Aren't you listening? I won't spend ten minutes with you, much less a night. You are *not* my choice."

Luciano darted across the room and grasped her right arm, too quickly for her to dodge. A gasp caught in her throat. His eyes locked on hers. He placed a fingertip on her lips, while the thumb of his other hand caressed her wrist. "Why are you fighting me, young one? I can give you what you need, and it's only for one night, after all."

"Are you trying to seduce me like a human female? You know that won't work. I'm immune."

"You won't be, two or three nights from now." He leaned over to sniff her hair, his breath tickling her ear. An unpleasant shiver ran down her back like a trickle of water, yet she couldn't force herself to pull away. "Yes, you smell like sweet musk. It won't be much longer."

Unwillingly she recalled what Volnar had said about Luciano's "experience." Thanks to their empathic perception, vampires normally couldn't lie to each other, and Luciano made no attempt to shield his emotions. He was telling the truth about the state of near-ripeness he sensed in her, and his eagerness was sincere. Her stomach knotted, and something deeper inside quivered. She shook her head.

"I know how to satisfy you." His tongue flicked her earlobe. "You feel the craving already, don't you? Do you think you can relieve it by yourself? Don't bother trying.

Artificial aids won't help, either. You'll need a live male inside you."

The image generated a rush of heat in her lower abdomen. She involuntarily swayed into Luciano's embrace, going rigid when she realize what she was doing. *No! I don't want him!* She wouldn't allow her body to trick her into surrendering to a creature who felt nothing for her but contempt. She stepped back, trying to tug her hand free.

He squeezed tighter and closed the gap between them. His other arm wrapped around her. Too astonished to evade him, she felt his open mouth cover hers. She had never seen any vampire kiss another. Maybe some of them toyed with that human custom, but none she had ever met.

When Luciano's tongue probed between her lips, she whipped her free hand up to scratch his face. He sprang back with a snarl. Blood beaded on his cheek. Rather than attack her again, he shut his eyes in a moment's concentration. The thin slashes closed.

He glared at her, the red sparks in his eyes more prominent than before. "I won't waste time fighting you now. You'll beg for my touch soon enough. I'll see you then." He stalked out and slammed the door.

Chapter Seven

Shaking, Gillian fastened the deadbolt and chain, then reset the alarm. *That does it, I have to get away!* The sensations that still stirred in the pit of her stomach told her that she didn't dare let Luciano within reach when she entered estrus. Her instincts would give in to him no matter how much she loathed the idea. She had to hole up somewhere until the hormonal storm passed.

Where? Roger or his brother Claude would give her sanctuary at a moment's notice. Her mother would probably do the same, though with more of an argument. And those were the first places Volnar would look. Gillian knew that hiding in plain sight would only delay the inevitable by a few hours.

Leave town and check into a motel hundreds of miles away? Using her credit card for airfare and lodging would leave a trail Volnar could follow. If she withdrew cash, she would still have to buy a plane ticket, and her adviser need only cover the concourse at LAX and interview one reservation clerk after another, using his hypnotic influence, until he discovered Gillian's destination.

Could she evade him by car? But where to go?

She collapsed onto the couch, her hands still trembling. Paul had invited her to his cabin. She could take him up on that offer. She'd never visited there before. Volnar and Luciano had no way of knowing about the place's existence, much less its location. All she had to do was get to Paul without alerting the two older vampires. *As if either one of them would stake out my house, anyway.* But just in case, she would behave as if they did.

After tossing a few clothes into her overnight bag, she stuffed the inside zipper compartment of her purse with hundreds of dollars in various denominations, thankful for Volnar's training on this point, at least. He'd always insisted that she keep plenty of emergency cash tucked away. Ready to leave, she turned off all the lights except for the porch lamp, then peered between the curtains to survey the street out front. No sign of Luciano, no wisp of a vampire's aura lingering in the dark. If he lurked out there, he'd veiled himself from her sight. Most likely, though, he wouldn't have bothered to hang around.

Still, she exited through the back door and didn't head for her car. On the threshold she paused to wrap an illusion of invisibility around herself, a psychic shield to deflect any eyes that glanced her way. Only a member of her own species powerful enough to penetrate that shield—such as Volnar, who was nowhere near—would see her. To ephemerals and lower animals, she flitted through the night like a wisp of fog.

She walked four blocks to the nearest Seven-Eleven, where she called a cab on the pay phone. When the taxi pulled up, she remembered at the last minute to make herself visible before stepping to the curb. She gave the driver Paul's address. Only when she was walking up to his door did she stop to think about the lateness of the hour. Paul would think she had gone crazy. No matter, he wouldn't shut her out.

Seconds after she rang the buzzer, she heard his footsteps on the carpeted floor. Why wasn't he asleep at this hour? Lying awake fantasizing about her, maybe? The thought gave her a frisson of guilty delight. He cracked the door a cautious inch, then unhooked the chain and flung it wide when he saw her.

"Gillian? What in the world are you doing here?"

He wore only a pair of running shorts. The fragrance of his clean flesh with a residue of sexual musk and a trace of aftershave swept over her.

After a quick glance toward the street, she said in a strained whisper, "Let me in. Please."

Without waiting for an answer, she shoved past him into the living room. He closed and locked the door, turning toward her with a puzzled frown.

Her courage dissolved. She dropped the overnight bag and purse, flung herself upon him, threw her arms around his neck, and shuddered with tearless sobs. After a second of astonishment, he wrapped her in a hug. Her fear melted in the warmth of his aura. His body heat and the smoothness of his back against her palms woke her hunger all over again. His heartbeat revved up, and his unguarded human emotions bombarded her with worry, affection, and lust. With the close fit between their heights, she felt his response physically, too. For a second she yielded to the impulse to press against the hard bulge.

Shocked at her own behavior, she pulled back, panting like some ordinary human female with her pulse and respiration not even under conscious control. Paul's flush of embarrassment quickened her appetite. *What's wrong with me? I fed on him just a few hours ago.* To her relief, he pretended to ignore her lapse and his own excitement.

"Gillian…shh, it's all right. You're safe." He led her to the couch and made her sit down. He sat beside her with an arm around her shoulders, a safe enough position as long as she remembered not to let her mouth stray too near his chest or neck. "Now tell me what's going on."

Ashamed of her panic, she managed a calm tone. "Earlier, you invited me to your cabin."

"Yeah? Does this mean you've changed your mind? I'm glad, but you could've told me tomorrow. It's not like the invitation was going to expire." The tenderness in his voice softened the teasing.

Noticing her fists clenched in her lap, she uncurled them and drew a deep breath. "I have to go right now. Please." Though she could have short-circuited all argument by hypnotically overriding his will, her human part couldn't accept treating a friend that way. Using her power to feed on a man who desired her anyway was one thing, but she couldn't bring herself to force him something he might not want to do.

The trace of humor vanished from his tone. "What's wrong, Gillian? Are you in some kind of trouble?"

"Sort of. I need to hide." She realized she should have concocted a reason to give him.

"From who?"

"A man." She sensed a spark of anger in Paul's aura. "I'm not hurt, but I need to get away for a while. It's a—a guy who's interested in me and won't take no for an answer."

"He's stalking you?" Paul squeezed her hand tightly enough to cause pain to a human female.

"You could say that. I want to go someplace he doesn't know about. Your cabin sounds perfect."

"Say no more—*mi casa es su casa*. But shouldn't you report this creep to the police?"

"No! No police!" At his bewildered look, she said, "I can handle this myself. All I need is a temporary hideout."

"Won't he just start harassing you again when you go home?"

"There's a good reason why he won't." She stood up, sizzling with impatience. "I can't explain the rest of it. Please trust me." Her eagerness to get moving almost overcame her scruples about mesmerizing him.

He got to his feet, took her hand, and lightly kissed it. "Of course I do. Maybe you can bring yourself to tell me later, but if not, that's your choice."

The brush of his lips on the cilia in her palm made her teeth tingle. She forced herself to retrieve her hand. "Thanks…I'll never forget this."

"Good thing I'm done with classes until September," he said over his shoulder as he headed for the bedroom. She heard him opening drawers and rummaging through clothes. A minute later, he reappeared with a small suitcase. "We can work on the books while we're up there."

She followed him into his home office, where he grabbed his laptop computer and piled manuscripts and diskettes into a briefcase. "Oh…you're planning to stay there with me?"

He turned to her with a look of faint surprise. "Did you think I was just going to abandon you in a strange place, with some jerk trying to hunt you down?" Snapping the briefcase shut, he walked over to her and cupped the back of her head, his thumb tracing absentminded circles behind one ear. "Don't worry, I won't try to take advantage of the situation. Separate rooms."

She acknowledged the pledge with a nod and glided out of his reach. Whether she wanted him to keep that promise, she still wasn't sure.

Minutes later, she sat in the passenger seat of his car, speeding northeast on Interstate 15 toward Big Bear Lake. He didn't try to talk much on the long drive, for which she was grateful. The farther they got from the city, the more her mood lightened. Surely neither Volnar nor Luciano had any way of finding her at Paul's vacation cabin. All she had to do was ride out a few nights of estrus and keep him from noticing anything abnormal about her.

Yeah, all! a sardonic voice in her head taunted her. She told it to shut up.

They drove straight through except for a short break at a convenience store, where Paul filled a bag with miscellaneous groceries. By the time the car pulled into the driveway of the cabin, the sky was turning gray with a hint of dawn. The small house with a fake log facade stood in a clearing at the end of a narrow gravel road, surrounded by trees. Gillian stepped out and stretched her cramped legs, inhaling the clean scent of pine and the cool breeze from the lake. *Good hunting here, I'll bet.*

Carrying the grocery bag, Paul led the way inside. The front of the cabin consisted of a living room and an eat-in kitchen. Down a short corridor to the rear of the building, he showed her to the guest room, with a bathroom sandwiched between its door and the one that led to his own bedroom.

"I guess you'll want to get some sleep. I sure do." He paused in the hallway, his eyes not quite meeting hers.

Not wanting to linger long enough for awkwardness to melt into temptation, she said, "Thanks for taking me in. It won't be for long."

"Long as you need. I just hope you'll be safe here."

"I will. Don't worry." Brushing aside her scruples, which became more insistent and inconvenient by the hour, she locked onto his gaze and said, "Don't worry about me. A few days from now, it will all be over, and I won't have to hide. Believe that."

His eyelids drooped, and he leaned against the nearest wall. "I believe you."

A problem she'd temporarily forgotten came to mind. "Listen carefully. I like to sleep most of the day. Don't let it bother you, and don't try to wake me. Don't disturb me at all. Okay?"

"Okay," he mumbled. His drowsiness added to the effect of her hypnosis.

"And don't worry about what I eat or don't eat, either. I'm fine. Understand?"

He nodded.

"Okay. Goodnight, Paul."

After his answering "goodnight," she slipped into the guest room and closed and locked the door. She hardly trusted herself not to take advantage of his delicious pliability.

Chapter Eight

Gillian awoke disoriented. Weak rays from the setting sun filtered through Venetian blinds. Paul's scent permeated the air around her. It triggered the memory of driving up from San Diego the previous night. Extending her senses, she heard Paul rummaging in the kitchen. She stretched, shrugging the sheet and patchwork quilt away from her naked body. A bird chirped outside the window. Wind rustled pine needles against the glass.

I'm safe here, really safe. Well, safe from everything but her own desire for her host. And surely she could control herself for a few days. *Oh, yeah? Your record hasn't been great so far.*

She reminded the voice that she had satisfied her hunger, and therefore her curiosity. Now that the mystery was gone, self-restraint should become easier. Would her hypnotic commands of the night before hold firm? She would find out in a few minutes, when she faced Paul.

At the last second she remembered to throw on a terrycloth beach wrap before opening the bedroom door. She was so used to living alone that she had almost stepped into the hall naked. For another vampire, a glimpse of her in the nude wouldn't have much effect without the heat and aroma of her own arousal, but human males reacted strongly to that visual stimulus. She tended to forget how bare female flesh excited them.

In the shower she scrutinized her body, wondering whether she needed to worry about a glance at it driving

Paul mad with lust. She didn't conform to contemporary human standards of beauty, with her height and small breasts. For a bleak moment, she speculated that without her vampiric allure, he might not find her attractive at all.

The aroma of broiling meat greeted her when she emerged from the bathroom and scrambled into jeans and a T-shirt. She didn't bother with a bra; with her breast size, she seldom did. In the kitchen she found Paul, dressed in a T-shirt and Bermuda shorts, scooping a couple of hamburgers out of the oven onto paper towels to drain. His aura brightened when he saw her. "Good, you're up. I hope I brought enough stuff you can eat. There's broth and vanilla ice cream and milk—"

"Milk is plenty for now," she said, opening the refrigerator to pour herself a glass.

"Okay," he said cheerfully. So far, her "don't worry" command was working.

She sat at the table and watched him load up his hamburger buns with ketchup and mustard. "I'll just watch you eat," she said, sipping the milk.

Conversation about the book project kept them going through dinner, after which Paul inserted a disk into his laptop and showed her outlines for future installments in the series. "I know we have to anthropomorphize the animals somewhat, to keep the kids interested," he said. "But I don't want to go too far and mislead them. It's too easy for people to fall into the trap of thinking animals' minds—if any—work the same as ours."

"Such as?" She hovered over him, too restless to sit.

"For instance, when a cat plays with a mouse, some people think she's being cruel. In fact, the releasing and recapturing behavior is just an instinctive response to the stimulus of the prey's movements."

"Okay, maybe we should write a story about feral cats."

"We've already made a good start on demonstrating that predators are a vital part of nature, with the coyote book."

"I like a man who appreciates predators," she said, wishing she were free to explain why she felt that way. "How about bears next?"

"Whoa, I don't even want to think about you trying to sneak up on a bear. I'd have too hard a time finding a new partner. Now, here's my raccoon plot—"

His nearness, the rhythm of his heartbeat and breathing, the radiant heat of his flesh all conspired to distract her. She would have to hunt for animal prey soon, just to take the edge off her appetite. She was thankful that Paul, being only human, couldn't sense her craving.

"I think we've done enough for one day," he finally said. After switching off the computer, he opened the curtain to reveal the fading light of a summer sunset. "How about a drink outside?" A thread of nervous anticipation underlay the simple words.

He opened a bottle of white zinfandel, and they took their glasses onto the wide deck at the back of the cabin, facing toward the mountains. They sat in a pair of deck chairs with the bottle on the floor between them. At least, Gillian thought, they weren't sharing a bench, where physical contact would add to the temptation she had to resist.

She quickly realized, though, that Paul had no intention of resisting. After a few minutes of silent companionship in the fading daylight, he carefully set his glass down on the other side of his chair, leaned toward her, and took her hand.

She could already hear his heartbeat clearly, of course, yet the sensation of his pulse racing under her fingers sent electric shocks through her nerves. When she didn't retreat, he lightly brushed her hair away from her forehead and stroked down her cheek and jawline. Her teeth tingled. He had no way of guessing how provocative that gesture was.

With her chin cupped in his palm, his fingers caressing her neck, he bent over to nibble the corners of her mouth. She could stop him anytime. She knew she ought to do that, should hypnotize him to forget any desire he felt for her. The command would work, if she really wanted it to, if she exerted her will firmly enough.

Instead, her lips parted to welcome the probe of his tongue. Her gasp of surprised pleasure encouraged him. His arm slipped around her shoulders. He tasted like beef blood and vanilla ice cream. She wanted him for dessert…

When his hand left her neck to explore the front of her shirt, a flimsy shield for the bare flesh underneath, Gillian recovered her senses. She pulled back. Taking the hint, Paul let go of her.

"You must know how I feel about you," he said. His rapid breathing and pulse gratified her, despite her better judgment. "I want us to be a lot more than collaborators or even friends. Tell me honestly, what are my chances?"

She gazed into his eyes. She wanted to answer rationally, but the hammering of his heart deafened her thoughts, and the pulsating glow of his aura fogged her vision. *Here's the perfect time to mesmerize him, make him to stop wanting me.* She couldn't bring herself to speak those orders. Instead, she stood up so abruptly she almost knocked the chair over.

When he got up, too, she backed away from him. "I'm sorry, Paul. I can't talk about that now. I need to get some fresh air." Silly excuse, when they were already outside. She sensed his surprise and hurt but hardened herself against the silent appeal. "Exercise, I mean. I need to go for a walk, alone. Please." She hurried down the back steps and into the dark woods.

* * * * *

From the deck, Paul watched Gillian rush into the shadows under the trees. What scared her so much about his question? She should know she didn't have to run away from him. All she had to do was say no, and he would respect her decision.

No matter how much he ached for her. Hell, how was he supposed to understand the workings of a woman's mind? He was a zoologist, not a psychologist.

Taking another sip of his wine, he grimaced. Suddenly it tasted sour. Dinner felt like a heavy lump in his midsection. Might as well admit to himself that he'd ridden along on this trip not just to protect her, but in hopes of seducing her.

So does that make me a sleazeball? I don't think so. After that kiss, he knew she wanted him, too. For some reason she fled in panic from her own desire. Should he chase her or wait for her to return on her own? She was running around by herself in the woods—

His frustration evaporated in a surge of fear for her. *What if that guy who's stalking her somehow followed us? I can't let her wander out there alone.* He dashed inside, grabbed a flashlight, and plunged into the forest in the direction Gillian had taken.

He didn't have any trouble tracking her. She'd left a trail of broken branches and trampled undergrowth. After a few minutes, he noticed a crumpled ball of cloth on the ground. When he picked it up, he recognized Gillian's shirt.

What the hell--?

Paul increased his pace. Seconds later, he slammed to a halt at the edge of a clearing. The flashlight reflected off a pair of red eyes.

The world tilted under his feet. *I don't believe this!*

Chapter Nine

Muscles twitched under her skin. Frustration made a knot in her stomach. She stormed through the undergrowth, heedless of the noise she made. Her peripheral vision caught glimpses of the auras of small animals that skittered out of her path. She growled aloud. Her nerves crawled like a swarm of ants. *How many nights of this can I take?*

Panting like a panicked animal herself, she leaned against a tree and skimmed her hands down the front of her body. The friction made her nipples peak. The burning in her throat and the pit of her stomach sparked a similar fire between her legs. One hand, almost without conscious direction, plunged into the V and began rubbing. An unfamiliar wetness welled up. Wrapping the other arm across her chest to press on her taut nipples, she vigorously massaged the source of the moist heat. After several minutes, though, she still felt no relief. Snarling, she shoved herself away from the tree.

There was one thing she could do to work off these unwelcome urges. The need to change boiled up from deep within her. Fur sprouted on her arms, neck, and face even before she stripped off her shirt and tossed it aside. The wings burst from her back. Her teeth elongated into fangs, her nails into talons.

Though she had no room to fly under the trees, she could run. Her feet skimmed the ground, hitting the mat of pine needles every couple of yards. Again, she made no attempt to glide silently or avoid the weeds and fallen branches in her path. When she blundered into a clearing and sighted the halo of a deer's life-essence, she was nearly as surprised as the animal.

The doe, nibbling on the leaves of a sapling, whipped her head around to fix on Gillian. Gillian sprang too fast for the victim to flee. No subtlety; she just crashed into the doe and knocked her down, with a blow to the head to stun her. Straddling the unconscious prey, Gillian sank her fangs into the softness of the abdomen. The gush of blood granted momentary relief for the fire in her stomach.

After a few swallows, she became aware of her surroundings again. That was when she heard human footsteps approaching. She raised her head and confronted the glare of a flashlight.

Behind it, she saw Paul staring at her, as stunned as the deer had been a minute earlier.

Gillian's body melted back into human shape. She was still young enough to have trouble holding the winged form, and stress always made it unstable. She rose from her crouch, automatically wiping her mouth with her forearm.

The light beam shook from the tremor of Paul's hand. "You changed…you were biting—oh, my God!"

She tried to pitch her voice to a calming tone. "Don't be afraid, Paul."

"Afraid?" He sounded hoarse. "Good Lord, your eyes shine red. No way—I am *not* seeing this."

She knew she had to erase his memory. But not here—back at the cabin, where he'd feel safer and she would have time to work on him. "I won't hurt you," she tried again. "Let's go back and…talk." The excuse for delay, she realized, meant she didn't want to make him forget. She enjoyed the idea of his knowing the truth.

"Talk," he said. "You bet we will." The fear he radiated ebbed as she stepped closer to him. He swept the flashlight over the ground while they strolled toward the cabin. "You bit that deer."

"I was hungry."

She sensed a renewed shock jolt through him, but he didn't show any signs of panic. "Either I'm crazy, or you aren't human. And I don't believe I'm crazy."

So far, he was taking the revelation better than she'd feared. "You're not."

"Let me get this straight. Wings—fangs—drinking blood—you're a vampire, right?"

Gillian suppressed the impulse to laugh. "This is one time I can be thankful for all those dumb movies. They save a lot of explanation."

"That explains the night-owl habits and the picky eating. If you sleep in a coffin, you forgot to bring it along."

She gave her head an impatient shake. "I didn't say the movies were accurate. I'm not supernatural. I don't sleep in a coffin, and I reflect in mirrors. We're another species, not undead."

"I saw you transform from a monster with fangs and wings to a human-looking female. That's not supernatural?"

"It's a kind of psychic power. We can shift into an ancestral form stored in our DNA. We don't think of it as supernatural. It's part of our biological inheritance."

"Oh, man, what zoologist wouldn't kill for a chance like this!" He added with a sidelong glance, "Not that I'd publish anything. Who'd believe me? And a headline in the *National Enquirer* would wreck my chances at tenure."

"Then you don't want me to leave?" she said as they reached the cabin and climbed the stairs to the deck.

"Hell, no! I want answers."

"How did you find me, anyway? And why?"

He shrugged. "I was worried, after you ran off that way. You weren't exactly hiding your tracks. Broken underbrush, not to mention this." She realized he was carrying her discarded T-shirt. "Uh...you might want to put it on."

"Why? You've already seen me."

He blushed and averted his eyes. "Humor me."

So she pulled on the shirt and followed him into the living room.

"Don't know about you, but I need a drink." His heartbeat spiked, and he threw her another dubious look. "Guess you already had yours." Detouring to the kitchen, he returned without the flashlight and with a gin and tonic on the rocks. "First question, just to get things clear. You don't do to people what you did to that doe, I hope?"

"I feed on human prey. I have to, two or three times a week, to stay healthy. But it's a small amount, and I don't kill them. They never know it, in fact."

They sat down at opposite ends of the couch. He gulped a swallow of his drink, obviously gathering courage. "Never know? Okay, next question. Have you done it to me?"

She nodded, igniting a spark of anger in his aura. "Once. Last night."

"I don't remember a thing. Well, except for a kiss. And a dream—a pretty hot dream." He scowled at her over the rim of his glass. "You caused it, right? You hypnotized me."

"That's what we do." Would he change his mind and throw her out now?

"Just routine, huh? So I'm just a snack?"

"No, Paul! We're friends."

She edged toward him, and he recoiled. "That's what I thought…until now. Friends don't do what amounts to rape."

"You're angry."

"Damn straight!"

"But you did enjoy the—dream. And you still desire me."

His face flushed a deeper red. "Now what, you're reading my mind?"

"Just your emotions."

Putting the glass down, he bowed his head in his hands. "Good God, this is worse than I thought."

"I don't understand what's so horrible. Now that you know the truth, I won't mesmerize you again without your permission."

"So you expect me to just let bygones be bygones? Oh, and have you pick up every feeling that pops into my head." The sarcastic edge in his voice stung her like a razor cut.

"What did you expect me to do?" she snapped. "Explain what I am and what I wanted? As if you would've believed me."

"You could have trusted me!" he yelled.

"Oh, you wouldn't have called the police or the men in white coats when I asked for a little sip of blood? Or thrown me out into the street, at the very least?"

He sighed. "You have a point. Truth is, I don't know what I would have done. And it's too late to find out now." The crackle of static in his aura quieted. "Trust me now. Why did you really ask me to bring you here? What are you hiding from?"

"A man actually is stalking me. But it's a little more complicated than I implied."

"I'd have thought you could protect yourself against any ordinary man."

"This isn't an ordinary man. It's one of us. As I said, it's a complicated story."

"We've got plenty of time, right? Tell."

"First off, I'm part human. You see, there aren't many of us, fewer than ten thousand worldwide, and our fertility rate has declined over the past couple of centuries."

"Are you immortal, like in the movies?"

"Movies again! Not exactly like that, but we do live a very long time and never die of old age."

"Interesting." He no longer emitted either fear or anger. "Then it would make sense for your species to produce very few offspring."

"Yes, that's how it works. Our females go into estrus only once every few years, and they don't ovulate every time. Males aren't fertile at all, except when stimulated by a female in estrus."

"That fits. Typical K-selected species."

"Say what?"

"Extended lifespan, only one or two infants per conception, long gestation, heavy energy investment in the young." The technical discussion seemed to calm him down.

"Uh—right. The trouble is, more often than not, heat periods are barren. The elders say it's been getting worse recently."

"So your population's declining—even if you don't die naturally, some of you must get killed."

Gillian reflected that Paul's doctorate in zoology saved a lot of time in explanations. "Right. Our Prime Elder got the idea for a breeding project, revitalizing our gene pool with human DNA. That's where I come in, being one-fourth human. He thinks I probably have hybrid vigor and might even be fertile at my first heat, which normally never happens. So he picked a mate for me."

"One that you didn't want."

She caught herself baring her teeth at the memory of Luciano's arrogance. "Not only is it our traditional right to choose our own mates, I can't stand this person. He doesn't like me, either. He's just trying to score points with the Prime Elder. I needed a refuge he wouldn't know about. Someplace to hide until I get through estrus."

"After that it won't matter, because you won't be producing the pheromones anymore. Is that how it works?"

Relieved at not having to spell out the details, she nodded.

"Okay, I admit I'd have thought you were putting me on or out of your mind, if you'd tried to tell me all this before. But now that I know, of course I want to help." Once again the blood suffused his skin, and his aura dimmed with embarrassment. "One thing, though…female animals in heat usually, uh…suffer."

"I had a theory that since I'm part human, it wouldn't be as severe. I thought if I stayed away from male vampires, I might be able to get through it on my own."

"You thought?"

"Well, it hasn't worked out quite the way I hoped. And would you please stop blushing like that?"

He picked up his half-empty glass and took a long swig. "It's not like I can control it. Anyway, why do you care?" His tone roughened with a blend of defiance and desire.

"The dilated capillaries and the rise in your skin temperature…watching that makes me thirsty, if you must know."

"Oh. Should I worry?"

"My self-control isn't totally shot!"

"Glad to hear it. Anyway, if you didn't rip out my throat before, when I was totally off guard, you sure won't do it now that I know about you." His eyes shifted away from hers and back again.

"Then what's wrong?" she said.

"I want to ask you something, and I'm not sure if it violates some vampire etiquette rule. I'd like to watch you change. I didn't get a good look out there in the woods."

Having expected something worse, she said, "Sure, I can do that, if you promise not to freak out."

"Freak out? Perish the thought. Cool, analytical man of science, that's me."

She stood up and peeled off her shirt.

Paul's eyes widened. "Do you have to do that?"

"I'm too young to include clothes in the change. What difference does it make, now that you've already seen me half-naked?"

"Nudity has emotional significance for human males. You must have figured that out by now."

She nudged her sandals off but didn't remove her jeans, in consideration for his obvious uneasiness. "You're not just any man, though. And what's the big deal about showing my breasts? I've seen those pictures in *Playboy*, and I don't come close to the American erotic ideal."

"Not all men have mammary obsessions, not even American men." He scanned her body, then hastily looked away. "And I like your breasts." The dilation of his pupils and the flare of red in his aura confirmed that claim.

With a sigh of pleasure, she unleashed the change. Again the silken fur, fox-red like her hair, spread over her body like flame over dry grass. Cream-colored, mothlike wings unfurled. She felt the tingling eruption of fangs and claws. The sensations eased a little of her tension.

Stunned, Paul gaped at her. After a brief silence, he stood up. "You can't fly, can you?" His hand reached for hers but dropped halfway. "You're too heavy for those wings to lift."

"We levitate. The wings provide balance and steering."

"Levitate." He shook his head. "Another psychic power, like hypnosis and shapeshifting? Sure looks supernatural to me."

Gillian reined her irritation. With so much to take in at once, he had an excuse for thickheadedness. "Our powers evolved like any other animal's special abilities."

Gathering his nerve with obvious effort, he circled around her. "May I touch?"

"Go ahead." Exactly what she wanted but knew she ought to discourage. "Take it easy, though. We're sensitive in this unstable condition."

When his fingers skimmed her wings, the membrane quivered, and she drew in a hissing breath.

"Sorry…does that hurt?"

"Not hurt," she breathed.

His hands swept over the curves of the wings. He stroked down her spine between them. The heat of his palm made her back arch. "Like velvet," he murmured. He repeated the caress. She responded with an involuntary growl-purr.

"Kitten." He clasped one of her hands and fingered the claws. "Tiger kitten." His other hand reached toward her cheek.

She grabbed his forearm.

He winced, though not in fear. "Good Lord, you're strong."

"I didn't mean to hurt you." She unclenched her grip. "You shouldn't touch my—teeth." Her jaws already ached. She couldn't rely on her self-control if he teased her there. His tangy scent and the pounding of his heart made her dizzy. The waistband of her jeans constricted her breath. She normally transformed completely nude.

"I thought I could handle this. Maybe not." She slithered away from him and melted into fully human shape. Her clothes still felt tight enough to make her stomach cramp. She fumbled at the snap and zipper, wiggled out of the jeans, and kicked them away.

Paul's breathing quickened when she stood before him in nothing but bikini pants. "What do you think you're doing?" Though his voice held an edge of anger, the emotion he radiated felt more like desire.

"I couldn't stand it anymore—my skin's crawling..."

"Look, you can't just strip naked in front of a man. Not even a close friend." She felt him tremble with the effort of staying motionless. "It's not fair."

"Then I'll get out of here." She didn't turn to leave the room, though.

"Don't do that. I mean..." He raked his fingers through his hair. "You're driving me crazy. Do I have to say straight out how much I want you? How beautiful you are?

Would he lust for her, though, if she were only human? Gillian knew perfectly well that her figure didn't match the Barbie doll ideal. "That's an illusion," she said. "It's the vampire allure you're responding to, not the way I look."

"Hold it—you aren't hypnotizing me right now, are you?"

She emphatically shook her head. "I won't hypnotize you or drink from you again without your permission. Word of honor." Luckily, it didn't seem to occur to Paul that she might influence him to accept her word, and he would never realize it. She didn't want to complicate the discussion by reminding him of that possibility. "It's a kind of magnetism we have. Involuntary, unless we suppress it deliberately, and it gets stronger the more excited we are."

"You're saying I can't help being attracted to you. Any man would."

She nodded. "Sexual polarity makes it more intense, but it can work on same-sex targets if we want it to."

"I don't believe it's just that." Now he did allow himself to inch closer to her, as if he expected her to bolt like a deer. "I like you for yourself, your mind, your personality."

"I'm glad," she whispered. If she let herself think too much about his claim, she would doubt it all over again. In her overwrought condition, she couldn't be sure, herself, how much she was lulling him with her innate power.

"Because I need a favor from you."

The musky aroma of his arousal made a fire smolder in the pit of her stomach. The antlike prickle under her skin was back, stronger than before.

Chapter Ten

"What kind of favor?" The tremor in his voice underscored the queasy excitement he radiated. A touch of anxiety made his pulse race, yet her heat vision showed blood pooling in his loins.

She snaked her arms around his waist and undulated against him. "I'm in estrus. I recognize the symptoms, from the descriptions I've heard. And I won't be able to ride it out alone, after all. I tried, and it didn't work. Something about needing a live male body in direct contact with mine, I guess.

He hugged her close and massaged her shoulder blades. "You mean you want me to—Good grief, do you know what position you're putting me in?"

"What's wrong?" She sensed waves of lust emanating from him. Why did he hesitate? "You said you wanted me."

"If you can read emotions, you know I do. Hell, you should be able to tell without that." His arms tightened around her, and he nuzzled her neck. "That's just the point. This is the stereotype of every man's ultimate fantasy, a woman in heat who can't get enough of him. I'd be taking advantage of your…predicament."

Ephemerals! Their logic completely eluded her. "Taking advantage of *me*? Don't be ridiculous, it's the opposite. I'm taking advantage of *you*. I need a male, and you're the only one around." She drew a deep breath. "And the only one I want."

He gazed at her, their eyes meeting almost level. "Really?"

"Yes. I certainly don't want any of the eligible males of my own species. If I have to choose anyone, it's you."

"All right." His voice shook. To her ears, the thunder of his heartbeat almost drowned out the words. "If you're sure, I'm not about to pass up the opportunity."

"Wonderful!" She decided not to mention the literal truth of the "can't get enough" clause. With luck, her human heritage meant that her needs wouldn't rage beyond the limits he could handle. She slipped out of his arms and stripped off her panties. "Take off your clothes."

"Whoa—" He backed up a pace. "We don't usually rush into things so abruptly."

"Oh. I guess you have plenty of experience with sexual relations." Her eagerness shaded into trepidation as she speculated that her ignorance of mating etiquette might offend or bore him.

He shrugged, his aura wavering with a hint of discomfort. "I'm no Don Juan. I've been celibate since my last relationship ended six years ago. So you don't have to worry about catching anything."

That point hadn't even occurred to her. "I'm immune to infectious diseases. And since I've never had intercourse, I can't be a carrier."

"Never? Not even with the men you've fed on?" His aura dimmed, then flared a lurid red.

What did that momentary flash of darker emotion mean? Jealousy? "It's not necessary. I get my satisfaction from them without allowing that intimacy. This is different."

At the word "different," she sensed a tinge of doubt in him, but he didn't pursue the point. "I almost forgot, what about pregnancy?"

"I don't expect to ovulate. That's just a far-fetched idea of my mentor's. If I do, I have enough control over my body to prevent a fertilized egg from implanting."

"That's all right, then. If you aren't worried about—"

"What's wrong?"

"Nothing." He exhaled a deep breath. "No problem."

"So what are you waiting for? Get undressed." She reached for the snap on his shorts.

Paul grabbed her wrist. "Hold it. I'm used to a little more in the way of preliminaries." To her dismay, the level of his arousal dropped slightly, tainted by confused hesitance.

"Why? You've acknowledged that you desire me, and I need a male. The seduction process is unnecessary."

"Another male fantasy, a woman who's as ready as a man. You make it sound so, well, mundane."

Gillian shrugged. "It's a biological process, after all." Though she enjoyed his ardor, at the same time it made her prickle with uneasiness. Personal involvement with a human donor meant a risk she'd always been taught to avoid.

"At least let's go into the bedroom. More comfortable."

"Very well." She laced her fingers through his. "Yours or the guest room?"

"Uh…mine, I guess." His thumb traced a circle on her palm. The cilia bristled, making her shiver with pleasure. "Hey, little hairs. Interesting."

"And sensitive. Come *on*." She led him into the bedroom and lay down on his unmade bed, still holding his hand.

Sitting on the edge of the mattress, he stroked down the front of her chest, between her breasts. "Interesting hair growth pattern."

"Speaking as a zoologist?" she whispered.

He grinned. "Right. Got to make careful observations." He traced the outline of the inverted triangle of fine hair that covered her torso from the underside of her breasts down, with its apex at her navel. "Like silk." The painless burning of his hand on her bare flesh made her squirm. Every nerve sizzled, and her nipples hardened.

Paul freed his hand from hers and skimmed over both peaks. Ordinarily, that caress would have made her salivate and the roots of her teeth ache. It did, but instead of the whole-body arousal that normally accompanied blood-thirst, she felt fiery darts shooting straight from her nipples to her loins. Crossing her legs and squeezing them didn't help. "Take off your shirt," she whispered.

After he pulled the shirt off, she raked her nails lightly over his chest, careful not to scratch him. When she played with the tight curls of hair and flicked one of his nipples, as taut as her own, he gasped.

"You're sexually aroused," she said.

"How'd you figure that out?" he said with a wry smile. "Oh, yeah, you sense emotions."

"Not only that. I see into the infrared, so I know your skin temperature is rising. And your scent has changed, too."

He flushed a deeper red and bent to take off his shoes and socks. "Good grief, I can't have any secrets around you, can I?" But embarrassment didn't stop him from bending to kiss her, while one hand returned to fondling her breasts. Even though she avidly drank in his taste and aroma, she writhed with impatience.

He paused to catch his breath and ran his hand down the front of her body, this time not stopping at the navel. She arched her hips to meet the hand cupping the soft triangle of pubic hair. "Do you have an erection?" she said.

"Are you kidding?"

"No, I'm asking. My knowledge of human male sexual physiology is only theoretical. I can see a concentration of heat at your groin, but that just tells me blood is rising to the surface there."

"It sure is." His breathing came heavy and ragged.

"Show me."

With shaking hands, he unfastened his shorts and dropped them to the floor, along with the briefs underneath. His erection jutted out at a ninety-degree angle.

Bracing himself with both hands on either side of her, he licked first one nipple, then another. Heat pooled between her legs. She dug her nails into his shoulders, only the scent of blood reminding her to exercise restraint. "What are you waiting for? You're obviously ready to copulate."

Paul gazed into her eyes. "I don't want to start before you're ready, maybe hurt you."

"You can't hurt me. I'm not human, remember? No hymen. Besides, I can suppress pain."

"Still, most women like to take it slowly, get warmed up, so to speak." His fingers toyed with the silken hair at the apex of her thighs.

"I don't need warming up. I'm hot." She meant the term literally; her normally cool skin felt scorched. "And my vagina is lubricated. I'm ready for intromission."

One of his fingers dipped into her wet heat, then stroked slowly up and down between the folds. "Unbelievable, you've got me incredibly turned on by talking like a textbook." He circled the firm bud at the top of her labia.

She couldn't suppress a moan. "That tickles."

"How's this?" His fingertip flicked back and forth over the sensitive spot. "Or this?" He swept down the insides of both thighs, then back up to her burning center.

"Tickles," she whimpered.

"Then I'd better stop." She heard the humor in his tone.

Her hips involuntarily rocked against his hand. "No! Stopping makes it worse." She wiggled, her attention torn between the slowly building pressure in that location and the hot flood deeper inside.

She gripped his shaft, fascinated by the texture, hard, yet satin-smooth on the surface. He groaned and thrust into her clasp.

"You're ready to penetrate, aren't you?"

"You bet," he said through gritted teeth.

"Then do it. Now!"

He knelt between her spread legs and probed at the welcoming portal. She arched up to draw him in. For a second she felt tightness, almost pain, but as she'd expected, it disappeared when he began to move. She caught her breath in astonishment. The sensation was so focused, so unlike the whole-body climax of feeding on aroused prey. Fire consumed her. She undulated with the rhythm of the contractions that convulsed her inner flesh.

The convulsion happened twice more before Paul plunged in to the full depth and groaned aloud while his whole body shook. She felt the hot eruption of his release inside her.

Breathing hard, he eased down on top of her. After a couple of minutes he said, "Oh, Lord, that was incredible. Too bad it was over so fast."

"We can take a slower pace next time, if that's what you want."

He raised his head to stare at her. She felt his surprise. "You're expecting a next time?"

"I'm in estrus, remember? Normally this continues for a full night."

"Yeah, that would be the usual pattern for animals like cats and such. You, too?"

"So I've been told." Did he think of her as an exotic specimen to study? Why did that idea disturb her? She wanted an uncomplicated mating, didn't she?

"Well, as long as I've waited to have you like this, one time couldn't wear me out." He planted a light kiss on her parted lips. "Just give me a little while to recover."

She already felt the insistent need coiling in the pit of her abdomen. Trailing her fingers down the front of his body, she curled over him to circle each of his nipples with her tongue. The salty flavor reminded her of blood, but the urgency that drove her felt different from bloodlust. Her fingertips brushed his genitals, and she felt a twitch of response. He caught his breath.

"I'm getting wet again," she murmured, nibbling her way down his chest, grazing the skin without scratching it.

"I don't think I'm ready—" He gasped as her nails found a sensitive ridge in the perineal area. "Or I could be wrong about that."

Alert to the changing nuances of his emotions and sensations, she followed the shifting pattern of his arousal until he hardened, and she sensed his passion building toward explosion. By now she was writhing with impatience. "Come on," she growled, rolling onto her back.

This time she enjoyed six orgasms before he reached his.

Struggling for breath, his head on her breast, Paul said, "Oh, God, how do you do that? Know exactly how to touch?"

"Empathic perception, remember? That includes physical sensations as well as emotions."

"I can see where it has advantages."

She felt the rhythm of his heartbeat and respiration decelerate as his emotional high faded toward sleep. She dozed awhile, too, although she couldn't really sleep after dark. Within less than half an hour, the craving seized her anew, as fierce as thirst.

She pushed Paul onto his back and lay on top of him. "Wake up."

"What—?" His eyelids barely opened.

"I need you again." She licked and nuzzled him, meanwhile rubbing her insistent heat against his dormant penis.

"Gillian, I'm not sure I can."

"You have to." She raised up to straddle his hips, stroking down his body in ever-lengthening spirals. As she'd expected, his nerves and blood vessels responded to the power of her touch. Finding the trigger points, she worked on them until he sprang erect under her.

"I don't believe this—how—" He was already thrusting even before she impaled herself on him. "You promised you wouldn't hypnotize me."

"This isn't hypnotism, just encouragement. I influenced your body, not your mind."

"Well, it's…definitely—encouraging!"

This time she lost count of her climaxes. Since even vampiric seduction couldn't completely overrule human male physiology, Paul lasted over fifteen minutes before he spent.

The aftershocks of their shared ecstasy left him trembling. "That's absolutely incredible!" he said when he could speak again. She purred with delight at his reaction.

Several minutes later, he stumbled to the bathroom and back, then collapsed into sleep. She watched him for a few minutes, smoothing his damp hair, before she, too, dozed off.

Again, though, she didn't stay zoned out for long. Her body demanded relief. When she woke Paul this time, he sighed. "You know I want to, but there are limits. I'm only human."

"Don't worry, I'll…encourage—you." Her nails raked over his chest. He shuddered. Blood beaded along one scratch where she'd miscalculated and broken the skin. Her tongue flicked at the tantalizing drops. Further aroused by the taste, she intensified her caresses. Inevitably his body responded to her urgency. She climbed on top while he lay with his eyes shut, his body slick with sweat. The prolonged coupling that followed gifted her with a continuous stream of orgasms, each peak almost overlapping the one before it.

After nearly half an hour, he pulled out and demanded in a passion-roughened growl, "Roll over."

"What?" Her head reeled, a crimson fog clouding her vision.

"My turn." He prodded her until she lay face down. Grasping her inner thighs, he shoved her legs apart.

"Paul, what are you doing?" She flexed her fingers and dug her claws into the sheet, fighting the panic incited by this moment of helplessness.

Silently except for the rasp of his breath, he hammered into her. With her legs splayed, she arched her hips like a cat in heat to match his pounding rhythm. He rammed more deeply, stretched her more fully, than she had ever imagined possible.

Wide open to him, body and mind, she found herself swept into the whirlwind of his passion, as if they were bonded. She drowned in his emotions.

He shuddered with the thrill of her wet heat rippling around his rigid shaft. The climax building in his loins felt like a flood of molten lava ready to erupt. He panted in time with his thrusts, and on every exhaled breath he groaned aloud. Gillian moaned in chorus with him. Her cries made his heart race even faster, and he pounded harder to match the speed of their synchronized pulsebeat.

He exulted in the frantic pumping of her hips. He'd unleashed this wildness in her—she wanted him and only him.

"Mine," he breathed. "You're mine. Come with me," he urged, clamping her wrists to the mattress. "That's it, let go, come now—" Seized by a savage impulse, he sank his teeth into the nape of her neck. With a keening moan, she convulsed beneath him. He roared in primal satisfaction.

After a few more strokes he spasmed in release. She howled like a she-wolf as his explosion ignited yet another one in her. Spent, she sank back into her own body.

When they parted and she stretched out beside him, he summoned the strength to put an arm around her. "Gillian, honey, that's the most mind-blowing thing I've ever experienced, but it's not exactly *fun* anymore. I may never move again."

"Rest, then," she whispered. "Sleep." A few seconds of stroking his forehead eased him into oblivion.

After that encounter, she hoped her need had exhausted itself. She got up to take a shower and drink three glasses of water. Though she didn't feel hungry now that the sexual drive had slacked off, the exercise had made her dehydrated. For a few minutes she stood on the deck, without bothering to dress, and watched the shimmering heat traces of insects and small animals in the dark woods. The cool air whispered over her bare skin and made the hair on her arms and torso vibrate along with the cilia in her palms.

She wandered back into the bedroom and looked down at Paul. His musky aroma stirred an echo of blood-thirst in the pit of her stomach. She knelt on the mattress and licked perspiration from his chest, savoring the salty tang. He shifted position but didn't wake. Gillian nuzzled his groin and lapped at the tip of his organ. The droplets that clung there tasted intriguingly similar to blood. Some other time, she looked forward to drinking from that fountain.

She felt her arousal reawakening. Sitting astride his legs, hoping the friction would provide some relief, she continued licking and kissing him until he struggled up to consciousness.

"Gillian, I can't," he groaned. "I'm sorry, but it's just impossible."

"But I need..." She hated to hear herself whimpering in frustration, but she couldn't help it, any more than she could help rocking against his legs to ease the burning that tormented her. Maybe it was true, after all, that a human mate could never satisfy her. If she'd been human herself, the thought would have made her cry.

"Gillian, come up here and let me try...please " Gathering her into his arms, he kissed her open mouth, then each of breasts in turn, while stroking her in long, languid caresses. She shuddered under his petting. Though his body heat felt wonderful on her hypersensitized skin, the fire between her thighs negated the pleasure.

To her surprise, he plunged two fingers inside her. She arched to meet his probe. Within seconds, she fell into a vigorous copulatory rhythm. It didn't seem to matter that his hand, not his erection, provided the stimulus. She had his warm flesh pressed against her and thrusting inside her, she had the comfort of his scent and taste, his thumb meanwhile teased the swollen bud that contributed more to her delight than she would have expected, and she was spiraling higher, higher...

"I know," he murmured, "like cats." She felt his fingernails scrape the inner wall of her canal. She screamed aloud in release.

He kept up the steady rhythm until her convulsions played themselves out. Finally she relaxed with her head on his shoulder.

"It worked," he said, his breath ruffling her hair. "We've found a solution."

"What did you mean about cats?"

"The tomcat has barbs on his penis. The stimulation seems to be vital to the copulation process. So I tried to imitate that, thinking it might be similar with your species."

"Interesting." She stretched and snuggled more comfortably against him. "Logical." She decided she was lucky, after all, to have picked a zoologist for a mate.

* * * * *

Over and over they fell into light sleep, then woke to repeat the operation as the peaks and valleys of her arousal demanded. The ability to please her seemed to satisfy him even though he could no longer share her climaxes. Waves of warmth emanated from him, enfolding her in a rosy cloud of sensual delight. Toward morning, the intervals lengthened. About five a.m., Paul had slept for almost two hours, and with the approach of dawn, Gillian felt the day-sleep beginning to overshadow her.

She was surprised to feel another surge of need. She caressed Paul awake. When he started to pet her, she whispered, "Wait. This should be the last time—I think you can..."

He lay back and let her vampire seduction work on him. For all her efforts and his willingness, though, his erection rose only to half-mast, while she moaned with impatience. "Let me try something," she said. "Trust me."

Often enough, she'd heard her elders refer to blood-sharing as the ultimate thrill. She'd seen evidence of it in the auras of her father and his lover in the aftermath of encounters she was expected to pretend not to notice. Now she slashed her wrist with her teeth and pressed the trickle of blood to Paul's mouth. For an instant he resisted, but the caress of her free hand lulled him, and he clamped his lips to the wound.

The flick of his tongue sent an electric shock through her. On top of it, she felt his emotions more keenly than ever, heard the chaotic riot of his thoughts—*what's she doing, that feels incredible, tastes like champagne*—and felt him stunned by the echo of her arousal in his own loins. Almost instantly his erection sprang upright. As she engulfed him and rocked through her climax, she felt her teeth tingling with thirst. She'd promised him, but—

"Paul, please!" she moaned.

His thoughts answered her, since his mouth was still occupied with sucking her blood. *What's wrong?*

"Please…I need to bite."

Then do it!

When her teeth nipped his throat, and his blood gushed into her mouth, she climaxed again, and he came with her.

For an unmeasured time afterward, they lay motionless, their thoughts so intertwined that Gillian couldn't tell his from her own. She hadn't realized how intimate the union would be. It frightened her, opening her thoughts to an ephemeral, and yet the joy of the sharing was worth it.

After a while Paul disengaged his body from hers and sat up. "Hey, what was that?"

"Bonding," she said, gazing at him from under half-open eyelids. "Two-way blood-sharing makes us telepathically linked."

"You didn't mention that." She sensed a wariness in him.

"I wasn't thinking. I just needed to be close to you and let you feel what I felt."

"And now you're in my head." He shakily stood up. "I'm not sure how I feel about that."

His withdrawal puzzled her. He had enjoyed what they shared as much as she had. Why didn't she feel the simple, pleasantly exhausted satisfaction she felt? "My cycle is finished now. We don't have to be inside each other's thoughts any more than we want to."

"Finished, huh?" A whipcrack of anger accompanied the words. "Just like that. You've gotten what you want, so you don't need me anymore."

"I don't understand...haven't you had more than enough of my demands? I thought you wanted it to be over—"

His irritation faded as quickly as it had sparked. He picked up his shorts from the floor. "Look, I'm worn out, and you probably need to sleep."

"Yes. Oh—when I'm asleep during the day, I look sort of, well, dead. Don't let it worry you."

"Yeah, right." His lips twisted in a wry smile. "After last night, I won't give a second thought to a little thing like that." He walked gingerly toward the bedroom door. Her own muscles reflected the soreness in his, and she wished he would let her massage the pain out. Instead of responding to that tentative thought, he said, "I'll crash in the guest room so you won't be disturbed when I get up."

Though she felt an emptiness when he'd left the room, her fatigue didn't let her brood for long. The daylight coma instantly overwhelmed her.

Chapter Eleven

The moment she woke, well into the evening, Gillian extended her mental antennae in search of Paul. When she brushed the fringe of his thoughts, he rebuffed her in a tone like a slap.

Stay out of my skull.

She curled up and hugged herself for a few minutes, until the sting of that command faded. She'd witnessed the profound union between Roger and Britt, seen the love flowing between them. Why did Paul react to the bond so differently?

Gillian showered and dressed, resisting the impulse to send Paul another telepathic greeting, but constantly aware of his presence in the house, moving from room to room.

She went into the kitchen, where he silently poured her a glass of milk. The aroma of bacon and eggs pervaded the air. Sitting at the table, she watched him serve himself a plate from the stove. Only when he sat opposite her with his food and a glass of orange juice did he finally speak.

"How often is this going to happen? Every seven years, like a Vulcan?"

She didn't pretend not to understand the question. "No more than twice a decade, normally."

"That's a relief," he said without a trace of a smile. "Any more would probably kill me. That's assuming we ever do it again."

She almost choked on a swallow of milk. "Why wouldn't we?"

"Next time you'll have plenty of warning to find a mate of your own species. I figure now that I've serviced you, we go back to being just collaborators, right?"

"Serviced? Is that how you see it?" His cold manner baffled her. "Why would you think that? We share a blood bond now. Our relationship can't be casual."

"A bond you created without asking me. That's a heck of a lot more serious than hypnotizing me a couple of times." She felt him bristle with outrage like a porcupine spreading its quills.

"You enjoyed it as much as I did."

"Damn it, that's not the point!" He shoveled in a few bites of fried egg. "You invaded my mind. Can't you understand why that bothers me?"

"I'm trying to. Paul, I didn't plot to take control of your brain and turn you into a zombie. I wanted to let you share what I was feeling. What's wrong with that?"

"You could've asked."

"I didn't think it out. I acted in the heat of passion. Plus, I really didn't know how intense it would be. After all, I don't make a habit of this."

"Yeah?" Chomping on a slice of bacon, he stared at her for a minute. "You never did this blood bond thing before?"

"Only with my mentor, and that's not the same at all."

"So maybe you have some excuse. But I'm still not sure how I feel. I need to think about it. This is a hell of an information load to process." He pushed his half-empty plate aside and stood up.

"You haven't finished eating. You need nourishment after last night."

"I can feed myself without you giving me orders." He headed for the back door. "I'm going for a walk."

"Okay, we can talk about—"

"Alone. I said I have to think, and that means without your…influence. My brain doesn't work right when you're around."

After he'd left, she drank the rest of her milk and fought the urge to follow him telepathically. Already his absence made her feel half-empty. How would she endure it if he continued to reject her? She wandered into the office and settled down to read some of his rough drafts. The thought of collaborating with Paul in this strained mode chilled her. Which would be worse, never seeing or touching him again, or working with him while this barrier separated them?

Oh, no, I think I'm addicted! She'd been warned about the risk of feeding too often from one victim or feeding at all from a donor she was emotionally entangled with. Yet the warnings hadn't given her any inkling of how fast and hard the condition could strike.

Giving up on work, she poured herself a glass of wine and sat on the deck in the deepening twilight. How long would Paul stay away? He couldn't hike around in the woods all night, could he?

She'd nearly finished the wine when a mental scream ripped through her brain. *Paul!* She leaped to her feet and extended her thoughts toward him.

Stay away from me, Gillian, it's a trap.

Ignoring his plea, she insinuated herself into his senses. For a few seconds she saw through Paul's eyes. A man led him to a car parked on an otherwise deserted dirt road. *Luciano.* Paul's mind still functioned, but his body obeyed the vampire's commands.

Relaxing the link for the moment, Gillian hurried into the cabin, scrambled into her shoes, and rummaged through the junk on Paul's bedroom dresser. She thanked the Dark Powers that he wasn't one of those men who automatically loaded their pockets whenever they dressed. She found his car keys almost immediately. Alone, she could have shapechanged and flown to intercept the pair, but she would need the car for Paul.

Of course he was right about the trap, but that fact was irrelevant. She couldn't leave him in Luciano's hands.

In the car she opened her mind to Paul's without making him aware of the contact. He drew her like one magnetic pole attracting its opposite. The only way she could lose the trail would be if her target drove out of telepathic range.

Despite her frustration at having to follow the windings of back roads through the trees instead of making a crow's-flight straight shot to the location, it took her less than an hour to catch up with Luciano. She found his vehicle, a rented four-door sedan, parked in the driveway of a cabin slightly similar to Paul's. She screeched to a stop on the side of the road, jammed the keys in her pocket, and raced toward the house.

Luciano stepped onto the front porch, leaving the door open behind him. Sensing Paul's presence inside—awake, unharmed—she itched to shove the other vampire out of the way and barge in. She knew, though, that Luciano's greater strength would make that difficult.

He greeted her with a gloating smile. "I expected to have to telephone you. I planned to let you suffer awhile, then tell you where I'd taken your pet. How did you get here?"

Her lips curled in an involuntary snarl. She had to inhale and exhale several times to bring her voice under control. "Never mind that. Let me see him."

"Only one way I can think of, but surely not—" He scowled, his aura darkening. "Don't tell me you bonded with this ephemeral!"

"None of your business." She would *not* allow Luciano to make her ashamed of sharing herself with Paul, yet his scorn showed clearly how most of her kind would regard the act.

"Well, no matter. However it happened, I believe you're actually addicted to him. If he's that important to you, all the better. You'll give me what I want, or he'll suffer."

She stalked toward him, pausing only when he emitted a warning growl. "How did you find me, anyway?"

"Naive child." He sighed in mock sympathy. "It was no trouble at all. I asked around until I discovered that you had only one regular associate, your professional collaborator. By questioning his neighbors, I learned that he'd vanished overnight and not come back. By further interrogation among his friends, I found out about his vacation property. Of course, all the people I talked to have forgotten they ever met me."

"Very clever. Now, what do you want?" As if she couldn't guess.

"You, of course, my promised mate. You'll be on the verge of desperation soon. After our night together, I'll return your pet to you."

"Forget about it, Luciano. It's too late for that."

"What the devil are you talking about?" He took a couple of paces away from the door.

"You've missed your chance. I'm not in estrus anymore."

Gliding closer to her, he sniffed the air like a dog. "Damn. You aren't. Who—"

In a dash almost too fast for her eyes to track, he sprinted to her side and grabbed her arm. He bent to inhale the scent of her hair. She flinched, and he squeezed her forearm.

"That ephemeral! I can smell him on you." He released her with a contemptuous shove. "You actually mated with that creature."

"Don't you dare hurt him!"

Luciano radiated disgust. "Begging, now? Incredible—you have tender feelings for him, don't you? The bond is more than lust? I knew all along this business of grafting human genes into our bloodline was a mistake."

Gillian's fists involuntarily clenched, and a crimson fog thickened before her eyes. The only thing that kept her from striking out was the fear that Luciano would inflict his wrath on Paul.

"If you had to get infected by this human disease called love," Luciano continued, "you didn't have to make it worse by going mad over a lower animal."

Gillian drew a long, shuddering breath to dispel the mist of rage that shrouded her brain. "Enough. Just give him to me."

Luciano's lips curled in a snarl. "I ought to tear him to shreds, just for the time I've wasted on you half-breed."

"If you kill him, I swear I'll—"

"Murder me? Break the most fundamental law of our kind?" He taunted her with a feral smile. "Oh, Dark Powers, girl, at least stop acting like a hysterical child. Why would I bother killing your pet? Come and get him."

He stepped aside with an ironic gesture of welcome. Gillian ran up the driveway to the open door. Why hadn't Paul come out already? What had Luciano done to him?

Chapter Twelve

The interior smelled dusty, shut up and unused. Luciano must have "borrowed" a cabin whose owners hadn't visited in some time. Tracking Paul's thoughts, she found him in a bedroom. He lay atop the rumpled covers of a fully made bed, his arms stretched to the sides and handcuffed to the headboard. His legs were hobbled by ropes tied around his ankles and the posts of the footboard. His eyes widened in alarm when he saw her.

The air rippled with the speed of Luciano's entry. He slipped past Gillian and appeared beside the bed. "Should I give him back to you right away or play with him a little? You arrived so fast I didn't have time for any recreation."

"If you hurt him, I'll rip your head off, law or no law."

"Don't worry, I don't consider him worth the trouble. I won't damage your pet."

"Stop calling him that!"

Luciano turned to Paul. "Think she protests too much? That's all you are to her, you know, a pet. We're superior beings, and your kind are our prey."

"It's not true, Paul!" she cried. "You know I don't feel that way about you."

Paul gave her a bleak stare.

Luciano bared his teeth at Gillian. "And you—do you really believe he's in love with you? Would he look twice at you if not for your vampire magnetism? That's the allure, you know. Without that, no human male would give you a second glance, much less get a cockstand for you. You don't have the kind of body they lust for."

"Stop it," she whispered. She knew he registered the impact of every barb he shot. Her agitation wouldn't allow her to guard her emotions from him.

Pulling down the collar of Paul's shirt, Luciano forced his head to one side and bent to lick his throat. "How does that feel? Not too different from the way she made you feel, I daresay?" He scraped a fingernail across Paul's neck. Blood oozed from the scratch. The vampire lapped at the drops, while his hand skimmed down his victim's chest and abdomen to the groin. Paul's body jerked, and a moan escaped from him.

Gillian felt his terror and revulsion at his own physical response. She stood panting, her hands curling and uncurling like claws. The scarlet fog in her brain almost obliterated thought, but not quite. She retained enough control to realize that charging the vampire would endanger her bond-mate.

"You like this, don't you?" Luciano breathed in Paul's ear, while his fingers danced like spiders over all the most vulnerable spots. "Doesn't matter which vampire is feasting on you, the sensations are just as keen." His tongue flicked the scrape again. "Ah, I notice you've recovered from Gillian's use of your cock. It's nicely stiffened. I could make you spend right now."

Paul closed his eyes and groaned, struggling to writhe away from Luciano's touch.

"But I won't." The vampire stepped back from the bed. "Take him, girl, and good riddance to both of you."

She pounced to the bedside and snapped first one ankle rope, then the other. Paul cast an agonized gaze on her when she approached the headboard.

"Here," Luciano said from the doorway. He reached into his pocket and tossed a key to Gillian. "Do you really want to release him? Now he knows what our kind are really like. Do you think he won't loathe the sight of you?"

He vanished, and as she began to unlock the handcuffs, she heard a car start and accelerate into the distance.

With his hands free, Paul hunched over, rubbing his wrists. Gillian watched, afraid to speak or touch him. His mind, boiling with turmoil and outrage, lay open to her. Finally he looked up.

"I have your car," she said. "Let's get out of here."

"Right." The word dropped from him like a stone.

When they got to the car, he walked to the driver's side and reached for the keys. She dropped them into his hand, catching a stray thought that letting her drive him home would be one thing too much to endure. The concept bewildered her, but she sensed that taking the wheel held a symbolic value for him.

Once they got on the road, she had to ask. "What's bothering you? Luciano's gone. It's all over."

"Can't you understand how I feel, being rescued by you? By a woman?" The anguish in his voice ripped into her.

"I don't believe you said that. I've never thought of you as a reactionary male chauvinist."

"Me neither, but it must have been hiding in me somewhere."

She swallowed her rising anger, recognizing it as mostly a reflection of his. "No, I don't understand."

"Then I sure can't explain it." Tight-lipped, he glared out the windshield.

They'd almost reached the cabin before he spoke again. "What that creep said. I'm a pet to you. How about it?"

"Paul, you know that isn't true. You never thought that way when we worked together or last night while we made love."

"Mated, you mean. You can't love a lower animal. Any man would have served the purpose."

His tone pierced her like an icicle to the heart. "You've known me for over two years. And now I've turned into a monster overnight?"

"I got a glimpse of your family background, so to speak."

Her jaws ached with clenching them in frustration. "How can I convince you I'm not like that?"

"I don't know," he said, "when you can hypnotize me into believing any claim you make."

"I promised not to do that again."

"Sure, but how can I believe your promises? Look what your vampire friend did to me. Controlled me like a robot."

"He's not my friend." She breathed deeply, striving to keep her voice level. "Yes, any vampire could do that, but I won't. Never."

He pulled the car into his driveway and turned to look at her. "But I'll never know, will I? I could be under your control without realizing it. And how do I know what I really feel for you? The way I reacted when that monster touched me..." She felt him swallow a surge of nausea.

She heaved an exasperated sigh. Put that way, the situation constituted an impossible Catch-22.

"And another thing," said Paul, opening the car door, "what did he mean by `addicted'?"

Too late to deny or evade; Paul would distrust her worse if she did. "It's a fixation, a physiochemical thing, that results from feeding on the same donor too many times, or feeding on a donor with emotional involvement."

"Wonderful." He stood upright and stared at her across the roof of the car as she got out. "So you can't be sure, either. For all you know, when you think you care about me, it might just be addiction talking."

Gillian shook her head. "It's not that way. I cared about you first—that's why I got hooked so fast when I tasted you."

He stalked into the house, and she followed. When he headed for his own room, though, she didn't pursue. Instead, she sat brooding in the unlighted living room.

* * * * *

Paul stood under the shower letting hot water flood over him. He leaned against the tile wall with his eyes closed, leaking tears. How could he ever face Gillian again, much less make love to her? She'd watched him get an erection for that monster. He felt as foul as if he'd had sex with a reptile. Even if she, with her nonhuman mindset, could put that incident behind her, Paul didn't believe he could. The humiliation of seeing her face while he lay there helpless would haunt him. He probably wouldn't be able to perform with her anymore, remembering that.

The worst of it was, Gillian didn't have a clue why he felt this way. Sure, she could read his emotions, but they obviously baffled her. Just silly human scruples, for all she understood. He must have been crazy to believe he could share love, or anything besides animal passion, with a woman of another species. Maybe, deep down, she really did regard him as a pet, a simple creature to be soothed into docility until the next time she needed its services.

When the hot water cooled to lukewarm, he turned it off, rubbed dry with skin-reddening roughness, and ducked into his room for fresh clothes. He had to get away from her as soon as possible. He could hardly abandon her here, though. Okay, so he'd drive her home. But after that he wouldn't see her again. This disaster didn't have to ruin their professional partnership. They could collaborate on their books by e-mail and fax. It would be a relief to escape the complications of emotional entanglement.

Dressed, he headed for the living room with a firm stride. Now that he'd made up his mind to treat everything that had happened this weekend like a surreal dream, he ought to feel at peace.

So why did he feel as if he'd been shot through the heart?

* * * * *

After a long time he emerged, having showered and changed. His clean scent, punctuated with traces of soap and shampoo, made Gillian's heart stutter. "That Luciano guy isn't a threat anymore, so you don't need to hide out." Paul said. "I guess I'd better drive you back to San Diego."

She stood up to face him, knowing that in the dark room he could see the red gleam in her eyes. "Please don't, not yet."

"Why the hell shouldn't I?" His folded arms mirrored the locked and barred gates of his mind.

She swallowed, groping for the words to explain her plan. It would work, if only he would agree to try. "I have an idea. I can prove my sincerity, if you'll let me."

"I can't imagine how, but go ahead and explain." He switched on a lamp and flung himself into the armchair.

"If you still don't believe I care for you—love you..." Her own words astonished her, but she realized she meant them. "After this, I won't bother you again. We can collaborate at a distance. You'll never have to see me."

His eyes followed her while she perched on the arm of the couch. "Okay, what's the plan?"

"You can enter my mind." She felt his instant recoil. "At your own speed, as deep or shallow as you want. We can drop our barriers, but I'll stay passive and let you do all the exploring." If he saw her as invading and overpowering him before, maybe this contact would make up for the indignity.

He gripped the arms of his chair. "Sounds reasonable. Go ahead."

She opened her mind and stretched an inviting tendril toward his. The gesture met a blank wall. "That won't work," she said. "You have to relax. Can't you trust me a little?"

He sighed, closed his eyes, and unclenched his hands. She closed her own eyes to concentrate, visualizing her inner self as an ivy-festooned mansion with the door ajar. *Come in,* she silently whispered.

She felt Paul's mind open with the creak of an unused gate. Then his thoughts brushed hers. He stepped into the entry hall of her mental house. She held very still, afraid of scaring him away.

Little by little, he inched his way to the inner rooms. She imagined his footsteps on the carpet of parlor and stairs. Quivering with her own kind of anxiety, she didn't make a move or a sound while he roamed through the bedrooms to gaze out the gable windows, up to the attic to survey her childhood memories. He caught glimpses of her confusion as a part-human girl, struggling with her vampiric urges, powers, and limits.

Step by step she guided him to a niche in the farthest corner of the attic. He opened a door upon a spiral staircase. With confident strides, he ascended. The stairs wound up, higher than Gillian herself had imagined, until they opened into a tower room lined with bookshelves. Paul roamed from shelf to shelf, taking down slim volumes and ponderous tomes to skim through them.

Leading him up a ladder, Gillian placed his hand on a brightly colored picture book. When he opened it, he saw a painting of tigers on a hillside behind a fence, one half-asleep, one pacing an endless circuit of the enclosure.

The picture cast Gillian back into the moment it portrayed. Volnar's fingers clutched her shirt and dragged her to the edge of the tiger pen. Midsummer sun beat down on her, only partly relieved by her baseball cap and polarized sunglasses. In contrast, Volnar's icy touch made her skin prickle. "You were careless," he said, his voice emotionless as ever. "You disobeyed me. You let yourself be seen."

"He was only a kid—"

"A child your own age. But human children prattle, and their parents sometimes listen. You let him see your strangeness."

She squelched a cry when his nails gouged her shoulder.

"Do you want to end up like them?" He pointed to the tigers. "A curiosity in a cage?"

The child Gillian shook her head.

"Then never let an ephemeral know what you are."

She snapped back to the present. Paul bent over the open book with moisture gleaming on his cheeks. *I see,* his thoughts murmured.

You're the only human being who's seen my true self, she silently replied. *I've put my life in your hands.*

She felt his dawning comprehension of her need for him and her longing to share the kind of love she'd witnessed between other bonded couples, as well as her fear of repelling him with her desperate craving.

His thoughts drifted through her brain like mist, no longer chill: *Then I'll put my life into yours. It's only fair.*

He clasped her hand and led her into his own mind-fortress, now with the gate open and the drawbridge down. She saw the depth of his affection for her and his hurt when he thought she'd been using him. Sweet warmth flooded over her.

Chapter Thirteen

She disentangled her thoughts from his, maintaining only a light sensory link, and opened her eyes to find him beside her on the couch. His aura pulsed with desire, tinged with a mixture of wonder and bewilderment. "I feel through your skin," he said, "the way I did this morning." A hot blush suffused his face. "I can even see myself through your eyes, if I concentrate. Weird."

"Yes, that's how it's supposed to work." She gently took his hand, ready to withdraw if he resisted. Instead of retreating, he drew her into an embrace.

"That feels great," he said, nuzzling her hair. "I'm already not sure why I fought it."

"I understand why," she said, "and I mean it when I promise I won't override your will ever again. Uh—I hope you don't mind some sensory 'encouragement' now and then, though?"

"You mean in bed?" His blush stirred her thirst despite her physical and emotional fatigue. "Or does no estrus for the next few years mean no sex?"

"Not at all." Her tongue lightly flicked his earlobe, then the side of his neck. "I get my satisfaction from your excitement. I'm looking forward to having you make love to me when I'm not in heat."

He stared intently at her. "Will you really enjoy it as much that way?"

"Sure. It's a different kind of pleasure, but just as intense, maybe more so because it involves my whole body, not localized."

"More intense? Are you sure I'll survive?" But this time he smiled, clearly teasing.

She answered the underlying doubt that remained, though. "You can go at your own pace, not mine. In fact, as soon as you've…recovered…we can try it. I won't make a move without your permission. You can guide me through the *Kama Sutra* page by page." She paused for a long breath, afraid he would hear the invitation as pressure. "Only if you want it, of course."

"You mean I could do this all night long?" He fondled her breasts. "Or this?" He kissed her throat, then nipped her earlobe. "How about this?" His fingers tickled between her legs.

"Yes." She drew a tremulous breath. "As long as I get my turn to choreograph…when I'm thirsty."

"Oh, yeah, I want." She heard his pulse quicken. By extending her senses only a little, she could feel the blood pooling in the dilated capillaries of his erogenous zones. He lightly brushed the tiny hairs in her palm. "Hey, that makes you thirsty, doesn't it? I can feel it in my own body. Incredible."

"Yes, so you'd better slow down."

"Why slow down? Why not give it a try?" Now he sounded only half teasing.

She stared at him in astonishment. "Now? Are you sure you're up to it?" When he laughed, she realized her unintentional pun.

"Oh, I think I might be up to it." His hands crept under her shirt. Warmth radiated from his open palms to spread over her breasts and make her nipples tauten before he even touched them. She stretched her arms above her head, and he slipped the T-shirt off her. With a purr vibrating in her throat, she lay back on the couch and luxuriated in the play of his fingers on her body. His tongue circled each nipple in turn. Each one caught fire, a flame that spiraled out to envelope every inch of her skin.

Opening her thoughts to him, she felt his mind leap to merge with hers. This time, rather than drowning in his passion, she swam in it as in a blood-warm river. She felt the glowing brand of his caresses. Yet she also felt her own curves under his hands, along with the satin coolness of her flesh. When she eased off his shirt and stroked his chest, the curly hair made the cilia on her palms tingle with delight. Through his senses, she thrilled to the way her nails skimmed down his torso and under the waistband of his jeans. The scratches burned him like impossibly painless razor cuts. There she stopped, waiting for his cue.

"Yes," he whispered. Pressure built in his stiffening organ. His pants felt tight. He guided her fingers to the zipper and lifted his hips to help her remove the rest of his clothes.

She withdrew slightly from the current of his sensations to savor his slow progress in peeling off her shorts and bikini briefs, inch by inch, nibbling his way down her flat stomach on the way. Waves of pleasure washed over her. Her clit throbbed, but the same electricity vibrated in her nipples, the erect cilia in her palms, and her lips and tongue that yearned to taste him. The ache between her legs and in the pit of her stomach, as well as the dryness of her mouth, felt like pleasurable anticipation rather than desperate need.

"Cover me," she murmured. He spread his body over hers, his blood-warmed skin like a silken blanket against the chill of her own. "Kiss me," she sighed.

His tongue parted her lips and fenced with hers. *You taste like spiced wine and something metallic,* came his bemused thought.

And you taste like salt and ripe fruit. The flavor thrilled her taste buds without slaking her thirst. Every nerve quivered with eagerness to melt into him and draw him into her.

She slid from her half-reclining position to lie flat on the couch. Without words he heard and accepted her invitation. He nudged at her portal, not quite entering. The moist petals opened to him.

A new thirst tantalized her. "Paul—I want to drink you." With his lips nuzzling her neck, he projected a silent question. "Not your blood." She sent him an image of what she wanted.

He gasped. His erection twitched as if zapped by electricity. While Gillian lay on her side to make room, he stretched out beside her, head to foot. The curves and hollows of their bodies fitted together, his heat branding her flesh, her chill sending delicious shivers through him. His pulse reverberated in her deepest core like the bass notes of an orchestra, and she transmitted the echo back to him, making his excitement soar higher and carry her to the heights with him. His lips nestled into the damp curls at the apex of her thighs. She closed her mouth on the head of his penis. His hips trembled with the effort of holding still while her tongue swirled around the swollen shaft. She ached with gratitude for the gift he gave her, allowing her razor-sharp teeth in such a vital spot without an instant of fear.

His tongue flickered like a flame over her throbbing bud. This time, instead of concentrating in that one place, her pleasure expanded in ever-widening circles until it was no longer inside her, but she was inside it. Her whole being melted into a scarlet fog of sensuality. With Paul, she tasted her metallic-tinged love-juice and felt the explosion ready to burst from his straining cock. With her, he plunged into the ecstatic whole-body rush of tingling heat that his embrace gave her.

Screaming out loud, he shot into her mouth. Her own body echoed the tremors that rocked him. She swallowed his salt-sweet essence. *Yes, it's like your blood! Oh, God, Paul, I do love you!*

With their senses still merged, the taste lingered on his tongue, too, blended with her intimate flavor. For both, the combination held the richness of vintage wine. *I love you, Gillian. Don't ever think of leaving me.*

Finally, he raised his head and wiggled around until she nestled against his chest. Long minutes later, their breathing calmed, and he could speak again. "Gillian, after all this, I really hate the idea of you drinking anything, even blood, from anybody else."

"Didn't I make that clear? No, I guess not. Part of what `addiction' means is that I can't stand any other human blood. I need yours. Animals provide the bulk nourishment, but for real satisfaction, I depend on you."

"Will that work? I mean, how much do you need?" The question carried no overtones of fear, only concerned curiosity.

"A few sips at a time," she said. "Your passion flavors it. Quality makes up for quantity."

"I just thought of something else. Pregnancy…did you ovulate?"

She turned inward to study the ebb and flow of the tides in her womb. "No. There's no pregnancy."

Paul hugged her closer. "Strange, I'm almost sorry. But with all the other adjustments we have to make, we're better off without that complication."

"True." She snuggled almost into his lap. "You know, most of my kin would say it'll never work. You'll get tired of serving as my ambulatory blood bank. Our circadian rhythms will clash. You'll want me to join you in daylight activities and lavish restaurant meals."

"So? You'll have to watch me turn into an old man, while you stay young and hotblooded forever. Right, it'll never work."

She heaved an exaggerated sigh. "Well, nobody ever accused me of obeying rules or acting sensible. Do you want to stay with me anyway?"

"Just try to stop me." Their lips met, and their hearts and minds echoed the union.

About the author:

Marked for life by reading DRACULA at the age of twelve, Margaret L. Carter specializes in the literature of fantasy and the supernatural, particularly vampires. She received degrees in English from the College of William and Mary, the University of Hawaii, and the University of California. She is a 2000 Eppie Award winner in horror, and with her husband, retired Navy Captain Leslie Roy Carter, she coauthored a fantasy novel, WILD SORCERESS.

Heart of Midnight

Written by

Kit Tunstall

Chapter 1

1903, Lasënbourg

Catriona shifted in the coach's seat, feeling the strain on her buttocks from the long ride since they got off the train in Munich. "Are we nearly there, Miss Otto?"

"Cease your prattle."

Her mouth dropped open at the sharp rebuke from the older woman. Catriona frowned, wondering what she had done to stir Miss Otto's ire. The companion had seemed like charm itself from the moment she arrived at her relatives' home in London to see Catriona to the special school. As the journey wore on, she had become less pleasant.

Perhaps she had asked too many questions. Her curiosity might have grated on the other woman's nerves. She bit her tongue, forcing back the sharp comment about Miss Otto acting as her eyes. Instead, Catriona smoothed her woolen skirt and shifted yet again, seeking a comfortable spot on the hard seat. The horses traversed the terrain at a brisk pace, rocking the carriage from side to side. She would be relieved when they arrived in the capitol, Stossburg, and her companion left her at the school.

She sighed and gave up trying to find a comfortable way to sit. Her thoughts wandered from the unpleasant journey to what awaited her at the small school in the heart of Lasënbourg. Aunt Victoria had assured her she would relearn everything she had so easily known before the accident claimed her vision. Uncle Frederick hadn't said much of anything, but she was used to that.

During the year circumstances had forced her to live with them, the only time he spoke to her was to remind her to be grateful to them for taking her in and to tell her how expensive she was to maintain. Her mouth twisted as she mused she must be, considering her relatives had already frittered away a large sum of her inheritance, mostly on her spoiled cousin Prudence.

Catriona was under no illusion that they were sending her to the school because it was in her best interests. They simply wanted her out of the way.

She stiffened as the horses stepped onto a different texture. It sounded like their shoes now rang out against cobblestone, rather than hard earth. She could also hear the bustle of a crowd and smell the underlying stench always present in a city. She risked incurring Miss Otto's wrath again. "Have we arrived in Stossburg, Miss Otto?"

"Yes," she said, and didn't bother to expand on her answer.

She hid a grimace at the woman's abruptness. During their ride through London and traveling via ship from England to Germany, Miss Otto had occasionally provided a visual commentary. Again, she wondered what had caused the woman to change so drastically in the last few hours.

The carriage ride lasted another ten or fifteen minutes, during which time Catriona repositioned her hat by touch and tried to banish the case of nerves twisting her stomach into knots. Her aunt had assured her of the school's fine reputation, letting her know it only accepted young women from the best families. Aunt Victoria had hinted there was trouble getting them to take her, but Catriona had ignored her aunt's implied insult.

She had grown a thick skin to their derogatory comments, having heard them so plentifully in the past thirteen months. Catriona knew a great deal of their bitterness sprang from the fact she was still more beautiful than their plain daughter could ever be, even without her sight. Part of it she attributed to sourness that she had survived the accident when her parents hadn't. If she had only had the good grace to perish along with her parents, their burdens would have eased.

Catriona sighed, reminding herself of her vow not to think of the Bonners again. This school was a new start for her. She had to focus on the positive, for she had dwelled in the dark pit of her memories long enough. She might go mad if she continued to live in darkness. She wanted to return to the self-assured woman she had been before the accident.

However, it was difficult to escape when darkness would be her companion for the rest of her life. It was impossible to forget when the knowledge pressed on her from the moment she opened her eyes in the morning—and saw nothing—until she eventually fell into a restless sleep at night.

The carriage drew to a stop near a noisy crowd, rich with bawdy singing, raised voices, and angry words. She lifted the curtain covering the window and smelled alcohol fumes, although she didn't know if she could have done so before losing her sight. Her other senses had sharpened to compensate, but it was little compensation. "Where are we, Miss Otto?"

"I don't want any fuss from you, Fräulein." The sound of the door opening accompanied her words, before Miss Otto slid her wide girth across the seat. Seconds later, the heels of her boots struck the cobblestone with a dull thud.

Catriona shook her head. "I don't understand."

"It's best you just accept things as they are," the woman said. "Come along now."

Fear paralyzed Catriona, making it impossible for her to slide across the seat. "Please, Miss Otto, what's happening?"

"Come out of there now," Miss Otto barked.

She shook her head. "I should prefer to go straight to the school." Catriona didn't know where they were, but she knew it wasn't any refined school for blind young women. Panic clawed at her throat as she began to wonder if there even was a school.

Miss Otto's cold laugh answered her internal question, even before she spoke. "You daft cow, there is no school. Your family wanted you out of the way. Seems the young man your cousin set her heart on has the eye for you."

She shuddered, imagining a life as Barnus Townsend's wife. She almost thanked her aunt and uncle from saving her from the fate of spending the next fifty years with that small-minded prig. Almost. "I still don't understand, Miss Otto."

"They sold you to me, Fräulein." There was a rustle of papers. "It's all legal and binding."

Catriona gasped, clutching her hand to her heart. "Sold me? Fo…for what purpose?" The sounds coming from the building increased in pitch, and she swallowed thickly. She had never ventured inside such places as this one sounded to be, but she knew of men's clubs and worse, where young men frittered away their purses. This seemed like that sort of establishment, judging from what she heard.

"To please the gentlemen. You'll adjust soon enough," Miss Otto said pragmatically. "You might even come to enjoy it, Fräulein."

Catriona shook her head. "I can't. Please, you can't make me do that."

The woman's voice was hard. "I paid good money for you. I've wasted enough time on this foolishness. Remove yourself from the carriage, or I'll have someone carry you in."

She dug her fingers into the bench, sitting tensely. Tears streaked down her cheeks, and she held her breath, listening for any sounds that might herald a way out. Instead, all she heard were heavy footsteps, followed by the coach dipping sideways as someone stepped inside. Catriona screamed when large hands fastened on her arms and dragged her forward. Her fingers slipped from their death grip on the seat, and she was soon out of the carriage.

The man holding her smelled of spirits and sweat. He had a large frame, and his unwashed hair brushed against her cheek as he slung her over his shoulder. Catriona kicked against him, but he seemed not to notice as he walked forward. The sounds from the tavern grew louder, then the fresh air disappeared, and the pitch of the sounds changed.

She choked on her first lungful of smoky air. The piano played a jaunty tune as two women sang a song she never would have heard in the salons of London. Whistles and catcalls intermingled with angry words and a lewd comment. She struggled to hide her fear as the man carried her through the room.

When he started climbing the stairs, she dared to hope she would receive a temporary reprieve. Surely, she could reason with Miss Otto. There must be some other duty she could perform instead of whoring.

The sound of his footfalls changed when they emerged onto the landing. She heard the sound of giggles and drunken male voices as the man's boots clomped down the wooden hallway, landing with a heavy thud with each step. He stopped walking, and a door opened. When he entered, she gagged at the odor in the room.

It smelled of unwashed bodies and something indefinable. She could smell cheap perfume, probably used in an attempt to mask the other scents, and the acrid smell of cigar smoke. It seemed to be a stale layer in the air.

"Please, sir," she said, trying to keep the tears from her voice. "Don't let Miss Otto do this."

His only answer was a grunt as he dropped her.

Catriona cried out, preparing for pain. Instead, she bounced against a sagging mattress. Her breath rushed from her, but more from surprise than any pain. His boots clomped away, and then the door closed. She heard the sound of the key twisting, and she screamed. "Please don't leave me here alone."

Her heart raced, and she clenched her hands together. She had no idea of the layout of the room, and she feared being alone in unfamiliar places more than most anything these days. Memories too easily encroached, and fear stole her courage before she could muster any. She knew from experience that the panic would only build, until she was sobbing and beyond coherence.

It was a relief when she heard the key turn again, seconds before the door opened. The hinges needed oiling, she thought disjointedly, listening to several sets of footsteps enter the room. "H-he-hello?"

"Aye, she's a pretty one, Fräulein Matilda."

"Yes, she is, Inga," Miss Otto said. "I paid a pretty penny for her, but it was worth it. She doesn't even need the surgery."

Someone gasped, and it was a high-pitched, girlish sound. "Why not, Fräulein Matilda?"

Catriona shrank away as they surrounded her, hovering too close for her comfort. Their perfumes clashed together in a disorienting cloud of stench, not adequately masking their unwashed states. They all smelled of that scent she couldn't identify. "What's happening?"

They ignored her. Miss Otto said, "She's blind. Some accident—I didn't get the specifics. All I know is it took her sight and her ability to provide heirs." She laughed, but it held little amusement. "She's a Godsend, right, girls?"

They made various sounds of agreement. Tears pricked Catriona's eyes at the reminder of her shame, and she bowed her head. She flinched when someone touched her cheek and tried to dodge as one took her hat, pulling out several strands of her hair by forgetting to remove the hatpin first. She whimpered.

"Can I have this, Fräulein Matilda?"

"You may, Bettina. Fräulein High-and-Mighty won't be needing it." The older woman cackled.

Fingers plunged in her hair, loosening the pins that held her knot. "She has pretty hair," the other girl said. "I've never seen a shade like this. What's it remind you of?"

"The bronze lions guarding Midnight Manor," said the girl she thought had stolen her hat, and there was a hint of fear in her voice.

Miss Otto made a strange sound. "Don't tell me you girls have been lurking around Midnight Manor, waiting for a peek of Herr Midnight. I thought you had better sense, Inga, Bettina. There's no accounting for the oddities of the wealthy. He's nothing but a strange fellow, wearing that mask. No mystery there, I'll tell you."

"Yes, Fräulein Matilda," the girl with the deeper voice said. "It's just—"

The other girl interrupted. "The Fräulein's eyes remind me of pennies."

"What is pennies?" the other girl asked.

"American money. A gentleman showed me one once."

"Bet that wasn't all he showed you." The girl snickered.

"Do you think Fräulein High-and-Mighty will faint the first time she feels a cock?" the girlish girl asked before giggling.

Catriona winced at the callous remark. She couldn't believe she was in a brothel, let alone the property of the brothel's madam. She knew the Bonners had little use for her, but she had never realized they hated her. How else could they have consigned her to this fate, if they didn't despise her?

"I think she has the makings of a fine whore," Miss Otto said. "There's something about her prissy attitude, something beneath the surface. I bet she'll be panting to fall back with her legs in the air in no time."

"You're wrong," Catriona snapped, pushed beyond her endurance. "I won't stay here, and I'll never be like you whores." The word burned on her tongue, and she added as much distaste as she could interject into the single word. She cried out when someone slapped her hard on the cheek.

"Keep a civil tongue, Fräulein, lest I cut it out. I think we'll give you a very special first customer, to show you your place." Miss Otto's pitch changed, indicating she had turned her head. "Is Freiherr Müeller coming tonight, Inga?"

"Yes, Fräulein Matilda. He comes every other Saturday, hoping for a new girl."

Miss Otto's laugh sent chills up Catriona's spine. "Excellent. Shall we prepare the Fräulein for her night of passion?"

Catriona tried to fight them as three pairs of hands pulled her from the bed. She grunted when they lifted her, and she started screaming.

"Keep practicing, Fräulein Catriona," Miss Otto said with evident relish. "The Freiherr loves to hear his companions scream."

"I'll be glad it's not me," the older girl whispered. "I didn't walk for near a week the last time I serviced the Freiherr."

Catriona's stomach tied itself in knots as they left the room she had been in and walked down the hall. The floorboards creaked under Miss Otto's weight, and she fervently prayed that the floor would break under them. Death didn't seem like a bad way of escaping her fate.

They entered another room, and Catriona was set on her feet. She uttered a protest when hands pulled at her wool traveling jacket, taking it from her. The indignities didn't end there. Between the three women, they soon had her stripped to her corset and drawers. Catriona tried holding onto the bone corset, but they removed it effortlessly. She grasped the waistband of her drawers, but someone ripped the fine lawn from her body, leaving her naked and shivering.

Something creaked, followed by the sound of water rushing into a porcelain basin or tub. She was surprised the whorehouse could afford indoor plumbing, but that thought fled from her when someone pushed her back into the water.

"Part her legs. Let's see what I paid for."

She screamed and thrashed against their hands, splashing water all over herself and the two girls as they pried apart her legs. Her screams intensified when fingers as thick as sausages invaded her pussy. One pushed inside her, making her gasp at the sharp pain accompanying it.

Miss Otto made a sound of pleasure. "She's pure, just as the aunt assured me. The Freiherr will be doubly pleased."

"She has pretty tits," the girlish one said. "Look at her pale pink nipples."

"The breasts of a fine *lady,*" the older one said, with a mocking inflection in her thick accent, before dissolving into giggles. She followed her comment by twisting one of Catriona's nipples hard enough to bring tears to her eyes.

"Freiherr Müeller will mark them with shades of black and blue," Miss Otto predicted as she withdrew her hand.

Catriona huddled in the tub, squeezed her legs shut, and gave in to the tears. The girls teased her for crying, but she ignored them. She wouldn't find sympathy with this heartless bunch, and what difference did it make if she showed her emotions? Once the dreaded Freiherr finished with her, she wouldn't be the same. He would ruin her, just as they were ruined.

"Finish her up, girls, and then get back downstairs. The men will be getting impatient with just Patrice and Marta entertaining them. Leave Fräulein High-and-Mighty locked in the room Hans put her in earlier, until the Freiherr arrives."

Catriona heard the horrible woman leave, but she didn't lift her head. She didn't try to plead with the girls as they went about washing her with strong-smelling soap, even when they invaded her personal areas. Whatever goodness might have once been in them had been burned away under the ownership of Miss Otto. She wondered if she would end up just like them. That thought frightened her almost as much as whatever tortures awaited her at the Freiherr's hands.

Chapter 2

Quintus could sense the pain rolling off the young woman before he even got close enough to see her. She had found refuge at the end of the alley, huddled on the ground, with her back against the sooty stones of the factory's wall. He could taste her tears in the wind, and he could feel the emptiness radiating from her. It was more than an unfilled stomach that caused the void in her.

His boots clicked on the cobblestone as he walked toward her. He felt a moment of guilt at having spent so much on footwear when this young woman didn't have enough to eat. He pushed it aside, having accepted long ago that he couldn't change the world. All he could do was relieve pain, a little at a time.

He knelt beside her. "What troubles you?" Quintus asked in a soothing tone.

She raised her gaze from the bundle in her arms. Her arms tightened around the bundle she held. "He isn't moving," she whispered. "He cried all day, but now he's quiet. I'm afraid to look." She sounded nervous, but deeper in her voice was a heart-rending layer of anguish. "Will you check him, Herr?"

With slow motions, Quintus reached forward and lifted the bundle from her arms. He frowned at the lightness of the bundle, and when he pushed back the top blanket, he found only a rag doll.

"My son," she said, rocking back and forth. "Tell me he is fine."

He touched her brow. "Shh. Look into my eyes." When she met his eyes, he used the connection instantly formed between them to send her into a trance. He set aside the blankets and leaned forward, pressing his mouth to hers. His lips didn't violate the young woman's. Instead, he sucked in her breath, but carefully. He didn't want her to stop breathing.

His eyes moistened as he absorbed her grief. She had lost her child to illness a few months ago, having been unable to pay for proper food for them, let alone a physician. Since then, she had left her job and now wandered the streets, seeking solace from her torment.

He couldn't take it all from her. He knew that. After a certain point, too many negative emotions began to poison him, rather than sustain him. His power reservoir refilled, and he knew it was time to break away. Still, her pain kept him inhaling her emotions long past when he should have.

It was only when a cramp hit his stomach that he was forced to break away. Quintus knelt on all fours, heaving. A cloud of putrid green emerged from his mouth, and he was strong again upon expelling it.

He turned back to the young woman once he was steady. She was still in the trance, and she would remain so for another minute or two. He grasped her thin hand in his, wincing at its iciness. "When you awaken, you will feel more at ease. Your guilt will have lessened, and it won't return to eat at you as it has. You must go on, as must we all."

Quintus kissed the back of her filthy hand, pressed three gold coins into her palm, and closed her fingers around them. As he rose and walked away from her, he reminded himself to find this girl again. He couldn't take on all of her pain and suffering, but he could help her deal with it. She need never know the part he had played when she recovered enough to resemble her former self.

He melted into the crowd moving through the streets. This was a dangerous area of Stossbourg, and he remained on alert. Gaslights at each intersection provided some illumination, but the pockets in between offered a host of opportunities for the thugs who preyed on others. Quintus kept the right side of his face hidden under the mask to the shadows as much as possible, while his wary eyes constantly scanned the milieu.

As he passed a brothel, a wave of terror and suffering jolted Quintus, causing him to stumble and jar the man he walked next to. He offered a hasty apology and moved deeper into the shadows, leaning against the wall of the building. Cautiously, he touched the bricks with his gloved hand, and the emotions threatened to overwhelm him again.

Their intensity surprised him. Rather, his ability to tune into the emotions so vividly surprised him. Normally, the pain surrounding him was a muted blur, unless he had need of sustenance. He couldn't remember the last time he had felt someone's suffering so strongly when he didn't need to feed.

He tried to walk on, to ignore what he was experiencing, but the terror suddenly increased, and his knees buckled. He barely kept himself from falling, managing to brace his hand against the wall at the last moment before his knees touched the dirty cobblestone.

Quintus knew he couldn't walk away from this misery. Surprisingly, he had never found a rich source of sustenance in the brothel before. A vague sadness clung to the building, permeating its very walls, but none of the inhabitants had the soul-deep pain he needed to feed on to survive.

Until tonight. Although he didn't require further energy, Quintus allowed his instincts to guide him to the woman whose heart was calling out. He couldn't turn his back on her suffering.

* * * * *

They had left her alone in the room for what she guessed to be at least an hour. Since losing her sight, she hadn't been able to keep track of time unless she heard a clock ticking off the minutes, so she couldn't be certain.

What surprised her was that she hadn't fallen into a sobbing heap of hysteria yet. Perhaps the fear of what was coming had obliterated the fear of the unknown she usually succumbed to when left alone. Somehow, the tortures she had imagined in the past didn't compare to those that loomed.

She had thought herself incapable of experiencing more terror, but when the key turned in the lock, her racing heart accelerated further. Her mouth became as arid as the desert, and she couldn't summon enough saliva to even whimper as the door slammed shut. She huddled against the headboard, praying for a way out.

She had a vague recollection of the girl she used to be—a spitfire full of energy, supremely confident in her own abilities. That girl would have tried to fight what was coming. This Catriona didn't know if she had the emotional strength, let alone the physical capacity, to even try.

When rough hands seized her, a spark of the old Catriona fired within her, and she lashed out with her fist, connecting with a fleshy cheek. She screamed when the hands clamped her to the bed, and she tried kicking out.

"If you don't settle down, Fräulein, I'll bind your feet."

A greasy hand caressed her calf, bared by the thin shift Inga and Bettina had dressed her in before locking her in the room. Catriona jerked away.

"Like that, is it?" He released his hold on her.

She seized the opportunity and tried to roll off the bed. She went too far and crashed onto the floor, landing with a hollow thud. She cried out at the pain, but she didn't let it slow her down as she tried to gain her feet. She settled for making it to her knees and started crawling.

Catriona didn't get far before the Freiherr caught up with her. Something whistled through the air before it struck her across the back. She screamed at the pain, unable to identify what the object was, and uncaring. She collapsed against the floor, but tried dragging herself forward. The article came down again, this time across her thighs, numbing her shaking legs.

"Just stay there, dove, and your punishment won't be so severe." Freiherr Müeller's accompanying laugh was cold as ice. "Fräulein Matilda tells me you're unspoiled. I want you able to perform before I introduce you to the delicious world of pain."

She tried to inch away, but the object landed against her buttocks. She tentatively identified it as a walking stick. Knowing what it was didn't alleviate the pain it caused as it connected with her buttocks and lower back again. Then he stopped hitting her.

She tensed, anticipating a massive blow, assuming he was gathering his strength. It never came.

There was the sound of breaking glass from the window, followed by someone stepping into the room, crunching shards under their shoes. Level footfalls crossed the floor, as the Freiherr squawked in protest.

As the feet paused near her, Catriona guessed the intruder was a man by the manner in which he walked and the impact his heels made against the thin floor.

"What's this now? You're interrupting a private session." The Freiherr seemed to be trying to bluster his way through, but the note of fear in his voice was unmistakable. "You can't just barge in here through the window, ruffian."

The other man ignored the Freiherr. He knelt near her. "Would you like me to leave, Fräulein?"

"No, please." Catriona shook her head. "I don't want to be here…to do this."

"I thought not." The man stood up. "How much did you pay for this evening? I will reimburse you."

"I don't want your money. I want what's mine." The trembling note in his voice had diminished under a barrage of outrage. "This whore's pure. I'll be the first to defile her."

"Never," the other man said with firm finality. "You can recoup your expense, or you can nurse your pain well into the night. I leave the decision with you."

The Freiherr's teeth clacked together several times. She imagined he was trying to swallow his anger so he could speak. His heavy footfalls moved to the door before it opened and slammed against the wall.

"We'll see how brave you are when I return with Hans." He didn't close the door behind him.

Catriona flinched when the man knelt beside her and touched her arm.

"I won't hurt you. Can you walk, Fräulein?"

She tried to get up, but her body wouldn't cooperate. Tears filled her eyes, and she cursed her weakness. "No, sir."

His hands were gentle as they lifted her into his arms. She liked the scent of his cologne, and she relaxed against him. Her nose wrinkled, and she struggled to identify the strange odor clinging to him. It wasn't like anything she had ever smelled before. It seemed to be a mix of bitter and sweet. That was as close as she could come to guessing it.

"Brace yourself for a drop. I don't think it's wise to try to leave by the front door."

Before she could reply, cool air caressed her face, and she became aware of his muscles tensing and relaxing as they slowly moved downward. She wondered if he was climbing down a trellis or pipe, but didn't bother to ask.

As soon as his boots clicked against the cobblestone, her mysterious rescuer broke into a run, holding her tightly against him. A feeling of protection washed over Catriona, and the accompanying sense of contentment nearly had her crying again. She hadn't felt so safe or cosseted since her parents last hugged her.

He stopped running and set her on her feet. His arms went around her, and she huddled into the wool cloak he wrapped around her frame. "How can I thank you, sir?"

"There is no need."

She titled her head. "How did you know to save me?" Catriona heard his indrawn breath, followed by the subtle timber of his voice changing when he answered, indicating he wasn't telling her the truth.

"I was walking near the brothel and heard you scream. I climbed up to see if it was a game among adults or the abuse of an innocent."

Her face heated with a blush, knowing how the scene must have looked to him. She wondered why he hadn't told her the truth, and then wondered if he were embarrassed. Perhaps he had been seeking out the services of a prostitute when he heard her cry. No matter. It wasn't her business. "I thank you again. It wasn't my choice—"

"I could tell." His voice was warm and encouraging. "Do you have a name?"

"Catriona Hathaway." His jacket rustled, and she wondered if he was tipping his hat.

"I am Quintus Midnight."

Her eyes widened, and she wondered if this was the man the girls had spoken of earlier. "Of Midnight Manor, sir?"

There was a pause. "How did you know that? Your accent is British. I would be surprised if you've been in Lasënbourg for more than a week."

Catriona shrugged. "I heard your name mentioned, and I've been here less than a day."

"Do you have a means of getting home, Fräulein Hathaway?"

She shook her head, feeling the cursed tears that always seemed to linger hovering on the tips of her lashes again. "No, Herr Midnight," she used the form of address the women had used, "I have no home to go to. My relatives sold me to that awful woman." She took a deep breath. "Do you know of anyone seeking help?" She wasn't sure what she qualified for, but she had to find some way of supporting herself. It wasn't as though she could depend on the Bonners to give her a share of the inheritance left by her parents.

"There is a factory looking for workers, but the conditions are deplorable."

Catriona shook her head. "That won't work, I'm afraid. I'm blind." She tensed when he swallowed, preparing for him to distance himself from her.

"I know of no positions for one such as you," he said gently. "However, if you would permit me to offer you shelter at Midnight Manor until you decide on a course of action, I would be happy to do so."

Catriona hesitated as an instinctive refusal rose to her tongue, but she bit it down. Her options were few. Could she afford to dismiss one because it wouldn't be proper?

He must have realized what she was thinking, because he said, "Fräu Markham is the housekeeper, and she would be there to preserve your reputation."

Still, she hesitated. What might come of her acceptance? She would be little more than a charity case. That didn't sit well with the remnants of her pride, especially after hearing the Bonners harp about keeping her out of charity. Yet, what choice did she have? "It will only be for a day or two, Herr."

His hand rested at the small of her back as he eased her forward, getting her to walk again. "My carriage is this way. We will soon be at Midnight Manor, where you may stay as long as you need to."

She accepted his gracious offer with equal graciousness. "Thank you for your hospitality, Herr." She was determined not to impose too much on the man's hospitality. She simply needed a plan of action for moving forward.

She used to be headstrong, as her father would often tell her with equal parts exasperation and amusement. Catriona had preferred to think of herself as a modern woman, who was secure in her independence. Why, before the accident, she had been a Suffragette. Somewhere deep inside her was that same woman. She just needed to find a way back to her, so she could stand on her own two feet again. She couldn't depend on others forever.

Still, it was nice to have his arm curve around her as they stepped down a curb. She allowed herself to relax in his light embrace and lean on him, just for a while.

Chapter 3

The sounds of Catriona screaming awakened Quintus late in the night, for the second night in a row. He threw on a silk robe and his mask before he hurried down the hallway to the bedchamber he had assigned her. He knocked loudly, but she didn't respond. Her cries went on, prompting him to turn the knob on the door. She had locked it, but it was a simple matter of applying his telekinetic powers to manipulate the lock.

As soon as it turned easily, he hurried into the room, glancing at the incandescent lamp to turn it on with his thoughts. The light illuminated the way Catriona thrashed in the bed, pushing against unseen bonds, as she cried out in fear. She was still asleep, despite her movements, and he was cautious when he sat on the bed and shook her gently. "Wake up, Catriona."

She let out one last blood curdling scream before her eyes snapped open. They weren't in focus when she gazed up at him. "Herr Midnight?" she asked after a long pause.

"Yes, it's Quintus." He stroked her back as she leaned against him. "You were having a nightmare. Were you back at Fräulein Matilda's?" When she awakened him screaming last night, he had checked on the bruises left by the Freiherr as he listened to her. Once she purged the horror from her system, she had fallen back into a deep sleep that lasted most of the subsequent day and into tonight.

She shook her head. "No. I dreamed I was lost in the forest. It was the darkest of nights, and I couldn't see. I kept stumbling around, but no one came for me." She shivered, seemingly unaware of curling closer to him.

"When our carriage overturned, I was delirious and wandered in the woods most of the night. When they found me, I slept three days straight. It was only when I awakened that the physician discovered I had lost my sight."

Quintus closed his eyes, feeling her pain inside him before she even spoke. It cut into him like glass, and he longed to ease her suffering. Although he had no need for more nourishment yet, he could safely take some of her distress into himself, to allow her to return to a peaceful sleep.

He eased her away from him, laying her back against the pillows, careful of the injuries that had faded to minor aches during her rest. She seemed confused as her unseeing eyes darted around the room. He leaned closer, not speaking as his lips neared hers.

"Quintus?" There was a note of fear in her voice, but an underlying thread of excitement.

"Shh, sweet one." Quintus placed his lips against hers. His eyes widened as she moved her mouth under his in a timid kiss. He had thought only to ease her suffering, but he found his mouth shaping to hers, returning the shy kiss with more passion than he intended.

She flinched as her cheek touched the cool porcelain of his mask. She withdrew a few inches, bringing her hand up to touch it. "What is this, Quintus?"

He pulled her hand away, holding it gently in his own. "It is nothing."

"Why do you wear a mask?"

"An accident," he said, trying to dismiss the subject.

"What sort of—"

He moved forward quickly, opening her mouth with his lips and sweeping his tongue inside. His intent may have been to distract her, but the first taste of her jolted him from his predictable world.

He had lived so long that the time tended to blur together, coming almost to a standstill for him. With one kiss, he was reminded of what it was to truly live. There was caution in her touch, but he also sensed unbridled passion and a thirst for life. The things she had endured had muted them, but those elements weren't gone.

Was it possible to fall in love at the first kiss? It had been a long time since he felt any emotion besides pity for another living being. The last time he had loved, he didn't remember feeling so invigorated. Every cell in his body tingled with life. His heart pounded in his ears, and his cock stirred to life. He had thought sex was nothing but a sweet memory, as the centuries settled on him. He wasn't old physically, but emotionally, he was as aged as the ancients.

To his shock, her passion increased and her sadness diminished as she kissed him. He hadn't yet taken any of her pain, and he couldn't remember having this effect on any of the women he had taken to his bed in the last few hundred years.

An image of her naked and writhing under him caused Quintus's cock to harden further, almost to the point of pain. His hands seemed to act of their own will as they cupped her breasts through the thin shift. She moaned as he thumbed her beaded nipples, and an answering cry rose in his throat.

She broke away, turning her head. "Wait. This isn't proper." She sounded as though the words had been torn from her with great reluctance.

Passion ruled his senses, a thing that hadn't happened since his youth. "I'll apply for a special license tomorrow. We'll be married in a week."

She gasped and tried to push him away. "No!"

He resisted her attempts, continuing to massage her breasts in lazy circles, not missing the way she arched her back to meet his touch, even as her hands pushed against his chest. "Why not? Heaven help me, but you've enchanted me."

"I can't."

He could sense her sadness welling again, and he released her breasts, embracing her instead. "It would solve your problems," he whispered into her silky hair. "I would take good care of you, Catriona." Her tears leaked through the silk of his robe, and he rocked her.

"It wouldn't be fair to you. I can't bear heirs." His robe muffled her words, but they were still distinguishable. "The accident, you see. Even if I could let you saddle yourself with a blind wife, I couldn't deny you children."

"I don't care about children." Quintus didn't even know if he could have offspring. In his time as an immortal, he had met only one other psychic vampire besides Lilly, whom he had turned, and that man had been his sire. The man had longed for the companionship of a son, so he had made one.

He hadn't taken much time to answer Quintus's questions about his new state. The old man had never wanted to discuss the realities of being a vampire, even one that was beneficial to humanity. Instead, he had spoken of his memories, keeping the young Quintus with him for two decades before he ended his long existence by greeting the sunrise. "I can't have them either," he added as an afterthought.

She lifted her head, and her shock was evident. "Truly, Herr?"

"Quintus," he said gently. "Yes, it's true."

"Was it your…accident?"

He shook his head. "No."

Her brow furrowed. "Then how do you know you can't? Have you tried before?" A blush tinged her cheeks. "Pardon my impertinence, but I must know."

"My first wife never conceived." He winced. To even think of Lilly was painful, and he almost touched his mask out of unconscious habit before forcing his hand to stay on Catriona's back and stroke her skin through the thin linen.

She stiffened in his arms. "You were married? For how long? Did she die?"

"I was married for several years." *More than a hundred,* he added silently, wondering how he had endured the vain Lilly for so long. "She grew tired of me." That was an understatement.

"You sound unhappy."

He shrugged. "Her leaving was a good thing, but she caused me much pain in the process."

Catriona sighed. "Yet, you would risk marriage again to protect me. You are a noble man, but I can't depend on others for the rest of my life."

A small chuckle escaped Quintus, and he was surprised to hear the sound. Although the negative emotions he fed on rarely stayed with him, he wasn't, by nature, a man of smiles and laughter. "It isn't nobility that prompts my offer. There is something about you that touches me."

"I can't marry you."

He didn't doubt her resolve to maintain her decision, but he could sense the yearning pulsing through her, even now. He knew he could turn that to his advantage and seduce her. He could be thrusting into her pussy within minutes, and she would be helpless in the face of her desires. When it was over, she would likely be crippled with guilt and agree to his proposal with haste, but he didn't want to trick her. "We'll speak more of this tomorrow."

She seemed to want to argue, but she finally nodded. She broke his embrace and lay back against the pillows. "Thank you for waking me, Herr…Quintus. The dreams endure sometimes even after I awaken. I can't dispel the images by opening my eyes."

He sensed sadness overwhelming her again, and he leaned forward, pressing a kiss to her forehead before touching his mouth against hers. This time, he breathed in, rather than giving in to the temptation to kiss her. A wealth of anguish flooded him, and he supped cautiously, not eager to poison his system. Her tense muscles loosened as he reached his limit, and he broke away from her. "Good night, Catriona."

Her eyes had closed, and she seemed to be near sleeping again. Her voice was little more than a sleepy blur when she said, "Good night."

He couldn't resist stealing a small kiss before he rose and left her. He paused to look back, intrigued by her air of innocence and the flush of desire still staining her cheeks. His blood pounded when he thought of making love to her, and the ferocity of the emotions overwhelmed him again. What was so compelling about this young woman to have drawn him to her so intently?

He exited her room, taking time to lock the knob again, before he returned to his room. As he neared his door, he froze in mid-step. A disconcerting thought entered his mind, and he struggled to dismiss it. Her blindness was an advantage, making her unlikely to reject his hideous countenance, but that wasn't why he wanted her. He hadn't known about her condition when he rescued her, he reminded himself.

However, it wasn't until after he found out she couldn't see that he had offered her sanctuary at Midnight Manor. Surely, he wasn't so desperate as to latch onto that broken soul to ease his own loneliness. No, he refused to believe he could have such nefarious motives. Something indefinable about her attracted him to Catriona, and he would do his best to persuade her to be his wife.

* * * * *

The memory of last night's events returned to Catriona as soon as she opened her eyes. Before she was even fully awake, she was thinking about Quintus's proposal. Part of her longed to accept the easy path, to allow him to be noble and protect her. A deeper part of her, one she had been more in touch with this morning than she had any time in the last thirteen months, resisted.

It told her she must learn to be independent again. She would never be any man's wife, for how could she bring the burden of infertility to a relationship? Despite Quintus's reassurance that he couldn't have children either, she refused to consign her mate to a barren woman. No, she must be strong and forge her own way. She firmly believed a woman could be happy with a career, instead of getting married and having children. She just needed to find a purpose once more.

As she slid from bed, her nipples brushed against the cover. They were still sensitive from his touch, and a corresponding ache between her thighs made itself known, as she remembered the way he had caressed her breasts.

Her mother had been strong and independent. Felicity had also been something of an eccentric, even among the rapidly evolving society of London. She had never doubted her equality to men, and she had passed those same beliefs on to her daughter. She had been the one to introduce Catriona to the Suffragette movement, and when Harry objected to her participation, she had ignored her husband and continued the fight for her cause, until he eventually stopped protesting her involvement.

There had also been a soft side to her mother. She might be at odds with her husband's decrees one moment, and content to fulfill his every whim the next. She usually had a dreamy expression on her face when speaking of her husband, and she often said she hoped Catriona would find the same degree of passion when she married. She had longed for her daughter to experience the melding of heart and mind.

Catriona's heart ached at never experiencing that special bond with a man. She was drawn to Quintus Midnight in a way that confused her. A year ago, she would have set her sights on winning him as her husband. That was impossible now, but she found herself contemplating a heady idea. A sense of freedom swept through her, and she was more light-hearted than she could remember being in recent months. All she had to do was convince him of the merits of her idea.

Chapter 4

Catriona sat tensely in the salon after dinner, sipping tea from a delicate cup, and listening to the ticking of the grandfather clock behind her. Quintus drew in a heavy breath every now and then, and she wondered if he were searching for a way to recant his proposal. Perhaps he was summoning his courage, as she was. Could that be why he had avoided her all day, having the housekeeper tell her he was conducting business when she hadn't heard him leave or return to the house?

She cleared her throat. "Quintus?"

"Yes?" He sounded startled.

She set aside the cup, fumbling to ensure it was secure on the table beside her before she released the handle. "I wish to discuss last night with you."

"Of course, Catriona." His voice deepened, and his cup clicked when he set it on a hard surface. "My offer is genuine."

"I know." She waved her hand delicately. "I appreciate your kindness, but I can't marry you."

"Catriona—"

"Please," she said firmly, "let me finish. It wouldn't be fair to you to marry me. I can't see, but I assume from my surroundings that you are well-off."

Quintus took a deep breath. "If you're worried about me providing for you, I assure you that you wouldn't want for anything."

She gave him a small smile. "That doesn't concern me. I know you must need an heir to inherit your position. Although your first wife didn't kindle, that doesn't mean you're unable to get an heir on another woman."

He sighed impatiently. "I don't care about heirs. I would like to be happy if I marry again. Therefore, I shan't marry anyone if I can't respect her and grow to love her."

She swallowed the lump in her throat, uncertain if it sprang from his words or her own nervousness. "That is an admirable sentiment, Quintus. I hope you can find the bride to suit you. I know I'm not her." She tried to be gentle, yet firm, when she uttered her refusal again. "However, that doesn't mean I don't want to become better acquainted with you."

Catriona could hear Quintus's puzzlement before he spoke. "I am afraid you've lost me."

She clutched her hands together and took a deep breath for bravery. "I would like to be your mistress."

He choked, and it was several seconds before he regained his breath. "You can't mean what you're saying, Catriona. You're free to stay at Midnight Manor for as long as you require."

Catriona grimaced. "I wasn't offering my body in exchange for room and board." There were tears at the back of her eyes, and her voice emerged as a rasp. "My mother often told me she hoped I found true love, matched with an equal passion. I had assumed I would find that in marriage, but I can no longer consider joining myself to a man in that holy state."

"Catriona—"

She ignored his interruption. "I am drawn to you, Quintus. I think I could experience perfect passion with you, and I see no reason to deny myself. I have no plans to marry, so I have no need to remain pure. I can't conceive, so there is no fear of an illegitimate child." She straightened the skirt of the dress borrowed from Fräu Markham, realizing there was a small benefit in being blind. She didn't have to attempt to evade his gaze to hide her embarrassment.

A harsh exhalation shattered the quiet. "This is insane. You can't dismiss the notion of marrying. You're a young woman. In time, you may change your mind."

Catriona shook her head. "Time can't restore the things taken from me. I refuse to bind myself to a husband I can't see, nor deny him children. I believe we could have a beneficial arrangement for however long it lasts, but if you don't want me, please just say so. I don't want to waste my time or yours." She was proud of the almost haughty note in her voice, and she was convinced no one but her could have heard the wobble of fear underlying it.

The ticking of the clock seemed to grow louder in proportion to the seconds it counted off. The silence in the room grew oppressive, and she shifted with discomfort, wondering if he would ever respond. Was he searching for a tactful way of refusing her offer? She squeezed her hands together with more pressure, waiting for him to speak.

"I can't believe I'm contemplating this," Quintus finally said in a soft voice. "Catriona, please discard this foolish notion. Let me give you the protection of my name before I bed you."

She shook her head more vigorously. "I can't marry you. I'm offering you all I am capable of giving."

Again, his silence stretched, until he broke it with a sigh. "When did you want to begin this *arrangement*?"

Catriona attempted to school her expression and tried to sound businesslike. "I see no reason to delay."

"Hmm."

She tensed as he stood and stalked across the salon. Catriona tilted her head when he walked away from her. She wondered if Quintus intended to leave without saying anything. She sagged when the door closed with a soft click, but her spine stiffened when the key turned in the lock. Her stomach clenched. "What are you doing?"

"Ensuring our privacy." His voice became clearer as he walked back toward her.

"You intend to begin now?" she asked with a little squeak.

There was a mocking inflection in his voice when Quintus asked, "Why delay?"

Catriona compressed her lips and nodded. She was determined not to show her fear of the unknown. She had an inkling he was determined to teach her a lesson, but she was equally determined not to falter in her resolve. She gripped the arms of the chair and nodded again. "I'm ready."

Quintus's laugh was low and sensuous. "We shall see. Can you undo your dress, Catriona, or do you require my assistance?"

She sniffed. "I managed to dress myself, didn't I?" He didn't need to know the housekeeper had helped her align the buttons going up the front of the shirtwaist. She tried to hide the trembling in her hands as she stood up and brought her fingers to the buttons. They opened with more ease than she would have imagined, and soon the dress gaped open, displaying her chemise. Fräu Markham hadn't had a corset in her size, so she had forgone one.

"Take it off."

Catriona obeyed his command with slightly less steady hands, pushing off the dress and letting it pool at her feet. "Satisfied, Quintus?"

He chuckled. "Not even close. Remove the chemise, drawers, and stockings."

Her eyes widened. "You wish me to bare myself entirely?"

"Yes." His tone brooked no room for argument.

She tilted her chin. "Will you be doing the same?"

Quintus's voice was a rough whisper. "Eventually."

She closed her eyes and summoned courage to strip off the chemise. When she bared her breasts, she heard him draw in an uneven breath a second before his hand cupped one, and his thumb stroked the nipple. Catriona stood still, biting back a moan as her breasts ached, and her body started tingling. Moisture gathered in her pussy. She took a step back and pushed down the drawers, letting them fall to the floor before she stepped out of them and the dress.

Quintus's breath hissed through his teeth with a whistling sound when she stood naked before him. "You're beautiful, Catriona."

She tried to drape her arms across her stomach, attempting to hide the scars there. A surgeon had cut her open to stop internal bleeding, removing her womb in the process. She had nearly died from the operation, but it had been crucial. Fortunately, she had no memories of the experience, having been unconscious during the procedure.

To her surprise, Quintus pushed away her arms, and he released her breast. His shoes creaked as he knelt. She started when the cool porcelain of his mask touched her skin, seconds before his lips traced the line of scars extending across her stomach. She tried to push away his head, but he ignored her efforts. She flinched when his tongue licked a patch of rough flesh. "Don't torment me."

His tongue withdrew, and he moved away. "I'm not tormenting you."

"Why do you focus on my scars? If it's to let me know you could never lie with me, don't be cruel about it." She couldn't hold back the tears, and one managed to trail down her cheek.

"I'm not being cruel. You are beautiful, Catriona—every inch, scarred or not." He spoke so firmly she couldn't doubt his sincerity.

She stepped back as he got to his feet. He followed, wrapping her in his embrace. She lifted her head, meeting his mouth as it descended. She opened her lips, remembering the pleasure of having his tongue stroke hers. When it touched hers, she couldn't help a small groan. She buried her hands in his hair, trying to pull him closer.

Quintus resisted, pulling away from her, causing her to loosen her hold on his hair. "Sit down in the chair, Catriona."

She didn't know if he was still attempting to dissuade her as she perched on the edge of the chair with his assistance. There had been a cool note in his voice before, but now his voice sounded ragged, and his breathing was faster than it had been. She sensed he wasn't completely in control.

"Lean back and spread your legs."

A blush tinged her cheeks at the impropriety of the position, but she surrendered to his orchestration as his hands draped each of her legs over the arms of the chair. Air caressed her pussy, and her flush deepened. "What are you doing, Quintus?"

"Shh." Catriona heard him walk away, pause, and then turn back. Then she was aware of his hand by her thigh as he knelt on the carpet near her, within touching distance, but not touching. "What—"

She started to repeat her question, but she broke off when something soft and silky stroked against her left nipple. The same sensation feathered across her other breast, and she tightened her hands on the chair's arms. "Quintus?" The scent of roses wafted to her.

"Just concentrate, Catriona." As he spoke, he sped up his stroke on her left breast, while slowing down the object caressing her right nipple.

She arched her back at the strange sensation. "What is it?" she managed to ask through gritted teeth as one of the objects trailed down her breast to flirt with her stomach.

"Roses. Fortunately, the gardener removed the thorns before filling the vase." One of the flowers stroked across her cheek, teasing her nose.

She inhaled the heavy perfume, squirming against the other rose as it moved down her stomach and stroked across her thighs. She got wetter as the petals trailed up her thigh, brushing against the outside of her pussy.

Quintus withdrew the rose from her face and returned it to her breast, alternating which nipple he feathered it against.

She could hear his heavy breathing, and she didn't doubt he was as aroused as she was. Catriona arched her hips as the satiny petals glided down her slit. He withdrew the other rose, and she reached for his hand, eager for him to continue teasing her breasts.

"Relax." Quintus evaded her hand.

Her eyes widened when his fingers stroked her pussy, near where the petals rested. "Quintus," she said with a sob, alarmed by how her lower body contracted. She cried out as one of his fingers plunged inside her. "What are you doing to me?"

"Making you burn." His voice was smoky with desire. He withdrew his finger and held open her lips with one hand. The rose teased across her clit seconds later, and she writhed against the teasing pleasure. It was too light, too delicate, to do more than inflame her senses.

Catriona arched against the rose as Quintus applied more pressure, filling her opened lips with the petals. A few strained at her opening, and she pushed down, instinctively responding to the idea of being filled. When he rotated the rose, more moisture drenched her pussy, as the petals brushed against her clit in a whisper-soft kiss. "Please."

Quintus removed the flower, and she shook her head. She hadn't wanted him to stop. She only wanted him to go further. Before she could explain, the fingers from his other hand explored her splayed pussy, and she wriggled against them. She gasped as one pushed inside her, bringing a burning sensation with it. The pain faded as his thumb circled her clit, and she relaxed again.

"Damnation."

"What? What's wrong?"

He sounded almost angry when he said, "I wasn't going to do this. I only wanted to make you come to your senses."

She giggled, startled by the sound of uninhibited joy. "What's changed?"

"Now all I want to do is make you come," he growled. "Right before I bury my cock inside you." Quintus's voice took on a serious note. "Be certain this is what you want, Catriona, before we continue."

She nodded eagerly, wondering if her sightless eyes displayed her enthusiasm. "I want you, Quintus. I'm not afraid." *Maybe just a little,* she added silently. She was afraid it would hurt, but she knew he would be gentle.

Quintus's answer was a kiss. Not on her mouth, but between her thighs. Catriona stiffened as his tongue swept into her pussy, swirling around her clit. His finger inside her moved in concert with his tongue, and she rocked her hips, feeling her desire swell as her movements brought his finger deeper inside her. Her hands moved from the chair arms to his hair, anchoring his mouth against her.

His tongue feathered across her clit before sweeping lower to plunge inside her, along with his finger. Catriona arched against him, crying out wordlessly as convulsions built inside her. She had never felt anything like it. Her muscles tensed unbearably, and her body shook. She sensed she was on the verge of something, but didn't know what. She released his hair and balled her hands into fists, struggling to find a shred of control.

Quintus's tongue swept back to her clit, and he sucked the bud into his mouth gently. His finger burrowed deeper inside her pussy, and all of her tense muscles released at the same time. Exhilaration swept through her, and she screamed her pleasure. Catriona was unable to prevent her hips from arching repeatedly as spasms rocked her pussy. A deluge of moisture saturated her pussy lips and Quintus's mouth as she stiffened once more before melting into the chair.

His mouth left her pussy, and she felt his mask as he laid his cheek against her stomach. She reached out to touch it, and he jerked away. She frowned. "You don't have to hide from me, Quintus."

There was a note of coolness in his voice. "I'm not hiding. I simply prefer to keep the mask on."

He got to his feet to shed his clothes. She could practically sense his emotional withdrawal, and she sighed. She didn't want to ruin the moment by pressing him about his mask. "If you wish."

Catriona stretched forward, seeking him. Her hand brushed against his chest, and she circled a hardened nipple with her finger and thumb. A shudder went through him, and she lowered her legs so she could sit up. She gasped as Quintus's hands tightened around her waist, pulling her forward, off the chair, and onto the carpet before he settled on top of her.

His mouth rested on hers. His lips were firm as he molded them to hers. She wrapped her arms around his shoulders as he settled between her thighs, and she returned his kisses with equal fervor. Her stomach quivered as his mouth softened, and he nibbled on her lower lip, drawing it into his mouth before releasing it.

Catriona shifted restlessly under his nude body, freezing when his cock pressed into her thigh. She had a rudimentary understanding of lovemaking, but she was about to experience it firsthand. It was suddenly less scientific and much scarier than it had been when her mother described the process a few years ago.

Quintus broke the kiss. "We don't have to go further if you're frightened."

Her smile felt a little shaky. "I don't want to stop." She arched her neck as he cupped her breast, lowering his head to lave the nipple. She spread her legs wider, bending her knees and putting her feet flat on the floor. When Quintus licked a trail from her breast to her neck, flutters of pleasure accompanied the motion.

She moaned as he sucked gently on her neck. His hand slipped between their bodies and parted her lips. She tried to stay relaxed, but she tensed when she felt his cock pushing against her pussy. She whimpered as he moved in deeper, bringing a dart of pain.

"Catriona?" he whispered against her neck.

She took his inquiring tone as a question of her resolve. She nodded her head, digging her nails into his back. "Make me yours, Quintus." She bit down hard on her lower lip as his cock surged into her. The pain was enough to make her cry out, but it didn't last long. When he thrust into her again, it still hurt, but not as much. Soon, she matched his rhythm, raising her hips to meet his as his cock filled her.

Catriona's muscles tightened around his cock, and she got wetter as he fingered her clit while sheathing himself inside her. She pushed her hips upward, taking in all of him, and she cried out as he pulled away before pushing into her again, filling her to the limits. Her juices soaked both of them as he pushed against her clit while thrusting into her again.

"Burn for me again," Quintus said against her neck, before nipping her. He sucked the sensitive flesh into his mouth as his fingers and cock worked their magic. Desire overwhelmed her, and the convulsions built again. As her muscles tightened and then released, his cock hardened before he filled her with his release. Their orgasms mingled, until she couldn't tell who was trembling.

He settled his weight on her carefully. As Catriona fought to regain her breath, she allowed the vibration of his racing heart against her chest to soothe her. Her entire body ached with the aftermath of release, but she didn't want to be parted from him yet, even if it would give her strained muscles a rest.

Quintus propped his hands on the carpet, lifting his torso from hers. His lips brushed against her forehead before he lifted his head. He sounded grim when he asked, "Do you regret your decision, Catriona? What I've taken from you can't be replaced."

"I know." She cleared the husky note from her throat. "I'm at peace with my choice."

"Won't you reconsider?" He sounded frustrated, and his muscles had tensed. "I still want you for my wife."

"Why?" she asked softly. "You don't even know me."

He made a sound low in his throat that sounded like a growl. "I don't know. I'm drawn to you, as you claim to be to me. I sensed a connection between us even before I kissed you last night. Something is urging me to hold you close and not let you go."

Catriona's heart stuttered at his blunt statement. She was too tempted to give in to his passionate words. She tried to wriggle away from him, to put some distance between them. "I do not intend to leave for a while, Quintus. Can't you be content with that?"

"Do I have a choice?" he asked with evident bitterness.

Catriona took a deep breath, steeling herself. "No. That's all I'm comfortable offering." He cursed under his breath as he got to his feet. She sat on the carpet, waiting for him to offer another argument, preparing to counter it. It wasn't fair that she had to fight both him and herself, she thought sourly.

Quintus sighed. "I'm sorry. I didn't mean to push you. I shall respect your wishes and not badger you."

"Thank you." She sagged as he walked away from her, but tensed when he turned around.

"That doesn't mean I've given up on the idea. I want you as more than my mistress, Catriona."

She shook her head, hearing his confusion. He seemed to be conflicted by this link between them, as she was. She wondered if the solution wasn't just for her to leave. Her heart seized at the thought, and she found it difficult to breathe. She couldn't stand the thought of leaving him after what they had shared, but if she didn't leave soon, she might never be able to.

Chapter 5

Early the next morning, Catriona heard someone ring the front bell. She had spent a sleepless night tossing and turning after Quintus escorted her back to her room. Her thoughts had turned to her parents, and she couldn't help thinking how disappointed her father would be that she had surrendered to her desires without benefit of a ring. She knew her mother would also be disappointed in her, but for a different reason. Felicity would consider it cowardly to hide from her feelings.

As she imagined their displeasure, her thoughts had turned to darkness again. She had relived the accident and subsequent shock of waking to find herself deprived of her parents, her sight, and the ability to have a family of her own. Her fickle beau at the time, Percy, hadn't even come to visit her. A week after she awoke, he announced his engagement to another woman. She hadn't been heartbroken, but she had been disillusioned.

Was it fair to paint every man with the same brush? She had to ask herself that question, and others. Was she really trying to protect Quintus from the burden entailed by marrying her, or was she trying to protect herself from pain and rejection?

The heavy thoughts had eventually induced tears, but her memory got hazy after that. She had a shadowy recollection of Quintus entering her room and kissing her, but she didn't think that had happened. More likely, she had finally fallen into an uneasy sleep and dreamed about him coming to her.

Now, she was awake, and she wondered who was at the door. She didn't know what time it was exactly, but she knew it must be early. The birds chirped outside her partially opened window, but the busy sounds of the city waking were just beginning.

She jumped with surprise when someone knocked on her door a few minutes later. "Yes?"

"May I enter, Fräulein?" Fräu Markham's voice was thick with an accent.

She pulled the covers to her neck. "Of course." The housekeeper entered. Catriona assumed she was a heavyset woman by the way her shoes landed with heavy thuds, and by the shapelessness of the attire she had borrowed from her yesterday. She smelled of lemon, and her voice was gruff, but warm with kindness. "Good morning, Fräu."

"Good morning." There was a thud as she set something on the floor. "Herr Midnight instructed me to order you some clothes yesterday, Fräulein. They have arrived."

She sighed with pleasure, happy she wouldn't have to borrow clothing from the housekeeper again. "That was thoughtful."

"Do you require assistance, Fräulein?"

"Yes, thank you." She felt a moment of discomfort at asking for aid, but she had to be practical. She didn't know what any of the garments looked like, and she wasn't able to deal with complicated fasteners these days. She hated her loss of independence, but the only other option was to remain in the thin shift from the brothel.

* * * * *

Later in the morning, Catriona sat downstairs sipping tea as she finished her breakfast of kippers and eggs. She couldn't help stroking the soft poplin of the lingerie dress she wore. The housekeeper had described the white lacy dress to her in detail as she helped her dress, and Catriona imagined it was lovely. She hadn't had a chance to try the new style before the accident, and there had been no funds for her to buy one when she went to live with the Bonners. She knew the housekeeper had also added a pastel sash at her waist, although she couldn't remember if Fräu Markham had said the color was lilac or peach.

Satin slippers encased her feet, and real silk hose and underclothes caressed her skin. She knew there was a matching hat, but she had no need of it while inside. For the first time in a long while, she felt like she used to, as the daughter of a prosperous merchant. The Bonners had taken most of her nice clothes and forced chubby Prudence into them, leaving her only a small selection of plain shirtwaists and one travel suit.

It was amazing how the touch of fine material against her skin could put her in such a cheerful frame of mind.

She frowned, realizing she had actually awakened feeling optimistic, rather than with the sinking awareness that usually accompanied her from sleep and haunted her during the day. She still felt an aching sadness when she thought of her parents, but it had dimmed these past two days. As had her depression over her future. Perhaps making the decision to be Quintus's mistress had revitalized her.

She grimaced, wondering why Quintus hadn't joined her for breakfast. Again, the housekeeper had dismissed his presence as saying he was attending to business, but she had been awake since early morning, and she hadn't heard him moving through the house. She knew the older woman was lying to her, but she didn't know why.

With a sigh, she set aside her cup and rose carefully. She had made a point of counting the steps as Fräu Markham brought her downstairs earlier, and she was somewhat confident she could make her way back to her room. Another day of boredom stretched before her. How she missed being able to read or take a walk without assistance. What she missed most was her set of paints. She had always found painting engrossing, and her mother had encouraged her, having been proud of her talent.

Harry had been oblivious to his daughter's pursuits, still somewhat old-fashioned and imagining she did nothing with her days but prepare to be a man's wife. A soft smile crossed Catriona's face as she marveled at the strong union her parents had built, despite how opposite their temperaments and beliefs had been.

She moved cautiously through the dining room, into the hallway beyond. She walked a few steps, trying to remember if they had turned left or right. She closed her eyes and tried to picture the route the housekeeper led her on, finally taking the right.

Her heart ached to experience the same intensity of love and passion her parents had shared. She already knew she could find that passion with Quintus, and her heart told her she could love him. It was her fear that held her back. How could she marry him as she was? What if he decided she was too much bother and sent her away?

Divorces were becoming less scandalous, and she knew marriage was no guarantee of a lasting relationship.

No, she was being sensible in her decision, Catriona decided, as her hand touched the banister. She gripped it as she walked up the curving staircase. She might not be completely satisfied with what she could have with Quintus, but it was better not to bind either of them into a permanence he might decide he didn't want.

She ignored the twinge of guilt that accompanied her resolve, knowing her parents would tell her she was cheating herself and Quintus. She had to make the decisions that best reflected her future as it was now, not the ones that would have suited her before the accident.

Catriona emerged onto the second landing and felt her way down the hallway. She frowned as she came to the door with the ornate handles. She hadn't expected to arrive at her room so quickly, and she wondered if she had taken a wrong turn. She mentally backtracked, eventually deciding she must have gone the correct way.

She turned the knob, finding it locked. She frowned. Had she locked her room? She didn't recall doing so. Catriona started to think she had wandered into the wrong section of the house, but didn't know how to find her way back. She tested the other knob, finding it turned under her hand. She breathed a sigh of relief. She and the housekeeper must have used only one of the doors to her room, leaving the other locked.

A small headache had built behind her eyes, and she knew lying down would relieve the pressure. It was a lingering effect from her head injury, and the physician seemed to think it would endure throughout her life.

She walked through the room, uttering an unladylike curse when her knee collided with a table. She sidestepped it, mentally castigating herself for forgetting the layout of her room. She had spent hours walking around it yesterday to familiarize herself with the location of everything. She imagined if anyone had seen her pacing the room, they would have thought her mad, but it was the method she had discovered that worked for her to memorize her surroundings.

She finally made it to the bed and sat down. She slipped off her slippers and thought about removing her dress. She decided it wasn't worth the bother to summon the housekeeper to undo the buttons at her back, and she stretched out.

Catriona froze when her arm brushed against someone. She inhaled and recognized Quintus's scent. "Quintus?" Had he come to her bed to wait for her? When he didn't answer, she touched him hesitantly. Her hand glided across his bare chest, and she couldn't resist tweaking his nipple. He still didn't awaken, and her hand traveled higher, noting the coolness in his flesh.

Her eyes widened when she discovered he wasn't wearing his mask. She ran gentle fingers over the puckered tissue, shuddering as she imagined the pain he must have endured. She wondered what had caused his injuries as she traced his high forehead, square jaw, full lips, and straight nose.

Her fingers stilled at the tip of his nose. "Quintus, wake up." She put her finger under his nostrils, frightened when she didn't feel his breath. Catriona rolled over and placed her ear against his chest, moving her head until she found his heart. It didn't beat.

"No," she cried out. He couldn't be dead. She knew he must be healthy and vital, after touching him yesterday. She had noticed during the past few months that those who were ill or old had a peculiar scent clinging to them, but he hadn't borne a trace of it. How could he be dead?

"Fräu Markham," she screamed forcefully. "Hurry." Within seconds, she heard the housekeeper's heavy tread rushing up the stairs. She cradled Quintus against her, noting he didn't smell of decomposition. It must have happened just a short time ago. Tears spilled down her cheeks, and sobs exploded from her. "Fräu," she cried again, but it was a low, mournful sound.

"What are you doing in Herr Midnight's room?" The housekeeper practically screeched the question. "This is most irregular, Fräulein—"

"I must have gotten lost. I thought this was my room." A wail broke from her. "It doesn't matter now. He's dead."

Silence descended, finally broken by the housekeeper muttering a prayer. "Have you killed him?" she demanded as she rushed across the room.

Catriona's mouth dropped open, and she sat up. "Of course not. I found him not breathing. His skin is cool to the touch. It must have happened just a short time ago."

The housekeeper breathed deeply and whispered, "*Danken Sie Gott.*"

Catriona frowned, wondering whom the housekeeper was thanking. If she remembered properly from her long-ago language lessons, *Gott* was God. Why would the servant be thanking God for Quintus's death?

"Come, Fräulein, I'll escort you to your room." The housekeeper sounded calm now. "Leave the master to his rest."

Catriona shook her head. "He's not resting. You must send for someone." She protested when the housekeeper's thick fingers fastened around her arm and pulled her from the bed.

"Herr Midnight will explain, if he chooses to." The housekeeper seemed to be keeping her tone deliberately distant. "He will join your for dinner, after sunset. You may direct your questions to him then."

She shook her head, trying to dig her feet into the hardwood floor. "You don't understand, Fräu. Quintus is dead. He isn't breathing. Please check him."

The housekeeper patted her hand as she forced her from the room, pausing to lock the doors behind her. "Have a rest, Fräulein. You'll feel better when you awaken and see the master safe and sound."

She continued to protest as the housekeeper half-dragged her down the staircase and through the hallway, to another set of stairs. As the woman pulled her up them, she tried to reason with her, to make her return to check on Quintus. The woman remained implacable as she took her down the hallway and opened her door. She firmly pushed her inside, ignoring Catriona's frantic pleas. Seconds later, the lock clicked, and the housekeeper moved down the hall.

She collapsed to the floor, beating her fists against the door. She wondered what the housekeeper planned to do with her, and she wondered why the woman had refused to check on Quintus. Coldness enveloped her as a horrible idea occurred to her.

What if the housekeeper had been the one to murder Quintus? If she had been, she would have no compunction about eliminating Quintus's guest to hide her crime.

* * * * *

When the key turned in the lock hours later, Catriona tightened her grasp on the vase she had taken from the table and propelled herself forward. As the murderous housekeeper entered the room, she ran to meet her, holding the heavy container over her head. She brought it down with a cry of satisfaction that turned to horror when Quintus grunted with pain. She clasped a hand to her racing heart. "You're alive."

"Of course—"

She hurled herself against him, cutting off his words. Catriona strained on her toes, covering his neck with kisses. Tears gushed from her, and she couldn't seem to stop babbling. "You were dead. I was so certain. I thought the housekeeper had murdered you." Sobs interspersed her words. "I kept thinking how unfair it was to have lost you too, after losing everyone else." A wave of sadness washed over her at the memory of the afternoon she had spent torturing herself, imaging the worst.

His hands soothed her as they touched her face, wiping away her tears. "Calm yourself, Catriona. I am fine. Fräu Markham didn't plot to do away with me." A thread of amusement underlay his mild tone.

"But she refused to check on you. She dragged me back to my room and locked me in." Her outrage was evident in her angry tone.

"I'm sorry she did that. She told me she didn't know how to deal with the situation, and she was frightened you would injure yourself if you had run of the manor."

She sniffed. "Still, she shouldn't have..." She trailed off, frowning. How could he be standing whole before her, speaking so calmly? He hadn't had a heartbeat. She took a wary step back. "What's happening?"

"Hmm?"

She caught the edge of subterfuge in his too-innocent tone. "I know what I felt. Your heart wasn't beating. Your skin was cold. You had no breath." Fear caused her throat to seize, and she clasped her hands to her chest. "What are you, Quintus Midnight?"

A sharp laugh escaped him. "A most appropriate question, dear."

The door closed right before the lock clicked, and she backed away, sensing his presence as he approached. She realized just how foolish she had been to entrust her safety to a mysterious stranger. No one knew where she was. A harsh sob escaped her when she more fittingly acknowledged no one cared where she was or what happened to her. She would be the perfect victim for this…thing.

"I can sense your fear. Please don't be frightened." His tone had reverted to soothing. "I won't hurt you." As he spoke, he approached her at a slow, steady pace.

Catriona continued to back away until her legs hit the edge of the bed. She plopped down, and the fight drained out of her as he closed the gap to sit beside her. She didn't try to pull away when he took her hand between his, squeezing gently. After everything she had been through this past year, it was the greatest of ironies to travel to another country to find death.

"Before I explain, I must swear you to secrecy, Catriona. If you can't vow to guard what I tell you, I'll have to send you away without an explanation."

His words surprised her, and her head snapped up. "Send me away…you mean…you aren't going to kill me?"

"Of course not." He sounded annoyed. "Haven't I just told you as much?"

She shrugged, disconcerted by the way her palm tingled where his hand touched her, even as her heart continued to race with fear. His hand brushed her cheek, and she automatically looked in his direction, though she couldn't see him.

"Will you promise me?"

She licked her lips, torn between the urge to escape and the need to know. "Whom would I tell?" she settled for saying. "No doubt whatever you tell me would be interpreted as ravings if I repeated them."

"Doubtless," he agreed smoothly. "How old do you think I am, Catriona? I know you can't see my face, but please guess."

She frowned at the odd question, taking time to formulate an intelligent answer. He had an air of wisdom about him that suggested he was wizened, but he had the physical prowess of a young man. His body was firm to the touch, and his hair was thick and full. He was a strange combination. "I don't know." She licked her dry lips. "Perhaps forty?"

"I'm so old even I don't have a precise count of the years any longer. I have even forgotten my original surname, so I took Midnight when I purchased this home." He delivered the statement without a hint of artifice. "I know I was born during the height of the Roman Empire, but I can't recall my own birthday."

She gasped at the ludicrous words, but she didn't doubt he believed them. He spoke with utmost conviction.

He seemed not to notice her indrawn breath, or he chose to ignore it. "I was somewhere between five-and-twenty and thirty when I met an old man." He hesitated. "He wasn't really that old, but he had a presence that suggested he was as aged as the gods. He took a liking to me and made me his son."

She frowned. "How did he make you his son?"

"He changed me to what I am now. He hungered for companionship, but not that of a lover. He wanted someone to pass along his memories to, someone who would remember and honor him." There was a thread of sadness in Quintus's voice when he spoke. "He made me like him, and I stayed by his side for two decades before he grew tired and met the sunrise."

Catriona shook her head, more confused than ever. "I don't understand." She fell into silence as he touched a finger lightly to her lips.

"He was a vampire, Catriona. He made me one too."

Her eyes widened, and she wrenched away. "You're mad! I've read *Dracula*. There are no such things…"

He laughed. "Mr. Stoker wasn't the creator of vampires. They have existed long before written history, in many varied forms. I think I am perhaps the most rare, for I don't feed on blood. I get my sustenance from emotions." He stroked the back of her hand with his thumb, seeming to realize she was having a difficult time comprehending. "I am a psychic vampire, Catriona."

She blinked, not at all sure what she should say. Part of her remained skeptical of his claims, and she thought to demand he take her to the train station. Yet, she knew he had been dead when she disturbed him earlier in the afternoon. No matter how she tried to convince herself otherwise, she knew what state he had been in. "Quintus—"

"Will you allow me to explain before you begin to doubt me?" he asked with gentle reproof. He must have taken her silence for acquiescence, because he continued. "Psychic vampires sustain themselves by drawing emotions from their victims. It can be any emotion, but I have always tried to take in suffering and pain."

His voice changed, became darker. "My first wife, Lilly, fed only on the pleasure of mortals, leaving them in despair. There is a certain bitter aftertaste associated with negative emotions, but one quickly adapts. Unless we draw in too much of the emotion, it doesn't actually elicit any response in us but a surge of energy. There is no discernable difference between taking in pain or joy, but she could never be bothered to acclimate herself to the taste."

He fell silent for a moment before saying, "In fact, she seemed to glory in leaving anguish in her wake." He sighed. "Almost as soon as I changed her, I knew I had made a mistake. One I couldn't correct unless I took her life. I wasn't strong enough to do such a thing, so I endured her poisonous presence for a century."

A confusing whirl of emotions swept through her, and she was discomfited to find jealously the uppermost among them. She didn't like him speaking of his first wife. "Why did you change her at all?"

He sighed again. "She was quite beautiful. I became enchanted with her when I fed on her. You see, she was dying, and there was no cure. I don't know what caused her illness, but it had something to do with her blood. She was so young, and had been so vital, that her disease brought on deep melancholy when she became confined to her bed."

"Did you know her…before?"

"No. Her suffering drew me to her. I thought she had a gentle soul, and I found my pity changing to love…or so I believed. I violated one of the few rules my father had imposed on me, which was not to reveal my powers to mortals. She embraced me." He sounded bitter. "I mistook her eagerness to be healed as a return of my affections. Like a fool, I married and changed her. It was only after she was well that I realized she wasn't the sweet woman she had pretended to be. She had used me."

Catriona's heart wrenched at the pain in his voice, and she cupped his hand between hers, rubbing gently. "What happened?"

"Our marriage was a period of Hell," he said bluntly. "She left for weeks and months at a time, only returning when her current lover ran out of funds or disenchanted her in some way. By the end of the second year, we didn't even make love when she returned to *try again*." He said the last part mockingly. "As the years passed, the span of her disappearances lengthened, until she didn't return for more than twenty years."

She held her breath, sensing he was about to reveal something terrible.

"I had convinced myself I didn't love her and never had." He exhaled before continuing. "However, it had been a long time since a woman warmed my bed. When she made certain overtures, I found myself responding. I don't think I ever fell in love with her again, but I did come to care for Lilly once more. I knew something had happened to her, and I thought it had changed her for the better."

"But it hadn't?"

"No." Heavy disappointment colored his voice. "There was a man she loved madly, but he had spurned her when he learned what she was. She decided he would accept her when he was like her, and she changed him without his consent. He rejected her again, and she came home to me to restore her confidence."

Her heart twisted, and she almost asked him to stop the tale. She didn't want to know how much he had loved his wife, or how Lilly had hurt him. Nevertheless, she couldn't deny the darker impulse that wanted to hear everything.

"I thought we had a chance to be happy, finally. She seemed more like the woman she had been before I transformed her." He sighed, and his hand shook in her grasp.

"A short time after her return, her lover came to her, telling her he'd changed his mind. He swore he wanted her forever, and he begged her to come with him. Lilly had no trouble choosing, but she couldn't just go. I still don't know why she did it, but she had to leave a mark. Maybe she wanted me to remember her, or perhaps she wanted me distracted while she fled. Maybe she just wanted me dead."

Nausea churned in her stomach. "She caused your accident?"

"Yes. Her servant branded me with the poker from the fire during the day, while I slept. It scarred me forever, because I was regenerating, and my body didn't have the strength to heal the wound.

"While her companion dealt with me, she and her lover fled. I went mad with anger and pain. I followed them after dealing with the servant, but they had a day's head start." His voice lowered. "I caught up with them at an inn, and I discovered her lover had played her false. He was a pious man, and he believed all vampires were an abomination. I think he wanted to save Lilly from herself. He destroyed the two of them by paying the innkeeper to open the curtains while they slept."

His pain drew her to him, and Catriona turned in his arms, pressing kisses across his face. "My poor darling." She smoothed her hands down him. "You must have been in such pain."

"It was almost anticlimactic. I had planned to kill her, but he had done it for me. When I saw her burned skeleton, I cried for the woman I had lost…the woman I suspect never existed anywhere but in my mind. I vowed never to love again."

Her lips on his muffled his voice, and it was a long moment before he drew away.

"I have kept that vow until I met you, my sweet one. I, of all people, know the folly of rash behavior, but here I find myself once again prepared to rush into marriage. I have fallen in love with you, Catriona. I know I'm not mistaken about your sweet nature." He kissed her again, thrusting his tongue inside her mouth and probing her depths. He finally withdrew. "Will you be my wife?"

She bit back a sob as confusion filled her. She ached to accept, but fear held her back. "I…oh, Quintus, kiss me."

He hesitated but, at last, his mouth touched hers. His lips were soft against hers as he moved his mouth. He caught her lip between his teeth, sucking gently, as his fingers toyed with the buttons going down the back of the dress. When he unfastened the last one, he pushed the dress around her waist. His mouth was hot through the silk of her chemise as he dipped his head to taste her nipple.

Catriona leaned back, pressing his head against her breast. She moaned as his teeth raked the bud. She didn't resist as he pushed her down on the bed, following her. He kept his mouth at her nipple, suckling with increasing pressure. He cupped her other breast in his hand, thumbing the hardened nipple.

She cried out as a tingle of awareness shot from her breasts to her pussy, causing it to spasm. She remembered the feel of his tongue against her clit, and she shifted restlessly.

Quintus lifted his head from her breast, and his fingers pulled at the skirt of her dress, bringing it up to her waist as she lifted her buttocks off the bed. He pulled her into a semi-prone position to remove the garment and her chemise before lowering her back to the bed.

"I want to touch you," she whispered shyly. Her cheeks flushed as he lay down beside her. She rolled onto her side, pulling at his clothes. He had forgone a jacket, and she was able to quickly strip him of his waistcoat. She fumbled with the buttons of his shirt, and in her frustration, she tore them open. Quintus chuckled as she darted forward to lick his chest.

His laugh turned to a husky groan when her tongue teased the nub she found hidden in his chest hair. She nipped him gently, mimicking the movements he had made on her nipples. He groaned again, and she moved lower, trailing her tongue down his chest to his hard stomach. She paused to write her name in wet swirls, and he shifted restlessly under her.

Her hands moved to his trousers, hesitating at the ties. His cock pressed against the material when she ran her hand lightly down the front of his pants. She wanted to touch him, but couldn't summon the courage to unfasten his trousers. Her eyes widened when his hands settled on hers, jerking open the ties. She drew her hands away. "I can't…" She trailed off, pressing her flushed face into his stomach.

"It's okay." He seemed amused. Quintus pulled away and stood up. The sound of him removing his clothing reached her ears, and when he returned, he was nude. He lifted her higher onto the bed before lying beside her. His mouth settled on hers as his hand slipped through the slit in her drawers to stroke her pussy. She barely noticed the cool porcelain of his mask as his mouth moved over hers.

Catriona's tongue stroked his as his fingers delved inside her, spreading her moisture. Her clit swelled under his caresses, and she arched her hips, wanting more. "Touch me." She spoke forcefully as she lifted her hips to bring his finger deeper inside her. There was a twinge of pain as he slipped inside her, but it faded when he rotated his finger in slow circles. Her clit pulsed, aching for his touch, and she squirmed.

"Will you touch me, Catriona?" He sounded husky and out of breath. He thrust his hips forward, pushing his cock into the soft flesh of her thigh. "Will you stroke my cock as I stroke your pussy?"

She groped for his cock, trailing her fingers across the thick head. He removed his hand from her pussy and wrapped it around hers, guiding it to cup his cock. He moved her hand up and down for a few strokes. His fluid leaked from the tip. He was thick and pulsing in her hands, and she tightened her hold as she raised and lowered her hand, mimicking the motion he showed her as he withdrew his hand. He moaned with pleasure as he thrust his cock deeper into her hand.

Quintus's hand returned to her pussy, and he slipped two fingers inside her. He plunged them into her pussy in rhythm with the thrusts of his hips. Catriona maintained a firm grasp on his cock as her hips rose to meet his fingers' thrusts. She hovered on the edge of an orgasm when he withdrew his fingers and pulled his cock from her cupped hand. She shook her head, aching for release.

"I want to be inside you," he said as he raised himself over her, parting her thighs. "Don't you want that, Catriona?"

She squirmed against his hand when he parted her pussy. "Oh, yes. I want you so much I think I might die." She raised her hips at the same time the head of his cock settled against her opening. He plunged into her as she arched against him, and she cried out at the mix of pleasure and pain. She locked her legs around him and thrust upward again.

His cock spasmed inside her, and Quintus withdrew before plunging into her again. He cupped one of her breasts in his hand as the other settled on her hip, urging her up to meet him. His thrusts were slow and deep, making her cry out with pleasure each time he buried his cock inside her.

Catriona strained against him, getting as close as she could. His hands moved to cup her buttocks, and she couldn't hold in a small scream as he drove into her while lifting her to meet him. Pain spread through her, but it only provided a sharp edge to her pleasure. The combination sent convulsions pulsing through her. As the walls of her pussy clenched around Quintus, she strove to take in more of him, until she was almost sobbing with the effort.

Release came quickly, causing the tiny tremors to lengthen and increase. Her pussy locked around his spasming cock as his ejaculate filled her. Catriona tightened her thighs, trying to keep him inside her just a little longer. It wasn't until her muscles ached with exhaustion and her pussy released that she relaxed, loosening her hold on him.

Quintus's cock was still semi-hard as he pulled out of her and rolled onto his side, bringing her with him. He tucked her close to him and pressed a kiss to her forehead. His heart hammered audibly, and sweat had given his body a slick feeling. The same sheen decorated Catriona's body. Her breath came in short bursts, and she could barely keep her eyes open.

"You delight me," he said in a low voice. "You're so passionate."

"Only with you," she said around a yawn that caught her by surprise. "I had never even kissed a man before meeting you." She curled her fingers into his chest hair. "You delight me too, Quintus. Your wife was a fool to not be content with what you gave her." Her last words emerged as a sleepy murmur, and her eyes closed. As they did, part of Quintus's explanation returned to her, floating across her subconscious.

I mistook her eagerness to be healed as a return of my affections.

Her eyes snapped open, but the ever-present blackness greeted her. "Quintus?"

"Yes, love?" He sounded as tired as she was, though he had spent the day in his deathlike slumber.

"You can heal me, can't you?" All traces of sleep fled, burned away by a burst of excitement. For the first time in months, pure joy swept through her. To not be confined to a life of darkness…she couldn't even begin to fathom such a thing after the last year.

His harsh tone chased away her joy. "Absolutely not."

She blinked with shock, and it was a moment before she could gather her wits. "I don't understand. If this gift healed Lilly, and it made you immortal, why won't it do the same for me?"

Quintus's silence filled the chamber. He exhaled harshly. "I didn't say it wouldn't heal you. I just won't do it."

A chill coursed through her. "What? I don't understand. Why not?"

"Because it's dangerous. The transformation is painful."

She shrugged. "I can endure more pain to regain my sight, Quintus."

"I won't do it! There are side effects, for one thing. You become vulnerable to enemies during the day. The trance you fall into is indistinguishable from death. Sunlight kills you. Can you imagine what it's like to not be able to see the sun anymore, Catriona? It's been hundreds of years since I saw anything but night."

"I can well imagine," she said in a cool voice, surprised by her equanimity. "I haven't seen the sun or *anything else* in thirteen months. You can change that, but you won't. Why are you doing this? I can hear the note of guilt in your voice. I know you're lying to me."

"I won't discuss this further." With jerky movements, Quintus rolled from the bed.

She could hear him gathering his clothes and dressing quickly before he strode to the door. Her heart clenched with fear. "Quintus, please don't leave me like this. At least tell me why."

His answer was the slamming of her door.

Chapter 6

Just a few feet from her door, Quintus fell to his knees, clutching his chest. Tears burned behind his eyes, and he struggled to suppress them. His breath emerged as harsh pants, and he trembled all over.

She couldn't ask it of him. She just couldn't. It was too dangerous. What if he lost her during the transformation? Why was her eyesight so important to her? He would love her for the rest of her life, despite the blindness.

Or because of it, a sly voice whispered in the back of his mind.

A gasp tore from him at the thought. No. He couldn't believe that was his only reason for wanting Catriona with him. He wasn't so selfish as to keep her blind just to save himself from seeing the pity—or, God forbid, revulsion—in her eyes when she looked at him without the mask.

When she was whole and restored, she wouldn't need to stay with him. She could take care of herself again. She would leave him. If his ugly face didn't scare her away, her own need for independence would. If he didn't change her, she would stay with him. She had nowhere else to go.

She would eventually die. His eyes burned, and a tear escaped, trailing down his cheek. He might be able to keep her with him as she was. He might convince her she had no other options, but unless he transformed her, mortality would steal her away…in fifty years, maybe. He knew how rapidly fifty years could pass to an immortal.

How could he even think about leaving her that broken creature she was when he had the power to restore her? He had chosen for more than a millennium to ease suffering where he could. How could he turn his back on his ideals now? Did he want her to stay simply because she had no alternative? Wouldn't it be better to have her stay because she made the choice, not because she had no other choice?

He was nauseated as he rose to his feet and staggered down the hallway to her room. He pushed open the door, finding Catriona attempting to dress herself. Emotion had flushed her cheeks, and he could feel the anger radiating from her. He sensed she was intent on leaving him. Not because he had refused to heal her, but because he wouldn't explain why. He sighed. "Don't leave, Catriona."

She spun in his direction angrily, though her gaze centered on the bust of a goddess on a pedestal beside him, rather than on him. "You can't make me stay. If I can't trust you not to lie to me, I certainly can't marry you. Why won't you explain? Damnation!"

"I'll transform you." He heard the weary defeat in his tone and winced. He made an effort to hide it. "If that's what you want, I'll change you tonight. You'll awaken whole and healed tomorrow night, after sunset."

She paused, and her brow had furrowed. She seemed shocked by his reversal. "Are...are you certain?" She licked her lips, betraying her nervousness.

"I leave the decision with you." He forced himself to sound impassive to her choice. He could sense her fear rising as she contemplated the change. Before, she had been too excited to consider the consequences.

"You said it was dangerous. Has anyone ever died?"

"I don't know. I don't remember anything from my own transformation except terrifying visions and unending pain. Lilly screamed for hours. Her heart stopped beating an hour before dawn, and I thought she had died. When she awakened at sunset, I was amazed." He shrugged, forgetting she couldn't see the gesture. "That may have been because she was ill before the transformation. I don't know," he said again.

Catriona fell silent, but her eyes moved back and forth rapidly. After several minutes of quiet, she nodded just once. "I want to try. I can't live like this for the rest of my life."

"Are you certain you're prepared for immortality?" he countered. "If you decide to end your existence as an immortal, the only way to do so is to let the sun consume you. My father screamed for close to an hour before the light finished him."

"I'm not the type to kill myself," she said brusquely. "Had I been, events of the past year would have driven me to do so already."

"I don't think we can have children." He made his last argument feebly. He really didn't know. Lilly had never been home frequently enough for them to try, and she hadn't been a virgin when he married her, so she might have known about birth control. Yet, his sire had never gotten a child on a mortal.

Her lower lip wobbled, but she shrugged. "I can't have them now either." She firmed her mouth. "What do I need to do?"

He accepted her decision with a heavy heart as he walked toward her. Quintus drew her into his arms. "You have to drink my blood." He turned her in his arms, pressing her back to his chest. "It's the only means of transformation for any type of vampire. Can you do it?"

She hesitated before nodding.

He closed his eyes as he brought his wrist to his mouth and slashed the vein. He quickly pressed it to her mouth. "Drink until the wound closes, but don't reopen it. You only need a little."

She gagged on the blood as it poured into her mouth, and he thought she might vomit. Her stomach quavered against his palm when he pressed his hand there. "Try to keep it down. If you throw up, you'll have to do this again." He interjected a lighthearted note into his voice. "I don't fancy the pain a second time, Catriona."

She didn't reply, but her throat worked as she audibly swallowed mouthfuls of blood. The wound started closing, and he eased his wrist away from her mouth, feeling her slump against him.

"My head." She sounded weak, and her body began to tremble. "Quintus, I feel…" She trailed off as shudders seized her. "So cold."

Quintus lifted her into his arms and carried her to the bed. He covered her with the blankets, forming a makeshift cocoon. "I'll do my best to ease your suffering. You'll soon pass out, but you'll still be aware of the pain. Do your best to endure it." He lowered his voice to a whisper as he pressed a kiss to her ear. "When you awaken tomorrow night, you'll be able to see everything you've missed for a year."

"Yes," she said with a soft sigh before her teeth clicked together. Convulsions seized her, sending her body flopping across the bed. Quintus crawled into the bed beside her, holding her close to him. It was just the beginning of a long night, but he knew it would be an even longer eternity if she chose to leave him when her injuries healed.

* * * * *

Catriona awoke suddenly the following night. Her eyes snapped open, and it took her a moment to realize she was staring up at a deep-red canopy and actually *seeing* it. She sat up so quickly her head spun, and she turned her head, eyeing the elegant room Quintus had given her. She was delighted with the unimaginative mix of maroon and cream. She had never seen anything so beautiful in all her life. A giggle escaped her, and she swung her feet onto the floor.

When she stood up, she realized she was nude, and a blush trailed across her face. When she hadn't been able to see her nudity, it had been easy to forget it. Now, she studied her body with intensity, trying to ignore her embarrassment. She touched her smooth stomach, pleased to find the scars gone. She winced when her overly long nails scraped her flesh, and she looked down at them. They had grown to talons during the night. Her hair had also grown, now touching her waist.

She cast her memory back to the night before, but she remembered very little except moments of terrible pain and strange dreams. Always, Quintus's voice was there to soothe her through the worst. She remembered him taking on her suffering several times, until he made himself unwell. Most of all, she remembered his tender touch as he held her against him. Everything else was a dull blur.

She frowned when she saw he wasn't in the room with her. Catriona went to the wardrobe and removed a dressing gown. She was about to go look for him when someone knocked on her door. "Enter."

She had expected Fräu Markham, but this man could only be Quintus. Her lips parted when she saw how handsome he was. His dark hair tended toward curly, but he had attempted to harness it by keeping it closely cropped. He was broad-shouldered and narrow-hipped, and he stood at least half a foot taller than her own average height. He wore an immaculate suit, and he had a well-formed face, with pleasing lines. She ached to draw him.

There was an air of hesitancy about him when he stepped into the room. He kept the masked side of his face averted, and he sounded distant. "How do you feel?"

A smile she couldn't contain burst across her face as she rushed across the room to throw herself into his arms. After a hesitation, his arms held her loosely. "I am wonderful, my love. You have given me back everything."

"You're strong, then?"

Catriona nodded, frowning when she saw the sadness in his green eye. The other was turned away from her. "I haven't felt so strong in a long time. I can do anything." She grinned up at him, hoping her excitement would be infectious. The air of melancholy clung tenaciously to him. "Are you well, Quintus? I remember you took too much of my anguish and became ill."

He nodded. "I am fine." He cleared his throat. "I suppose it would be polite to hold off on this conversation, but I find I can't wait another moment."

She frowned at his seriousness. "What conversation?"

He began pacing. "What will you do now, Catriona?"

She tilted her head, considering. "Before I accepted there would be no miraculous recovery, I often envisioned what would be the first thing I did when I regained my sight. I always thought it would be to go to my parents' graves to bid them a proper goodbye."

He nodded. "I can arrange that for you."

She shrugged. "I would like to in the near future, but I find myself too happy to mourn right now. I know my parents would understand this feeling. I have the urge to paint." She walked over to him, stopping him in mid-step. "I want to capture you on canvas, if you'll permit me to."

He flinched, but didn't answer. "My question referred to your long-term plans. Will you return to England and attempt to reclaim your inheritance?"

It was her turn to flinch. "I thought…" She trailed off, frowning. "Did you change your mind?"

He cocked a brow. "About what?"

"Your marriage proposal." She tried to keep her tone polite and emotionless. "I'll understand if you wish to withdraw the offer. After all, we don't know each other at all. I suppose it would be scandalous to marry so quickly—"

"No more scandalous than having made you my mistress," he said. His hands trembled as he lifted them to his face, where they paused. "Do you want to marry me, Catriona? You never answered the last time I asked you."

"I wasn't certain then." She gave him a tentative smile. "I wanted to be with you, but I didn't want you to be burdened by me. I didn't know if I was drawn to you because of my dependence, or for another reason." She hesitated. "I wasn't even certain how you really felt about me, until last night. I can't doubt your feelings after the way you stayed with me, sharing my pain. Now that I can meet you equally, I would be honored to be your wife."

Quintus shook his head. "You mustn't decide until you see my face." He fumbled with the black porcelain, removing the mask slowly to reveal his ravaged face.

She bit back a cry when she saw the pale, puckered flesh. Sections of pink scars furrowed his countenance, and the injury was a hideous irony to the left side of his face, which was so handsome. She clenched her hands together, trying to examine him dispassionately.

She could sense his fear and nervousness—the first indication of her new powers. She knew he wouldn't want pity or coddling. Her best reaction was calm acceptance, and she struggled to hide her anger. Her voice still trembled when she repeated, "I would be honored to be your wife."

She reached out to touch his face, and he jerked away. "That bitch." The anger exploded from her, and Catriona could have throttled his first wife if the sun hadn't already consumed that cold-hearted fiend. "I could kill her for the pain she's caused you."

"Catriona—" He took a step back, seemingly intent on keeping her from touching him.

A surge of strength filled her as she stepped forward and pressed her body close to his. Catriona clasped her hands around his neck and forced his neck to bend, lowering his head toward hers. Her gentle kisses across the marred flesh were in direct contrast to the rage still flowing through her. She felt his bunched muscles slowly relax, and his mouth softened when she touched her lips to his.

She drew him into her arms, feeling his pain sweep through her. It struck her that Quintus was more of a broken soul than she had ever been, and he needed her. She acted on instinct as she stopped kissing him and instead inhaled. His breath flowed into her, but more than that, his torment filled her. It tasted bitter, almost enough to make her choke, but she persisted.

Slowly, the taste dissipated, and her energy skyrocketed. Quintus's pain lessened, and she continued to drink until her stomach churned with nausea. She broke away, coughing until a cloud of green escaped her.

When she looked up, tears streamed down Quintus's face, and he wore an unguarded expression. She touched her palm to the scarred side of his face, caressing gently. "I love you, Quintus. Will you marry me?"

He turned his head as he captured her hand. He kissed her palm, nuzzling his mouth against her skin.

She closed her eyes, enjoying his touch. A sense of peace filled her as he pulled her into his arms for a long kiss. There was no sharing of pain this time. This kiss was all about pleasure and love. It was a healing touch, for both of them.

Epilogue

50 years later…

Catriona studied the portrait in the artificial light of the lamp. The only time she truly missed daylight was when she was painting. Electric light didn't compare to the softness of natural light. She chewed on the end of her wooden brush as she struggled to identify what was missing in the painting of Quintus.

"The sun will rise soon. Are you coming to bed?"

His voice caused her to jump with surprise as he entered her studio, and she turned her head to smile at him after pulling the paintbrush from her mouth. "I'm sorry, love. I lost track of the time." She gestured to him to approach. "Tell me what's missing in this painting."

She held her breath as he studied the image. She had been trying for fifty years to capture his exact visage, but each painting always fell short of her mental picture.

He shrugged. "It looks like me…or how I used to look."

She shook her head. "There's still something missing, Quintus."

He put his arms around her, bracing his hands around her distended stomach. "I agree. My wife is missing from my bed. She needs to rest, for the baby's sake."

His cock poked into her back, and she couldn't hold in a throaty chuckle. "Somehow, I think you have more than sleep planned for me."

He thrust against her gently. "How perceptive. Baby needs rest, and Daddy needs loving."

She nodded. "I'll be there as soon as I put away my supplies."

Quintus heaved a sigh, but nodded. "Very well. Don't take too long."

As he walked away, she started to put her brushes away. As she did so, she looked up at the painting. It suddenly struck her what was wrong about it. In each rendering, she always showed him looking solemn and stern. He wasn't like that anymore. It was seldom that a smile wasn't on his face, and he was quick to laugh. The pain he used to carry had faded to a distant memory during the past half-century.

With deft strokes, she painted over the expression she had captured, putting a smile in its place. She fixed the eyes and grooves around his mouth quickly, before stepping back to survey her work.

She nodded, satisfied with her attempt for the first time in five decades. The man smiling back at her from the canvas was the man she knew and loved. Yes, that was her Quintus, with the name Midnight, but a heart of sunshine.

She dismissed her silly musings and rushed through cleaning up. She was anxious to join her husband, to share with him her victory and her passion. Most of all, and always, her love.

About the author:

Kit Tunstall lives in Idaho with her husband. In addition to books available through Ellora's Cave, her shorter works have appeared in more than a dozen markets, including Sex on the Edge, Boise Weekly, Epiphany Magazine, BloodLust-UK, and Bridges Magazine.

Also by DOMINIQUE ADAIR:

- Tied With A Bow

Also by MARGARET L. CARTER:

- Things That Go Bump In The Night 2
- Virgin Blood

Also by KIT TUNSTALL:

- A Matter of Honor
- Blood Lines 1: Blood Oath
- Blood Lines 2: Blood Challenge
- By Invitation Only
- Phantasie
- Playing His Game

Dominique Adair, Margaret L. Carter and Kit Tunstall welcomes mail from readers. You can write to them c/o Ellora's Cave Publishing at P.O. Box 787, Hudson, Ohio 44236-0787.

Why an electronic book?

We live in the Information Age—an exciting time in the history of human civilization in which technology rules supreme and continues to progress in leaps and bounds every minute of every hour of every day. For a multitude of reasons, more and more avid literary fans are opting to purchase e-books instead of paperbacks. The question to those not yet initiated to the world of electronic reading is simply: *why?*

1. *Price.* An electronic title at Ellora's Cave Publishing runs anywhere from 40-75% less than the cover price of the exact same title in paperback format. Why? Cold mathematics. It is less expensive to publish an e-book than it is to publish a paperback, so the savings are passed along to the consumer.
2. *Space.* Running out of room to house your paperback books? That is one worry you will never have with electronic novels. For a low one-time cost, you can purchase a handheld computer designed specifically for e-reading purposes. Many e-readers are larger than the average handheld, giving you plenty of screen room. Better yet, hundreds of titles can be stored within your new library—a single microchip. (Please note that Ellora's Cave does not endorse any specific brands. You can check our website at *www.ellorascave.com* for customer recommendations we make available to new consumers.)
3. *Mobility.* Because your new library now consists of only a microchip, your entire cache of books can be taken with you wherever you go.

4. *Personal preferences are accounted for.* Are the words you are currently reading too small? Too large? Too...**ANNOYING**? Paperback books cannot be modified according to personal preferences, but e-books can.
5. *Innovation.* The *way* you read a book is not the only advancement the Information Age has gifted the literary community with. There is also the factor of *what* you can read. Ellora's Cave Publishing will be introducing a new line of interactive titles that are available in e-book format only.
6. *Instant gratification.* Is it the middle of the night and all the bookstores are closed? Are you tired of waiting days—sometimes weeks—for online and offline bookstores to ship the novels you bought? Ellora's Cave Publishing sells instantaneous downloads 24 hours a day, 7 days a week, 365 days a year. Our e-book delivery system is 100% automated, meaning your order is filled as soon as you pay for it.

Those are a few of the top reasons why electronic novels are displacing paperbacks for many an avid reader. As always, Ellora's Cave Publishing welcomes your questions and comments. We invite you to email us at service@ellorascave.com or write to us directly at: P.O. Box 787, Hudson, Ohio 44236-0787.